RISING STORM

THE LAST SANCTUARY: BOOK ONE

KYLA STONE

CONTENTS

Rising Storm

This book is a work of fiction. Any references to historical events, real people, or real places are used fictitiously. Other names, characters, places, and events are products of the author's imagination, and any resemblances to actual events or places or persons, living or dead, is entirely coincidental.

Printed in the United States of America

Cover design by Deranged Doctor Designs

Book formatting by Frostbite Publishing

First Printed in 2017

ISBN 978-1-945410-10-9

Paper Moon Press

Atlanta, Georgia

www.PaperMoonPress.com

❀ Created with Vellum

To my Dad, for teaching me to read and write,
but more importantly, to love reading and writing.
And for always believing in me.

1

AMELIA

Terror coiled in the pit of eighteen-year-old Amelia Black's stomach. Sweat beaded her forehead. The fabric of her dress clung damp and chilly against her skin.

The polished marble corridor stretched ahead of her, silent and empty but for the bodies.

In just a matter of minutes, the whole world had fallen to pieces.

It was hard to believe that only a few hours ago, the *Grand Voyager* was a glittering jewel of crystal and glass, a lavish fulfillment of every wish and desire, a shimmering promise of dreams come true.

But it was all a lie. This wasn't a dream; it was a nightmare. And with the nightmare came the terror, the shrieking and running, the beautiful bodies falling, limp as dolls.

Now, there was nowhere to run. Nowhere to hide.

Amelia strained for any sound over the crashing thunder of the storm. She crouched behind the counter of a coffee bar along the corridor of Deck Ten of the *Grand Voyager* luxury liner.

The display cases were all smashed, glass shards littering the marble floor. A humanoid service bot slumped against a bank of storage cabinets, smoke hissing from the bullet hole drilled into its forehead. Above the sink, the broken holoscreen flickered.

The voices came again. Two or three of them, from somewhere down the corridor.

She didn't know who they were. Terrorists, pirates, hired thugs, or private militia. It didn't matter. They were ruthless killers. And they were hunting her.

Because of her father, the powerful leader of the Coalition. Because of what he'd done.

If they found her, she was dead. They would use her as a bargaining chip, a pawn to get whatever they wanted from her father. They'd torture her. Then, they'd kill her.

But she was sick of being a pawn. She'd die rather than give in. She had her own plan, if she could live that long.

She'd thought the terrorists were the deadliest threat on this ship. She was wrong.

Thunder crashed. Waves rocked the ship. The floor tilted, and she stumbled, glass fragments jabbing into her bare feet. She sucked in her breath. She had to ignore the pain, the mind-numbing fear. She had to *think*.

Her family was still out there, trapped somewhere on the ship. Her brother, Silas. Her mother. And Gabriel. She winced. She couldn't think about him. Not now.

She'd done something, too. Something she couldn't take back.

Lightning shattered the night sky through the floor-to-ceiling windows on the far side of the corridor. Rain lashed the glass. The awful rat-a-tat of gunfire exploded from somewhere above her.

The voices grew louder. They'd be on her in thirty seconds or less.

Her heart leapt into her throat. She was cornered. Trapped.

Out of time.

2

AMELIA

Two Days Earlier . . .

For Amelia, the decadence of the *Grand Voyager* was nothing new. She was used to luxurious opulence. Only the setting changed. What never changed was the pressure, the expectation, the anxiety that always snarled in the pit of her stomach.

People only saw the beauty and the glamour, the illusion of a perfect life. They didn't see the cracks—or what lay beneath them.

"Are you all right?" her mother asked, her elegant brow furrowing in concern.

"I'm fine," Amelia lied. They were almost halfway through the fourteen-day cruise. Tonight, they were preparing for yet another dinner at the captain's table in the Oasis dining room.

Her father, Declan Black, slid open the glass doors of the veranda and strode into the Infinity Suite, the most extravagant stateroom on the ship. He'd been deep in a tense conversation on his Smartflex. A line like a scar appeared between his eyebrows. It hadn't gone well.

She tensed. "Who were you talking to?"

3

Declan tapped off the platinum earpiece curved around his right ear and slipped it into the pocket of his tuxedo. Her father's presence was regal and commanding, drawing all the energy in any room he entered. His brown hair and spade-shaped beard were threaded with silver, his magnetic, iron-hued eyes dark and cunning. "Just confirming the last few details of the Safe and Secure Act. Nothing to concern your pretty little head about."

He was one of the wealthiest, most powerful men in the country. He was the founder and CEO of BioGen Technologies as well as the chairman of the Unity Coalition, a conglomerate of powerful biotech, communications, and defense corporations that advised the government on pretty much everything.

His critical gaze swept over his wife and daughter, his eyes narrowing as he appraised them, searching for imperfections. It didn't matter how perfect they looked. There was always something wrong.

Amelia's gut tightened as she smoothed her dress, the shimmering scales shifting with her every movement. She stood taller, forcing a smile.

"Not the pearls." Declan fingered the array of necklaces, earrings, and bracelets spread over the vanity. He picked up a necklace with a half-carat benitoite gemstone haloed with diamonds. "Blue is her color."

He was right, as always. The benitoite glistened at her throat, highlighting her white-blonde hair and bringing out the ice blue of her eyes.

Her father turned to her mother. "Wear your hair down. That up-do ages you."

Her mother flinched. She was beautiful and elegant, from her sculpted cheekbones and arched brows to her flawless posture. Obediently, she unpinned her mass of auburn curls.

She always did what Declan wanted. They all did. Except for her brother, the black sheep of the family.

"Get up, boy," her father snapped.

Sixteen-year-old Silas was sprawled sullenly on the ivory settee, his legs slung over the velvet arm, his expensive tuxedo already rumpled.

"Stand up straight. And fix your damn clothes."

4

Behind her, Silas unfolded his lanky limbs and stood as slowly as possible. He stared at her in the mirror, a smirk playing at the corners of his mouth. He shared their father's lean, wolfish face and cruel, smoke-gray eyes.

The beginnings of another headache pricked the back of her neck. She winced.

Amelia's mother peered into her eyes. "Are you dizzy? Tingling or numbness anywhere?"

Maybe this once, she could be too sick to play her part. "I don't feel well—"

"Are you taking your medication as directed?" Declan asked.

Amelia nodded. They never spoke of her illness, the one they kept secret from everyone outside the family.

"She could have caught that terrible bat-flu," her mother said. "If she was infected before she received the vaccine—"

"She wasn't," Declan snapped. "I would know."

BioGen's new universal flu vaccine promised to eradicate the bat-flu epidemic plaguing the country. Last week on National Health Day, BioGen had inoculated over forty million citizens in a well-publicized display of goodwill. Amelia's inoculation was captured by the most popular vloggers and shown repeatedly on the newsfeeds.

Her mother frowned. "But a fever could trigger another episode—"

Declan raised a hand dismissively. "Last year was an anomaly. Her dosage was corrected. Do you doubt my abilities?"

Her mother blinked, her hand fluttering to the hollow of her throat. "Of course not."

Declan rounded on Amelia. He stared at her with hard, unflinching eyes. His gaze always unsteadied her. Like he could look straight through her and see every pulsing organ, her vulnerable, trembling heart. "Your mother treats you like you're made of glass. Is that true?"

Her mouth went dry, her heart thudding in her ears. It was like this whenever she did something wrong, whenever he made her feel small and stupid.

She lowered her gaze and stared at the digital ocean drifting across the wall opposite the veranda. The suite's polymer walls were embedded with photo-synthesizers, surrounding the occupants with whichever environment suited them—jungles and waterfalls, a sleek cityscape, or the black velvet of outer space.

The ocean usually calmed her—but it did nothing to calm her now. She opened her mouth, but the words curdled in her throat.

"Speak, girl," Declan demanded. "I asked you a simple question."

"Mr. and Mrs. Black, I detect an increase in stress indicators," the room AI said in a smooth feminine tone. "How may I make you more comfortable? May I suggest—"

"Activate privacy mode," Declan snapped. The AI fell silent.

Before her father could say anything else, Silas seized an opened bottle from the liquor cabinet and held it aloft. "Who feels like getting drunk?"

"I must have misheard you," Declan said, wheeling to face him.

Silas took a long swig and wiped the back of his mouth with the sleeve of his tuxedo. "I think not."

"You will not attend dinner acting like a drunken, spoiled idiot," Declan said, his voice going cold. "Stop this infantile behavior at once."

"Who's going to make me?" Silas asked defiantly. He stood tall, his fists curled at his sides. He was all tight, bristling energy. Like he was waiting for their father's wrath. Like he wanted it.

Declan's face darkened in fury. He took a menacing step toward Silas. "You do not want to test me—"

Someone knocked on the door of the suite. Everyone froze.

Ed Jericho, her father's head of security, opened the door. "We're ready for you, Mr. Black."

"Of course, Jericho," her mother said brightly, instantly composed.

The tall, muscular Nigerian hesitated in the doorway. "Everyone good to go, sir?"

The tension in Declan's face melted away, the mask he wore for everyone else slipping into place. He grinned broadly. "Jericho! How are your sea legs?"

Jericho had been with Declan's security team for the last six years.

His clean-shaven, angular face matched his broad shoulders and confident swagger. He was cordial but aloof, always professional and all business, exactly the way Declan wanted him. Jericho frowned. "Fine, sir."

"Why the long face?"

"I'd feel better with my weapon, sir." He'd been in a foul mood since they'd boarded a week ago, when ship security had forced him to stow his drone and refused to let him wear his gun clipped to his belt. It was stored in the safe in the chief security officer's office instead. "Even with the private security detail, this ship is understaffed—"

"I've heard this complaint too many times already, Jericho. That's why you're here. Besides, these are our people. Let's go." Declan adjusted his gold cuff links and turned to Silas, the faintest flash of disdain in his eyes. "Don't bother coming to dinner."

Jericho followed her mother and father into the corridor. Amelia hesitated. She glanced back at her brother. She wanted to thank him for what he did, for drawing her father's wrath away from her.

But his face was closed, his mouth twisted in contempt. He raised the bottle in a salute. "Go on. You wouldn't want to disappoint dear old Dad."

She ignored him and checked herself in the mirror. Face. Hair. Nails. Posture. Dress. Check. She took a deep, steadying breath and pasted a smile on her face. And there she was. The dazzling girl her father wanted.

She left Silas behind, just like she was supposed to. She played the part of the good daughter perfectly.

She hurried from the suite as gracefully as possible, lifting the glimmering fabric of her mermaid gown so it wouldn't catch on her designer heels. In the corridor, two ship's security officers waited to escort them to the captain's table in the Oasis dining room.

She recognized the tall and handsome one who'd been on her father's security detail all week. He was Latino, with flawless bronze skin, a scruffy goatee, and dark, brooding eyes. Like every time she saw him, he met her gaze and flashed an enigmatic smile, a dimple forming in his left cheek.

Her stomach gave a little jolt. She was used to being admired, but this was different somehow, in a way she couldn't put her finger on. Instinctively, Amelia started to smile back.

Her mother caught her arm and gave a sharp shake of her head, her gaze flicking to Declan. Her father would disapprove. Of course he would. She swallowed her smile and looked away, focusing on her surroundings instead.

The *Grand Voyager* was the most opulent ship to sail any sea. Everything was gleaming marble, sparkling crystal, and shining glass. Glass elevators soared through the ten-story atrium. A curved grand staircase constructed completely of glass swept up to the second and third balconies. Radiant sunlight flooded through the transparent domed ceiling, making every surface glitter like diamonds.

Beautiful children tossed coins into the grand marble fountain. Turquoise water streamed from the mouths of gold-plated mermaids. Elegantly-dressed men and women murmured greetings to her father and shook his hand as they passed. Her father was usually delighted to oblige, but today he barely acknowledged them. He was tense and on edge.

Declan's SmartFlex blinked. He swiped the platinum band and the digital overlay appeared. He read the message, his frown deepening. He turned to Amelia and spoke under his breath, so only she could hear. "You're failing with Senator López. Turn on the charm tonight, as I've repeatedly instructed. Get him in a favorable mood."

"Yes, sir." She'd endured these types of political dinners a hundred times, charming senators and CEOs, investors and financial czars, including President Morgan and Vice President Sloane. Her father paraded her around like a prized possession, a beautiful doll who performed on command.

"I will announce his support—and the success of the bill—at the Prosperity Summit gala tomorrow evening." He snorted in derision.

"It's ridiculous that we even need his vote. The senate is obsolete. Those pompous asses are the only ones who don't know it yet."

"Yes, father," she said obediently. She rubbed the violin on her diamond charm bracelet, the one her father had bought for her thirteenth birthday. She longed to play her actual violin, which always soothed her. Her father had her play several times at dinner, showing her off, but it wasn't the same as playing for herself.

A white-gloved waiter greeted them at the entrance to Oasis. He led Amelia and her parents to the large round table on the dais in the center of the dining room. There were no bots allowed here, only human servers. The three-story ceiling glimmered with holo-stars like floating candles. The walls were diamond-glass, so clear it seemed the ocean was at her fingertips. The music of the four-string quartet swirled over the hum of voices and the clink of silverware.

Her father greeted Captain Liebenberg warmly as well as the others at the table, all members of the Coalition: the cocky entrepreneur Tyler Horne; Bradley Marx, a heavy-set international banking guru; Omar Ferguson, a black senator from Illinois; and the CEO of Yates Pharmaceuticals, Meredith Jackson-Cooper, with her helmet of glossy yellow hair and perpetually pursed lips.

"Hello, Amelia dear."

Amelia pasted a smile on her face and turned to Senator López. "Are you having a pleasant evening, Senator?"

Enrique López was a handsome Mexican-American in his sixties, lean and fit, with dark eyebrows and thick, silver hair. He shook his head and swiped the newsfeed holo from his SmartFlex. "Just checking the latest updates on the bat-flu outbreak. Three hundred thousand dead. Can you imagine?"

She couldn't. Not really. "Thank goodness for BioGen's universal vaccine."

He raised his eyebrows dubiously. "If it's as effective as claimed."

"The vaccine distributed on National Health Day will prevent millions of people from getting sick. And the Safe and Secure Act is the next step in protecting our citizens," she said, parroting her father's words.

"Your faith in your father is admirable." The senator swirled his wine. The lines bracketing his mouth deepened. "But I'm afraid I'm rather set in my ways."

"You don't think the VitaliChip implant will save millions of lives?" Amelia asked. "A simple, noninvasive scan at the checkpoints into every city will easily identify contagious individuals and minimize the spread of disease."

"Citizens do not want their every move tracked."

"But bio-identification will prevent terrorists from hacking Smart-Flexes and crossing state and city lines to evade capture," Amelia argued gently. The law would require citizens to receive VitaliChip microchips implanted on the underside of the wrist. Wirelessly connected to a neural processor embedded near the base of the brain, it couldn't be hacked or cut out without alerting authorities. The vote in congress was scheduled for mid-September, less than two weeks away.

"The Coalition may have hands in many pots, but they still need votes to change laws. There are many citizens concerned about the potential ramifications of this bill, including myself. And President Morgan."

"You may wish to reconsider with whom you align yourself, Senator López," Declan said from across the table, an edge of steel in his voice.

Amelia flinched.

Declan flashed a thin, flat smile that didn't reach his eyes. "President Morgan harms our interests with his anti-security state border policy. He allows disease and dissidents to ravage our beautiful country. He's done nothing to eliminate these so-called revolutionaries."

"We're one terrorist attack or plague outbreak away from the breaking point," Tyler Horne said, raking his hands through his styled blonde hair. He'd founded VitaliChip Technologies, one of her father's subsidiaries and the company set to manufacture and distribute the VitaliChip once the law passed. He was in his mid-twenties, with a square jaw, cultivated stubble, and a swagger to match his enormous ego.

Senator López frowned. "I hardly think—"

Declan cut him off. "The people respect strength. They always have. They always will."

Horne leaned back and crossed his arms over his chest. "Unity through might is the key to our country's restoration. Don't you agree, Senator?"

Amelia rubbed her charm bracelet uneasily. This wasn't going well. How could her father expect someone like Senator López to change his beliefs? It was an impossible task. Yet somehow, it would still be her fault. Her father expected things of her no one could accomplish, just so he had someone to blame when things fell apart.

Declan's lip curled in barely restrained derision. "Everything worthwhile requires sacrifice. These measures will usher in a new era of security, prosperity, and freedom."

"I'm afraid you and I have different definitions of freedom," the senator said stiffly.

"Would you like some more champagne, Senator?" Amelia asked, trying to hide her dismay. Every word he spoke only angered her father further.

Meredith Jackson-Cooper sipped her wine, leaving a lipstick stain on her glass. "What is freedom in the midst of chaos?"

"Here's the cold, unvarnished truth," Declan said, his face darkening. "The people don't care about freedom. They only care about one thing. Safety. The government has failed to provide this precious commodity. So the Coalition will do so instead."

"Just what are you suggesting?" López asked, his voice rising.

"Only this." Her father clutched the stem of his wine glass so tightly she feared it might break. He was incredibly stressed. He never spoke like this—not in public, at least. "The Coalition *will* ensure our country's future. Either with the Senate's help, or without it."

A strained silence settled over the table. Anxiety twisted her stomach. This would be her fault, somehow. She cleared her throat, resting her hand on the senator's forearm. "Senator, you clearly care about your constituents. I'm sure they're grateful for your leadership."

"Let's all drink to that," her mother said brightly, raising her nearly empty glass. "We're all working to benefit the people. This was the purpose of National Health Day, after all. Now, let's indulge in a bit more Château Le Pin, shall we?"

Just then, the waiter returned, pausing at the captain's side. Amelia only half-listened as the other guests ordered braised veal chops, fresh lobster served on a bed of steamed asparagus, and seafood salad.

"I'll have the chilled Malossol caviar." Declan inclined his head toward Amelia. "She'll have the poached blue lobster tail, hold the caramelized butter."

She didn't even like lobster. The dull roaring in her ears intensified. She was hot all over, her skin prickling. She needed air.

She rose quickly from her seat. Across the dining room, the handsome security officer caught her eye again. He cocked his brows—in concern? Mockery? Something else?

"Amelia," her mother said under her breath, her brow furrowing as she gave her a warning glance. "Be careful."

She heard everything her mother didn't say. Be careful not to displease your father. Be careful not to shame your family. Be careful of your illness, your *defect*. Be careful of that boy, he's not like us.

"I am," she said.

She was always careful, every minute of every day.

3

GABRIEL

From the outside, twenty-one-year-old Gabriel Ramos Rivera was a tall and handsome Puerto Rican with a charming smile. His white security uniform accentuated his broad, muscled shoulders.

He made sure that the elites saw what he wanted them to see: a charismatic ship's officer eager to serve their every beck and call. Nothing more, nothing less.

They couldn't see what lay within him—the burning, barely contained anger, the explosive hatred just waiting to be unleashed.

Gabriel gritted his teeth. *Soon.* Soon, the truth would be revealed to the whole world. Soon, this glass monstrosity would topple, this decadent symbol of greed and corruption brought to its knees. After months of preparation and planning, everything was almost ready.

Outside on Deck Five's jogging track, the sky was clear, the blue sea rippling like silk. This high, on a ship like this, on a bright, pure day like today, Gabriel could almost believe the world was beautiful and whole. Could almost believe the ugliness back home was just a bad dream, a nightmare he would wake from.

Almost.

"Gabriel!" His younger brother, Micah, leaned against the glass railing, waiting for him. "Where've you been? I've been messaging you."

"Too busy with Teresa Velasquez in the Oceanarium." A girl was always an easy excuse, and one Micah never hesitated to believe.

Micah adjusted his glasses. "Is there some magical aphrodisiac in that place that I don't know about?"

Gabriel grinned. "That's a trade secret."

"Leave it to you to find the best spot to seduce a girl."

In truth, the Oceanarium *was* perfect—but not for the reason Micah thought. Gabriel had stored the smuggled weapons—gleaming automatic rifles and illegal pulse guns—in nondescript cardboard boxes inside the darkened, half-finished theater. The Oceanarium was still under construction, but the artist hired to paint the bioluminescent mural had fallen ill. "I can't help it if the ladies can't get enough."

Micah rolled his eyes. He and Gabriel shared the same dark curly hair, full lips, and bronze skin, but where Gabriel was sharp and hard-edged, Micah was soft and boyish.

Gabriel tilted his chin at the tattered paperback in Micah's hand as they started walking. He was the only person Gabriel knew who still read books you could hold in your hands. "What're you reading this time?"

"Joseph Conrad's *Heart of Darkness*."

"You ever read anything fun and lighthearted?"

Micah shrugged. "Hey, it could be worse. I also have *Moby Dick*."

Gabriel laughed. "Okay, you win."

A metalhead brushed past Gabriel. "Excuse me," it said as it swept the jogging track. The service bot was eerily realistic, with poreless skin made of silicone, synthetic hair, and metallic ferrofluids that allowed its smooth, human-like movements.

Pretty soon, these metalheads would take over every ship position. They'd already stolen half the jobs in the EpiPen. Another metalhead bussed a newly vacated table in the outdoor seating section of the Italian bistro, stacking plates still half-full of real caramelized quail and honey-glazed salmon with avocado salsa.

Gabriel's stomach twisted in revulsion. So much wasted food, each plate worth three hundred dollars or more. Avocado was a delicacy even on the *Grand Voyager*. He hadn't tasted one in over six years. These rich scumbags simply trashed anything they didn't like. The food on that table alone could feed a family for a week.

A thrum of hatred beat in tandem with his pulse. He gritted his teeth and pushed the dark thoughts out of his mind. He only had to be patient a little longer. *Soon.*

"You hear that?" Micah tilted his head as they rounded a corner of the track.

The sound of a violin rose above the roar of the wind. A girl in a filmy dress stood at the railing, facing the sea, a violin tucked beneath her chin. The music was hauntingly beautiful, the sonorous notes soaring into the air, only to be caught and whipped away by the wind.

She paused and turned toward them as they approached. Gabriel recognized her with a jolt. Amelia Black, the Coalition chairman's daughter. She was beautiful, with delicate features, milky-white skin, and long white-blonde hair swaying to her waist. Her every movement was filled with elegance and grace.

He fought down a surge of resentment. She was a mission. One his mentor, Simeon Pagnini, had assigned him two days ago, after Gabriel had secured the weapons and provided the room numbers and entrance codes for all private security on board the ship.

"Let's put those handsome features to good use," Simeon had said as they strolled past the plasma art gallery and the designer boutiques on Deck Eight. "You might extract some valuable information from the daughter."

Gabriel had grimaced. "You can't be serious."

In his late forties, Simeon gave off the air of a favorite uncle, with his soft cheeks, receding chin, and amiable expression. It was easy to miss the dark gleam in his eyes, the sharp, thin-lipped smile. "It may be beneficial."

Gabriel was used to groveling to the strutting elite, pandering to their every whim and desire, a forced smile always on his face. It was his job as a ship security officer. But the daughter of Declan Black?

Black was the founder of BioGen Technologies and the chairman of the corrupt and powerful Unity Coalition. Some said the Coalition wielded more power than the president.

After the Second Great Depression crippled the economy a decade ago, it was the Coalition who bailed out the country, ensuring their position of influence on the national and global stage. And now their ID-chip implant would track every citizen, especially those who disagreed with the increasingly brutal restrictions placed on those citizens' freedoms.

And Declan Black was the worst of all, epitomizing ravenous corporate greed and government malfeasance. He and his Coalition would destroy the country if they weren't stopped.

A hot spark of rage ignited inside him. Declan Black was the reason both of Gabriel's parents were dead. For that and a hundred other reasons, Gabriel would utterly destroy him. "What possible purpose could it serve?"

"We don't always see the entire board before we begin to play," Simeon said. "The more pieces we have, the stronger our position. When our friends arrive, we want to be ready."

He gritted his teeth. "I don't need to babysit some filthy rich princess." Their mission was to take the ship hostage, demand billions in ransom to support the coming war, and assassinate the Coalition leadership—Declan Black first and foremost.

They would not be tagged and tracked like dogs. They would not watch their families sicken and starve while the elites lived in obscene decadence. It was a first shot across the bow, a statement the world would hear loud and clear: the second American Revolution had begun. "I'm here for the mission. To *do* something."

"I need you to trust me for just a while longer." Simeon's voice was firm. He expected obedience. "Do you trust me?"

Simeon had never let Gabriel down, never lied to him or disappointed him. Simeon was the one who gave him a purpose, who brought him into the cause. Gabriel trusted Simeon with his life. "Of course."

Simeon had paused, turning to face Gabriel. He placed his hand on

Gabriel's shoulder. "Do not let yourself become distracted," he had warned. "A pretty façade is their weapon, their disguise. Remember who these people are, what they've done. Remember your reason."

Gabriel never forgot, not for one minute of one single day. His hatred was always with him, his anger a live wire, sparking and dangerous.

He looked at the girl, her delicate fingers grazing the strings of the violin as she met his gaze. Another jolt shivered through him. He ignored it. If Simeon wanted this of him, he would put everything into it, whether he saw the purpose or not.

Gabriel flashed a slow, languid grin, the one the girls all seemed to adore. He'd never had a hard time getting girls. But he didn't care about any of that. He couldn't afford to. "Nice instrument."

"Thank you." Amelia trailed her fingers along the violin's delicate stem. Her expression was coolly reserved, her eyes the color of blue ice. "It's an 18th-century Guarneri."

Gabriel had no clue what that meant, but he nodded along anyway. "The song was pretty good, too."

Her face brightened. "You enjoy Barber's *Adagio for Strings?*"

He shrugged. "Never heard of the guy. Do I have to be a classical music snob to enjoy great sound?"

"No, of course not. I'm glad you liked it," she said politely.

"I'm partial to good ol' rock 'n roll myself. Some Queen, Guns 'N Roses, Aerosmith."

"Sorry, never heard of them."

"What? They're classics!" He raked his hand through his hair. His father had loved those old bands, back before it all went to hell.

She shook her head as she tucked her violin back in its case. Her posture stiffened again, her expression reserved and carefully blank. He was losing her.

"You shouldn't have to play up here in the cold wind. Meet me in the Jazz Lounge on Deck Four in an hour. I'll get with the concierge and set up a daily schedule for you to practice."

She blushed, the hint of a real smile creasing her lips. "How thoughtful of you, but I enjoy playing out here."

He shrugged and flashed another cheek-dimpling grin. "Suit yourself. My name is Gabriel Ramos Rivera, by the way."

"You're part of my father's security team," she said, as if that dismissed him. She dipped her chin and slid elegantly past them.

Gabriel ran his hand over his scruffy goatee, fighting back a surge of resentment. He watched her duck into one of the side doors. He would just have to work harder to win her over. "Be careful of beautiful things, brother. They're not what they seem."

"That one didn't seem so helpless to resist you."

Gabriel's lips quirked into a half-smile. "Just give me a few days. You'll see."

Micah laughed without a hint of resentment or jealousy. He was loyal to the core.

An Indian couple strolled past, their boisterous twin girls scampering ahead of them.

"Gabriel," Micah said hesitantly, his tone growing serious. "This afternoon, I thought I saw—Is Simeon Pagnini a passenger?"

Gabriel's shoulders tensed. He quickened his pace. "I told you he had connections in high places." His brother had never liked Simeon. But it was Simeon who had stepped in when their dad died six years ago, ensuring their cold, indifferent aunt actually took care of Gabriel and Micah.

It was Simeon who paid for years of specialized tutoring and training, who taught him how to hack government servers, how to handle a gun, how to wage a war.

It would have been better if Micah hadn't noticed him at all. Nine months ago, when Simeon had helped push through Micah's application, Gabriel hadn't known the mission, hadn't known what was about to happen. He never would have allowed his brother on the ship.

But it was too late now. Their plans were in motion, only days from playing out. Only days from changing everything.

"But it seems odd that—"

Gabriel whirled on him. "What's there to talk about? He's on the ship. So what?"

Micah stared at him, hurt and confusion in his eyes. He didn't understand what Gabriel needed to do. He'd always been more concerned with being good than doing what was necessary to right the wrongs of the world. It was better to keep him in the dark—for now.

Gabriel rubbed his goatee and sighed. It was his job to keep his brother safe. He'd protected Micah since they were little kids. He pushed away his irritation. His brother was everything. "I'm sorry. I'm just stressed right now."

"No problem," Micah said.

Gabriel knew it was true. Micah would forgive him anything.

He made his voice light and teasing. "You always worry too much."

"Yeah. Okay."

"Just us?" *Just us. Always.* The phrase they'd used as kids, when they took turns keeping watch at their mom's hospital bed, making sure she was still breathing. And still later, when their grief-stricken, drug-addicted father wouldn't drag himself off the couch.

And still later, when it literally was just them. They had each other's backs.

Micah smiled. "Always."

4

WILLOW

Seventeen-year-old Willow Bahaghari still couldn't get used to the opulence that greeted her everywhere she looked, even after six days of the *Grand Voyager*'s sumptuous luxury and ridiculous extravagance.

"Lo Lo!" Her eight-year-old brother, Benjie, tugged on her hand. His black hair stuck up all over his head. "Can we go swimming, now?"

Her thirteen-year-old sister, Zia, fluttered her eyelashes and gave her best pleading, puppy-dog look. "Pretty please?"

"Oh, all right. It's not like I have a million better things to do," she grumbled.

Willow let her siblings drag her through the cavernous atrium and Royal Promenade. She caught sight of her harried reflection in the glass walls. Dark circles rimmed her eyes. She looked as exhausted as her mom. *Relax.* She was supposed to be having fun. Not just fun: the time of her life.

Willow's family was only on this swanky ship because her mother basically won the lottery. Once a year, all the *Grand Voyager* employee-of-the-month candidates got their names thrown into a hat. The one that came up this year was Marisol Bahaghari.

Willow's mom worked her butt off for Voyager Enterprises as

Associate Director of Housekeeping, overseeing all the sani-bots. For the last five years, Willow and her siblings lived with their *lola*, their Filipina grandmother, in a cramped one-bedroom apartment in Newark, seeing their mom only a few months out of the year.

As soon as they'd arrived, her mom had pulled out her red staff wristband and checked in with Housekeeping. Instead of relaxing with her kids, her mom was off working. Apparently, the sani-bots had been hacked. Some anarchist's idea of a joke. "Imagine the outrage if a rich elite doesn't get her eighty-dollar bottled water restocked or her perfectly folded octopus-shaped towel draped across her bed," Willow had snapped.

Her mom had grabbed her hands, her skin creased, her eyes weary. "Benjie can go to the Kid Zone on Deck Fourteen to give you a break, but Zia's too old. But she's not old enough to be by herself, do you understand?"

"Okay, whatever," Willow said, biting back her frustration.

"Please, Willow. You're *Ate*," she'd said, using the Filipino term for eldest sister. "They're your responsibility. Take care of your siblings. Do this for me, okay?"

She was sick and tired of being *Ate*, of always being the responsible one. But it didn't matter what she wanted. Just this once, she had hoped things would be different. That they could all be a family again. That she could be happy, free of the anxiety that always plagued her at home, where worries about bills and work and feeding hungry mouths never ceased.

Some vacation.

They strolled through the glass doors to the outside deck, which seemed to go on forever. On the upper deck, filmy-curtained cabanas offered massages from a service bot with arms tentacled like an octopus.

Two men strode toward them with their heads bent, walking so swiftly she had to grab Benjie's hand and jerk him out of the way.

"Watch where you're going." One of the men glared at her. His brow was furrowed, his jaw clenched, his eyes dark and furious.

Instinctively, she stepped back, a sudden unease jolting through her. "Um, sorry?"

The man scowled and brushed against her shoulder as he stalked past. The other man didn't glance at her at all. The first guy had looked almost . . . hateful, like she'd personally offended him.

She shivered, though the September sun was hot. "Have a great day to you, too," she said to their retreating backs.

"Don't let them bother you." Zia was always the one to look on the bright side. Her eyes shone with excitement. Her turquoise-tipped pixie haircut accentuated her heart-shaped face. She was younger, but already as tall as Willow's five-foot nothing. "What should we do after this?"

Benjie didn't bother to answer. He shoved his ratty Star Wars backpack into her hands, dashed off, and jumped into the massive infinity pool before Willow could say a word. He was a sweet, goofy kid, always leaping into trouble headfirst.

Zia stared at the ship's map, a hologram she brought up by clicking her wristband twice. "How about cryotherapy? The glass-floored tapas place? The Gilded Coral Spa?"

"Anything you want." Willow had already spent the last six days being the patient big sister: she'd taken Zia and Benjie to the Xtreme Worlds virtual reality center, managed not to freeze to death in the snow room, and glided around the low-grav center, where they slurped up floating spheres of lemonade over and over.

Zia studied her, wrinkling her nose. "Are you okay? You're acting strange."

Willow stiffened. Zia always seemed to sense her moods. How could she explain her guilt at enjoying this opulence, then her shame for feeling guilt in the first place? Or how she loved her family but at the same time wished they would all disappear, at least for awhile?

"I'm fine," she muttered. "Just go swim with Benjie, okay?"

"Be that way." Zia stuck out her bottom lip in a pout and and stalked off. Zia was usually good-natured, exuberant and giddy about absolutely everything, especially on a ship like this. She'd get over it quickly.

Willow sighed and glanced at the humanoid bots straightening cushions and delivering fresh towels. They zipped between the rows of lounge chairs, carrying frilly, fruity drinks on trays. They still gave her the creeps, no matter how normal everyone treated them.

Rihanna would understand. She smiled at the thought of her best friend since fifth grade. She ran her fingers over the third-gen Smart-flex she'd borrowed from her mom earlier. It was old and scuffed, nothing like the gorgeous SmartFlexes the elites wore, with their cuffs of smoky platinum, shimmering gold, and silver filigree edged in tiny rubies.

They looked like designer jewelry until you activated the digital overlay or holo-ports. At least her mom's SmartFlex featured a holo-port, unlike her own ancient version. She tapped the cuff and swiped Rihanna's avatar. A moment later her image appeared, shimmering above the holo-port. "Please tell me you're already engaged to a wealthy playboy CEO-wannabe."

Willow grinned. "Hell no. They're all stuck-up jerkwads. Well, most of them, anyway."

"Their loss." Rihanna coughed and pulled a pink polka-dotted blanket tighter around her shoulders. Usually all bright-eyed and bursting with energy, her brown skin looked faded, her eyes glassy, her braids frayed and unkempt.

Willow was about to tell Rihanna about the boy she'd met a few days ago, the only bright spot other than the food, but Rihanna's ragged appearance unnerved her. "Are you okay?"

"Got that Armageddon bat-flu thing the media keeps going insane over. For days, it was just a stupid cold that wouldn't go away. Then, bam. Woke up yesterday feeling like I've been smashed into a blender. This thing is malicious."

"You don't look so hot."

"Funny you should say that. I'm actually dreadfully, horrendously hot. You ever have a fever of one hundred and five?"

"Seriously? Shouldn't you be in a hospital?"

Rihanna grunted. "They're sort of full right now."

"What do you mean *full?*"

Rihanna waved her hand. "Everyone here is sick. And those stupid border checkpoints won't let you outside the city limits without a medical clearance. We're stuck here."

A pang of guilt struck her. Here she was, drinking champagne every day and sunning on Bahamian beaches while Rihanna was puking her guts up. "I'm so sorry. Did you get out of that physics test, at least?"

Rihanna coughed. "They shut down every school in Newark yesterday. Lots of other places, too. Voluntary quarantine or something. It sure doesn't seem voluntary, though."

Nervous energy prickled up and down Willow's spine. Schools shut down for a few days or weeks every year due to the flu or whatever new disease was all the rage, but never so many of them. Not all at the same time. That was weird.

She tapped the top left corner of the SmartFlex. The home page appeared alongside Rihanna's face, the various newsfeeds reporting the latest on the mandatory microchip debate, the near-constant weather record-breakers, and the corn and wheat blights still spreading throughout the southern States. 'Vice President Sloane Claims Epidemic Concerns Overblown,' one headline stated. Another posted, 'Universal Flu Vaccine Declared a Success.'

"The news says things are getting better. Lots of doom and gloom over nothing."

Rihanna snorted. "I'm about to hurl all over your doom and gloom."

"Love you, too. But didn't you get the free shot?"

"A useless five hours standing in line, if you ask me. A pointless publicity stunt."

"You must have already been infected."

"I guess." Rihanna's face turned an unhealthier shade. She swallowed several times. "Seriously, though, the toilet and I have a date. Go kiss a hot rich guy for me, 'kay?"

Willow swiped off, missing Rihanna like a physical pain in her chest. Rihanna was funny and irreverent and always up for a dare. This cruise would be a radically different experience with her best friend here.

With anyone her age who didn't look at her like she was a pariah or a communicable disease.

There was that boy, Finn, that she'd run into on her first day, literally bumping into him on the Royal Promenade. He'd been sweet and kind and treated her like a normal person. She'd been so busy watching her siblings, she hadn't gotten a chance to see him since.

But she always had terrible luck with boys. An opulent ship brimming with beautiful people wasn't going to change that.

Willow sighed and shielded her eyes to check on Benjie and Zia frolicking in the pool. At least the ship was free of surveillance drones, stupid border checkpoints, and those irritating holo ads everywhere in the city, always scanning everyone's SmartFlex's for purchasing history and consumer index records and vying for attention: "Willow, try a sample of Desire, our new pheromone-engineered formula guaranteed to make your guy blah, blah, blah for you." And, "Our new Allure has all the taste of real, soil-grown food with none of the calories, so you can finally lose those fifteen pounds, Willow!"

Like calories were the reason no normal person could eat cheeseburgers anymore.

Willow took a step closer to the glass railing but stayed a good five feet from the edge. It was a long way down. The ocean stretched in every direction, an expanse of blue that went on forever.

She'd stood right here six days ago as the ship set sail from the Manhattan Terminal, the bay shimmering far below, the glittering skyline soaring above her.

Everything had appeared so perfect—until she'd glanced down at the loading docks. The gangway was closed. Dozens of security bots had patrolled several areas blocked off by old-school barbed wire fencing. Armed security dressed in black combat gear guarded a crackling plasma fence. Drones zoomed back and forth, a silent but menacing warning.

Beyond the fence, a mob of people shook their fists and raised signs and holo projections. The waving signs were too far away to read, though they likely protested the impending mandatory implant chip and new surveillance laws, the metalheads stealing all the jobs, the lack of food stocking grocery store shelves, or the armed-guard checkpoints outside every city. The list went on and on.

She understood their anger. She felt it herself. Food and jobs were scarce. The Second Great Depression had dragged on for over a decade. The *Grand Voyager*'s gaudy extravagance was garish in the face of such hopelessness.

They had a right to be angry, unlike the rich jerks who'd nearly bowled her over a few minutes ago. What did the elites have to be upset about in their perfect, gilded world?

This extravagant cruise promised an unforgettable trip, the fulfillment of every lavish desire and dream one could imagine. But only for the elites, only for those rich and powerful enough to thumb their noses at everyone else.

She didn't belong on this ship. She belonged with the outraged mob below—exhausted and overworked just like her mom, consumed by worry and forever trapped in survival mode.

For Willow, the *Grand Voyager* was a glimmering dream slipping through her fingers, a reminder of everything she didn't have—and never would.

5

MICAH

"I need to talk to you," nineteen-year-old Micah Ramos Rivera said. A sickening sensation wrenched his stomach. He worked hard, tried to do the right thing, and more than anything, he loved his brother. He'd never had a single reason to doubt him.

Until now.

Micah faced his brother, his shoulders tensed, his voice hoarse. "Now, please."

Gabriel sat at a metal table in the officer mess hall. He stabbed a green bean with his fork and waved it at him. "Remember how Mom always made us eat a serving of vegetables at every meal, including breakfast?"

"I've been searching for you all over the ship."

"I've been busy." Gabriel grinned. "I still eat my vegetables, even when she's not here to make me. Silly, huh?"

Micah would not be pushed aside. Not today. "I know what you did."

A shadow crossed Gabriel's face, so quick he might have imagined it. Gabriel untangled himself from the chair and followed Micah into the corridor.

The beige walls were tacked with peeling posters of notices and safety policies, the bare floors and exposed piping a sharp contrast to the decadence upstairs. No one cared about the state of the crew quarters.

"Just what do you think you know?" Gabriel asked sharply.

The memory was still fresh. Micah had spent an endless shift catering to the elites fresh from another shore excursion. He'd served middle-aged men nursing hangovers and rich women giddy with the 'deals' they'd bartered off the impoverished in the bustling shops of Grand Turk. It was exhausting, but he tried not to show it. He was just grateful to have a job.

He'd gone below deck to the laundry area for a fresh load of linen napkins to reset the tables in the Oasis dining room where he served as a waiter. He'd seen something that made the hairs prickle on the back of his neck.

"What's that?" Micah had asked over the roar of the ship's engines. The waves lashed the hull. The stink of bleach and brine filled his nostrils. His stomach tightened.

A short, stocky Asian man stood in front of him, blocking his view of the pallet of fifty-pound bags of detergent the man had been unloading with two sani-bots. His name tag read Liu Wei Zhang. He wore a yellow bandana tied around his forehead.

"Napkins are over there." Zhang gestured to the left, where a sani-bot stacked folded towels, sheets, and table linens inside a yellow metal cage. "By the towels."

Micah pushed his glasses up the bridge of his nose and glanced at the blue powder dusting the cement floor. One of the detergent bags on the pallet was split open. He could just make out something white, square, and saran-wrapped poking out of the blue powder. "Look's like you've got a spill. Need any help?"

Zhang smiled wider. Sweat beaded his hairline. "We've got it under control. Here, follow me. I'll help you get those napkins."

But Micah wasn't fooled. He stepped around the man and brushed the powdered detergent aside with his hand, uncovering dozens of packages of white pills. His stomach sank to his toes. "You're smuggling Silk."

Zhang scowled. "Keep your voice down."

It made sense. Drug running was a huge business with any form of international transportation, including luxury cruise ships. Considering how little the crew was paid, an extra few grand a trip was plenty of incentive to look the other way.

But still, it was wrong. Serenaphin—Silk—was the worst of the synthetic drugs that had flooded the streets over the last several years. Micah's own father had been hooked on the stuff. Until it killed him. Fresh anger burned through his veins. "You know I can't do that."

"What are you going to do, then?"

"I have to tell Schneider." Franz Schneider was the chief security officer, a German guy in his mid-forties who always smoked cigars in the crew bar.

Zhang snorted. "You think he isn't in on it?"

"I don't believe you."

"Talk to him yourself. He's paid good, that's all I know. He'll cut you in."

"I don't want to be cut in." Micah thought about his father, his life force sucked out of him as he slumped on the couch day after day, his ribs growing more prominent, the hollows in his cheeks deepening until he resembled a living skeleton. Until he was one. "I'll go over Schneider's head. I'll go to the captain if I have to."

Zhang stared at him, incredulous. He stepped close and poked the brass name tag over Micah's chest.

Apprehension jolted through Micah. He hadn't thought to be afraid.

"Your name," Zhang said. "Rivera. Your brother is on the security crew, yes?"

Micah said nothing.

Zhang read the answer on his face. He smiled. "Do what you gotta do. You report the drugs, your brother goes with us. Thirty-year sentence for this many kilos. Maybe he'll get out in time to meet your grand-kids."

Micah went rigid. He watched two sani-bots feed sheets into the jaws of a machine that automatically pressed and folded the linens. He felt like a giant hand was crushing his windpipe. He struggled to find his voice. "What are you talking about?"

"Your brother. He's—how do you say it? He's in deep, *amigo.*"

A memory of his brother flashed through his mind. Gabriel carrying him in his arms as pain and blood exploded through him, murmuring, "You're okay, you'll be okay" over and over.

A crack of doubt opened inside him. Not Gabriel. It couldn't be Gabriel.

Zhang sneered. "What're you gonna do now?"

Micah had wanted to punch the man in the face. Instead, he bit the inside of his cheeks hard enough to draw blood. "Just give me the napkins."

"Ask him." Zhang's eyes glittered. "He'll tell you himself."

The crack of doubt had opened wider.

It felt like a crater now, a canyon separating himself from the one person he loved wholly and without reservation, the only family he had left in the world. The words were barbed wire in his throat as he faced his brother. "I know about the drugs you've been smuggling on the ship."

Gabriel smoothed a stray wrinkle in his security uniform. His movements were careful and deliberate. "What are you talking about?"

A fresh wave of anger swelled over him. Gabriel was a smooth liar. Always had been. But Gabriel wasn't supposed to lie to *him.* "Zhang told me."

Gabriel leaned against the wall and crossed his arms over his chest. His expression was placid, his eyebrows cocked in mild curiosity. "Zhang is a piece of trash. He's looking for someone to blame. I don't have a thing to do with any drugs. Why would I?"

Micah wanted desperately to believe him, but the evidence told him otherwise. It explained so much. The hushed conversations. The way Gabriel's face would harden at some innocuous question or comment, shutting Micah out for no reason. "Then you won't have a problem when I report this to the captain."

"You need to follow the chain of command and report to Chief Security Officer Schneider."

"Schneider is in on it." Micah watched his brother's face. There was the barest twitch of the muscle in his jaw, a hint of anxiety around his eyes. "But you know that."

"I know nothing of the sort. It's against protocol to break the chain of command. You'll be disciplined—if they don't just kick you off at the next port."

Micah bit the inside of his cheeks. He forced his voice to sound confident. "I'm going to Captain Liebenberg tonight. If you're clean, you don't have anything to worry about."

Two crew members walked by. Micah edged out of the way to let them pass.

Gabriel's hands balled into fists. The harsh florescent lights flickered, highlighting the shadows beneath his eyes. "You know how many people would be affected by this? A dozen crew fired, and what are their families going to do? They'll starve. These guys are just trying to earn a living, Micah. You know what it's like now."

"I know." He remembered how hard their parents worked just to keep the electricity going and food on the table. But even at the worst times, his mom never hurt anyone. Even his father, always so angry and defeated, only took Silk, never sold it. "It's breaking the law."

Gabriel made an exasperated sound. "You don't get it. The law is nothing but a weapon the elite use to oppress the rest of us."

"Don't you remember Dad?" Micah's voice cracked. "I'm going to report it, with or without you."

Micah turned and walked away. He prayed his brother would stay silent. He clung to a thread of hope that he was wrong, that somehow Gabriel wasn't involved. Maybe Zhang was lying. Everything could continue as it had been, his brother still his best friend.

He hadn't gone five steps when Gabriel spoke. "Stop."

Micah turned and faced him.

"You turn in those drugs, and you're turning me in, too."

Micah's heart cracked open inside his chest. All the things he wanted to say—*Why? How could you do this? How could you lie to me?*—stuck in his throat. "I have to."

"You don't have to do anything, brother. I promise you, it's for a good cause."

"I have to," he repeated. The rest of the English language had suddenly deserted him.

"No, you don't. You're a good person, Micah. That's what I love about you. But I need you to trust that I'm a good person, too."

His brother *was* a good person. He knew it in his deepest heart. But Gabriel was also a hothead. He'd joined the New Patriots, always railing against the corrupt government. He got in fights at school. And he'd put that boy from the park in a hospital all those years ago.

Micah still winced at the memory of what Gabriel did because of him, *for* him. An act of violence Micah couldn't condone. But Gabriel's actions always protected something or someone else.

But this was different. None of it made any sense. "That doesn't make what you're doing any less wrong. Don't you see that?"

"It's easy for you. Some people can afford to only see things in black and white. The rest of us can't do that."

"Right and wrong *is* black and white." His mom taught him to do the right thing, even when it hurt. *Be good*, she'd tell Micah, squeezing his hand. *Be brave.* They were the last words she'd spoken to him in the hospital. *God has plans for you, my son. Be good. Be brave.*

Gabriel's mouth hardened. "Do you have my back or not?"

Micah hesitated.

Gabriel's gaze pinned him. "It's just you and me. Just us."

"Always," Micah forced out, his throat gritty.

"See? I knew you'd come through. You always do."

For a long moment, neither of them spoke. He stared at Gabriel but couldn't read him, not anymore. If he ever really could.

Gabriel rubbed the back of his neck. "Look. I've got work. I know you'll do the right thing. Trust in the greater good."

He spoke with such confidence, such certainty. But Micah felt anything but certain. He teetered on the edge of a gaping hole, about to fall. "Gabriel—"

But his brother's expression closed, slamming shut like a door. He sauntered down the corridor and disappeared around the corner.

Micah walked through the ship as if in a daze, smiling on cue, greeting the passengers, laughing at a crew member's joke.

And all the while, the secret smoldered like a burning coal behind his eyes.

6

AMELIA

S omeone was watching her. The back of Amelia's neck prickled.
She swung around, scrutinizing the dancing couples, the clusters of people talking and laughing, the circulating wait staff, everyone exquisitely dressed for her father's Prosperity Summit gala. It was in the Grand Ballroom, located above the bridge, over thirteen stories above the waterline. The room rotated, offering spectacular 360-degree views. On every side, the floor-to-ceiling windows revealed endlessly blue water, like the sky turned upside down.

She caught sight of Jericho standing stiffly near the entrance next to a few other security officers, his usual frown etched on his face. A few yards away, Gabriel Rivera chatted with a waiter. His skin was dark bronze, and his straight black eyebrows and scruffy goatee gave him a serious, brooding look. He met her gaze for a moment and flashed her a simpering grin.

She looked away, heat creeping up her cheeks. She'd seen him a dozen times over the last few days. Each time, he'd sauntered over to chat, so handsome and charismatic, his gaze intense and disconcerting. She kept thinking about that lopsided grin, that dimple in his left cheek.

The feeling came again. Stronger, and deeply unsettling. Someone was watching her. And it wasn't Gabriel Rivera. She turned with a frown, searching the room.

A burly ship's officer leaned against the wall near the entrance. He had a smug, oily face and reptilian eyes. He smiled at her, slow and lecherous, his mouth bristling with teeth. His gaze slithered up and down her body.

Her stomach lurched. She was accustomed to a certain amount of looking. She was used to being scrutinized, leered at. But this was different.

This man's gaze was a cold blade sliding between her ribs. It felt like he was invading her, opening her up, turning her inside out. This guy didn't want her; he wanted to *hurt* her.

A sinking sensation gripped her. She smoothed her cream chiffon gown with trembling fingers. She was surrounded by people. She had no reason to be afraid.

A floating tray laden with delicacies drifted by. "Would you care for some prosciutto cheese and melon appetizers?" offered the tray's cultured, disembodied voice. Amelia waved it away with a flick of her wrist. Her appetite had disappeared.

"I hope you're enjoying our sixth annual Prosperity Summit," her father boomed to the expectant crowd. He stood proud and commanding on the raised dais in the center of the ballroom as he gave his speech. Amelia barely listened. She'd heard it all before. "To BioGen, to the Coalition, to the Safe and Secure Act and to the prosperity of this great country!"

Everyone applauded enthusiastically. Yet tension buzzed through the room like an electric current. Shame gnawed at her. She'd failed with Senator López. She'd done her best and still screwed up. She felt brittle, hollowed out. Like everything was all her fault.

She forced herself to return to her duties, drifting around the room, extolling the virtues of her father's leadership and singing the praises of CEOs, financial czars, corporate sponsors, and senators. She giggled enthusiastically at jokes, pausing to bestow compliments and accept them with fluttering lashes and flushed cheeks.

She knew how to act. She was her father's daughter.

She scanned the ballroom for that awful man again but didn't see him. He must have slipped out. The thought of his malevolent gaze made her skin crawl. She pushed thoughts of his viper eyes out of her mind and paused to refill her drink.

Declan Black strode across the room and seized her arm. His expression was flat, his mouth pressed into a thin, bloodless line. "Come with me."

He squeezed her elbow as he escorted her out into the foyer, away from the crowd, before whirling on her. "I had planned to announce the support of Senator López tonight. Did I not ask you to put him in a favorable mood?"

Her mouth went dry. "I tried. You heard him. He doesn't—"

"You tried? It was a simple request, Amelia. Did you really try?"

She went rigid. "I'm sorry, I tried to—"

His steely gaze bored into her. "Do you enjoy making me look like a fool?"

Her heart thudded in her ears. She could barely hear herself think. She could barely think at all. "No. Of course not."

"You're simply careless and irresponsible, then?"

"I tried to talk—"

His lip curled in derision. "You *tried*."

"He had his mind made up, how could I—"

"You thought you would play me for a fool, is that it?"

Her breath left her lungs. "Father—"

"Instead of charming Senator López, you turn him against me?" He towered over her, his nostrils flaring, contempt etched across his face. "Are you *trying* to sabotage me?"

She shrank back against the wall, wilting before his scorn, fear making her small and stupid. "I would never—"

"You've been such a disappointment to me. You and your brother both. Spoiled, ungrateful little—"

"Excuse me, sir," Gabriel Rivera said from the ballroom doorway. "Your head of security, Ed Jericho, is asking for you."

The mask slid into place, the disdain melting from Declan Black's face in an instant. His expression shifted to polite reserve as he straightened his diamond cuff links. "Thank you for informing me."

He strode back into the ballroom without a backward glance at Amelia.

"Are you okay?" Gabriel asked.

Her hands trembled. She hid them behind her back. "Sorry, ah—he's under a lot of stress. And I made a mistake—"

He cocked his head. "I didn't eavesdrop on your conversation. Just—you look miserable."

She blushed and rubbed her charm bracelet fiercely. "It's been a long day."

He shot her a questioning look. "Maybe you shouldn't go back in there."

"I have to."

"But do you *want* to?"

She stared at him, unable to answer.

"What's the point of all this if you're unhappy?" He gestured at the marble floors, the crystal chandeliers.

She shrugged helplessly. Because how could she begin to explain it? If only she were smarter, more talented. If only she were beautiful and charming and perfect enough, he'd change his mind. Her father would decide she was worthy of his love.

A deep, ugly shame filled her. She wanted to run away, disappear, sink straight down into the floor. But what she wanted didn't matter, had never mattered.

She opened her clutch and grabbed one of the cigarettes nestled next to her auto-injectors with trembling fingers. Her EpiPens, as she tried to think of them. They weren't EpiPens, and they weren't for allergies. It was what her father told her to call them, so no one would question her. She tapped the top of her cigarette until it self-lit.

Gabriel nodded at her cigarette. "You're not allowed to smoke inside."

She waved her hand, flustered. "Oh. Sorry. I'll just put it out—"

"You can smoke outside. I know a spot just around the corner on Deck Thirteen. It has the best views. You feel like you're on top of the world. I can show you."

She hesitated, then nodded. "Thank you."

She followed him into another alcove and through a set of glass doors to the starboard side of Deck Thirteen. The engine rumbled beneath her. Beyond the ship's lights, the water swirled black as pitch. The breeze pulled at her French twist, tugging several strands of hair free to whip around her face. She breathed in the salty air.

Gabriel leaned against the glass railing, facing her. "When I have a bad day, I always come out here and just relax for a while, you know?"

"I can't get enough of the ocean, how it goes on forever." Even as she said the words, she wondered why she was speaking so freely. It was the stress of the evening—her failure with the senator, her father's disdain, that man's malicious gaze. She felt off-balance. Vulnerable. "It gets inside you out here."

He nodded. "Yeah, I get that. Like your music."

She looked up, meeting his eyes. She took a long drag of the cigarette to steady herself. The intensity of his gaze unnerved her. "Yes, exactly like that."

He raked his hand through his hair. "How do you like the *Grand Voyager*? Is there any place you'd like to see? Backstage at the Galaxy Lounge? The bridge?"

"I've been to the bridge. With my father."

His lip curled. "Of course. How could I forget? You have access to whatever you want, whenever you want."

Her stomach twisted a little. He was subtly mocking her, or maybe not so subtly. It reminded her how little she actually knew him. "I should go back inside."

"But you don't want to." It was a statement, not a question.

She didn't answer, only breathed out a tendril of smoke. The breeze took it and flung it out over the vast, empty sea.

"I'm sorry. I shouldn't have said that." He took a step closer. He smelled like something musky and male, like cedar or pine, a deep and wild forest. "But you clearly deserve some fun. Come with me."

"Excuse me?"

He smiled, his eyes going darker. "Come with me. I'll show you the ship, her inner workings, her guts. The stuff you don't see on the official tour."

She didn't have a handle on this conversation. She didn't have a handle on him. He seemed to waver between friendly and slightly hostile. It made her nervous. He made her nervous.

And yet, he was incredibly attractive. She couldn't deny that. She couldn't deny the flutter in her belly when she felt his eyes on her. The way her own gaze kept straying to his lips.

Her father would hate Gabriel. Because he was a lowly security officer. Because he was unsophisticated, uncultured. Because he wasn't an elite, wasn't one of them. She dropped her gaze. "I can't."

"It'll be fun. And I'll be a gentleman, I promise."

She took a step away from the railing, away from him. The ship rolled beneath her. She fought off a wave of dizziness. "Isn't there some rule about crew and passengers not fraternizing with each other?"

He cocked an eyebrow, grinning mischievously. "Is that what you want to do? Fraternize?"

She blushed. For one second, she imagined what it would be like to take off, to defy her father. How furious he'd be when he realized his only daughter, his prized possession, had dared to disobey him. And with the likes of Gabriel Rivera.

But she didn't get to do whatever she wanted. She needed to focus on doing better. Being better. She needed to push this rakish boy and his dark, brooding eyes out of her mind.

"No, it's—I'm sorry. I have to go." She blinked back the wetness burning her eyelids and straightened her shoulders, steeling herself.

Her mouth formed a smile. But it was a smile about to shatter, a smile cracking her open from the inside.

7

MICAH

On the evening of the seventh night, Micah made his way to the lido deck after he'd finished his shift. The *Grand Voyager* had departed Ocho Rios several hours ago.

Further down the deck, couples in fine evening gowns and tuxedos preened for the photo drones. The wind whipped Micah's hair into his face, stinging his eyes. He stood at the glass railing and looked out at the vast and endless sea, the horizon bleeding into the darkness.

A pale strip of moonlight reflected on the water. In the distance, the lights from a sister luxury liner glittered like a star fallen from the sky. He was surrounded by so much beauty, but inside, he felt ripped in half.

Micah hadn't spoken to his brother since yesterday. Gabriel's parting words echoed in his mind. *It's just you and me. Just us. Always.*

Questions tore at him, jagged as glass. How could he betray his own brother? How could he live with himself if he didn't turn in the drugs? How could he live with himself if he did? Gabriel was his home, his compass, his fixed North Star.

All of his life, he'd tried to be good. What was he now?

Micah stared at the water until his vision blurred. A seed of loathing sprouted in his chest.

He knew what he would do. As soon as he'd spoken the word "Always", he'd known.

Nothing. He would do nothing.

And already, he hated himself.

8

GABRIEL

Gabriel stood on the glass catwalk on Deck Thirteen, anxiety and anticipation coiled in his gut. It was the eighth day of the cruise. Tomorrow, the world would change.

Simeon leaned against the railing beside him, along with Simeon's second in command, Alexi Kane, a huge white guy with a crew cut, a thick, bulging neck, and a body built like a bulldozer.

They looked over the deck of the Imagination Café at the passengers inhaling their decadent breakfasts, their plates piled high with exotic fresh fruits, all of them ready for another lazy day of gluttony and opulence.

Many of the passengers had already departed on their shore excursions to Grand Cayman, where they'd enjoy beach massages and jungle treks, explore engineered coral reefs on personal submarines, and ride modded killer whales. Scientists had genetically modified the animals to be dumb and docile, safe for the whole family to enjoy, at least according to the holo ads at the excursion center. Gabriel had his doubts.

On the starboard side, the sun was a white ball in the sky. He rechecked the CCTV feeds on his tablet. Everything under control. Everything normal. For now.

Kane flexed his bulging arms. "Enjoying your day?"

Gabriel had taken an instant dislike to Kane the moment he'd met him two years ago. He was one of those men who oozed violence, who took pleasure in causing pain and made no pretense of hiding it. But Simeon trusted Kane, which meant Gabriel had to endure him.

"Kane," Gabriel said as cordially as he could manage.

Simeon waved them to silence and brought the satphone to his ear. "What changes?" A long pause. His face darkened. "Yes, I understand. I'll contact the affiliate and arrange the rendezvous point." By the time he clicked off the phone and turned toward Gabriel and Kane, his face blazed with fury.

"What's wrong?" Gabriel asked.

"After you deal with monkey island and disable communications and the ShipLoc, I have another task for you. Get Declan Black's girl to a secure location until I contact you."

"Why? I want to be here, serving the cause."

"I'll do it." Kane sneered. "I'll give that girl more than she can handle."

"No!" Gabriel felt nothing for Amelia Black. She was a mark, part of his mission and no more. Still, the thought of someone like Kane touching her set his blood boiling. "Stay away from her."

Simeon shot Kane a warning look. "That's not what we're here for."

Kane laughed, a rumble deep in his chest. "We here for romance then? What the hell is this, Simeon?"

"Of course not!" Gabriel swallowed the words he wanted to say, but only for Simeon's sake. For the sake of the cause. He forced his voice to stay calm. "We're after her father, not her."

Kane leered at him. "You think just 'cause you got a pretty face, a girl like that's gonna let you in her—"

"Don't be crude!" Simeon said sharply. He turned to Gabriel. "Your fervor and patriotism are noted. But I need you to do this. All will be clear in due time."

"Understood, sir." Gabriel tried to keep the resentment from his voice. He was as much a fighter as Simeon and Kane. He'd trained for years. He was strong. He was ready.

"And the girl?" Kane's upper lip curled. "I could give her a grand time in the good ol' captain's quarters. You sure you don't want me to—"

"Can't you ever shut up?" Gabriel clenched his jaw, fighting to contain his anger and disgust. He was startled by the intensity of his reaction. He felt mild pity for the girl, a shock in itself. Before her, he never imagined he might feel anything but loathing for an elite. When Declan Black had laid into her last night, he'd wanted to kill him then and there.

Simeon put a restraining hand on his shoulder. "Our mission has changed. It is now essential we take Black alive. He has critical information—information he may be unwilling to give us."

"What do you mean? What's changed?"

"All in good time, my faithful friend. For now, obedience is what I need from you. This is it. This is our time. The world changes tonight."

"Tonight? I thought it was planned for tomorrow—"

"The schedule has changed. The *Grand Voyager* will be heading back to the mainland by this weekend, guaranteed."

Kane spat over the railing. "Why?"

"The flu that's not a flu. The underground's full of chatter. They're calling it the Hydra virus. It keeps popping up everywhere. The virus is infectious, virulent, and lethal. More people are dying than the media are reporting. By the hundreds of thousands, if you believe some vloggers.

"My source just confirmed. She believes an announcement should come tomorrow from the White House. Americans will be banned from all domestic and international travel. Every international port will be turning us away shortly."

Gabriel leaned against the glass railing, taking it in. He'd heard rumors, but he'd been so focused on the mission, he'd blocked most of it out. "What about—?"

"Our fellow Patriots are safe. For now. According to my source, the president himself may be ill. This information has not been released to the public. The average Joe believes he's on another golf vacation."

Kane whistled.

Gabriel wondered, not for the first time, how Simeon could possibly know so much. New Patriots were entrenched in the government. Even more were sympathetic to their cause, fellow believers in a new order, a new government that would actually serve the people. But he didn't know how many there were or how high their influence and power reached. He only knew the members of his local chapter.

"As for us," Simeon continued, "we need to act before the captain realizes the severity of the *Grand Voyager*'s situation and changes course. We must reach our rendezvous point off the coast of Puerto Cortés.

"One other thing. Tropical storm Wyatt is headed directly toward our path. Normally, the captain would skirt the storm. But we must meet our deadline, including our final extraction point. Everything is too finely calibrated to adjust now. The others are in position. We're prepared to neutralize the secret service and private security agents. Everything has gone according to plan. There was a slight snag with a crew member in the laundry, but it's been dealt with."

Gabriel took a breath. He hadn't told Simeon about Micah. But it didn't matter. The drugs were a cover. Micah had no idea what was really happening. He'd never turn Gabriel in. The mission was safe.

Simeon turned to Gabriel. "And the Coalition chairman's bodyguard?"

"Jericho is always with Black except for the dinners at the captain's table," Gabriel said. "Black doesn't seem to want him around for those. Jericho works out at the gym or spends time with the son, Silas."

Simeon nodded and held his fist over his heart. Gabriel and Kane followed suit. "For the honor of true patriots and the love of country."

The thrill of anticipation hummed through every cell of Gabriel's body. It was time. The country was about to change for the better. Everything started today. It started with them, with *him*.

Gabriel spent the early part of the afternoon crouched on monkey island, located on the roof above the Grand Ballroom, with the radar antennae and the satellites. He cut power to the VHF and HF radio phones and dismantled the satellite wireless and communication systems.

He deactivated the GMDSS, the Global Maritime Distress and Safety Systems, which would send long-range distress signals to a series of orbiting satellites if activated. The ShipLoc satellite tracking device was supposed to be in a hidden location, but in their arrogance, Voyager Enterprises just stuck it on monkey island with everything else.

He left the orange buoys with the Emergency Position Indicator Radio Beacon on the bridge wings. To move them now, in full view of the bridge, would only invite suspicion. If they hit the water, they'd automatically activate their satellite-relayed hourly position to NOAA, the National Oceanic and Atmospheric Administration headquarters in Washington, D.C. There was plenty of time to get those later.

Now, Gabriel strode the length of the glass catwalk, checking and rechecking the surveillance feeds. He'd copied several loops of undisturbed video last night, ready to hack them into the feeds.

"It's time." Simeon's voice crackled through the walkie-talkie. "Meet me on Deck Twelve in fifteen minutes."

He hurried to meet Simeon, who stood with Kane and another New Patriot named Vera Hollis, a thin white woman with a sharp, angled face and auburn hair pulled into a tight bun. Two other men dressed in crew uniforms directed a laundry hover cart into the alcove of the crew hallway.

"Our fellow comrades are en route," Simeon said. "Davison and Hernandez are outside the engine room, awaiting orders. The rest of the team are stationed and ready."

"And the surveillance?" Kane asked.

"The relevant CCTV screens are set on a loop, ready to remote activate." Gabriel glanced at the tablet in his hand. The ship's internal security system required two additional levels of access to hack, but he'd infiltrated them with ease.

Kane adjusted his body armor beneath his uniform. "Start the damn thing."

When Simeon nodded, Gabriel tapped the tablet. Eight of the surveillance screens flickered and activated the recorded loops. "Done."

Simeon nodded and put his right fist over his heart. The other men followed. Gabriel could feel his own heart beating through the fabric of his uniform. "For the honor of true patriots and the love of country."

"For the honor of true patriots and the love of country," he repeated.

He followed the men down a series of hallways to the central entrance to the bridge. They stopped before a reinforced steel door labeled 'Bridge: Authorized Entrants Only.'

Unfortunately, there was only the one corridor leading directly to the bridge. If a bridge officer was watching the security feed directly, he or she would simply see several crew and officers of the ship. The crew members and the laundry cart were odd, but shouldn't be alarming.

The two men in crew uniforms pressed themselves against the shallow alcove in the right wall out of sight of the camera over the door, which only captured the hallway itself. They dumped the layer of towels from the laundry cart and pulled out three subsonic automatic rifles.

Simeon and Hollis did the same on the left side of the door, pistols outfitted with silencers now in their hands. Both groups pulled black masks over their faces.

Gabriel stood beside Kane in front of the camera and pressed the metal switch recessed into the left wall. The captain and bridge officers accessed the bridge through a retinal bioscanner. Everyone else entered the old-fashioned way.

The bridge officer on the other side of the door would glance at the CCTV monitor and see only Kane, a radio officer, and Gabriel, dressed smartly in his security uniform with the black epaulettes on the shoulders. It was nothing out of the ordinary.

Reinforced steel couldn't protect against treachery. Gabriel's heart jolted at the word. This wasn't treachery. It was justice. Justice for the people. A new revolutionary war, beginning today. Beginning *now*.

The hatch swung open with a soft click.

Everything happened at once.

9

WILLOW

"Can we order dessert first?" Benjie asked, a goofy grin on his face. He pulled another pack of playing cards out of his Stars Wars backpack he carried with him everywhere. He was intent on practicing his latest magic trick, something about making a card disappear in his hands. "And breakfast for lunch!"

"Only if we eat broccoli last," Willow's mom said.

Zia wrinkled her nose. "No deal."

They were in the middle of an early dinner at the Imagination Café. Willow's stomach ached from stuffing her face every chance she got, but that didn't stop her from eating more. Every morsel was the real deal, not that prefab or reconstituted crap that looked and tasted like a cardboard box.

They'd spent the morning at a local beach in Grand Cayman, exploring the shops crammed with cheap island ware and trinkets made in China. It hadn't been as fun as she'd expected. Port security handed out respiratory face masks to everyone disembarking.

"Just a precaution," they'd said with huge, white smiles. Apparently, the bat-flu had sickened a ton of people in Grand Cayman, too. It was unsettling. It reminded her of Rihanna, sick and miserable with the same flu back home.

Zia swiped the menu embedded in the table and entered their orders. "After lunch, let's do low-grav karaoke again!"

"I'll pass." Zia could sing and dance, but Willow was about as graceful as a walrus on a trampoline, even when floating in midair. "How about we check out the sleep pods in the spa and take a nap? The simulation makes it seem like you're sleeping on silk, furs, velvet, drifting in water, or floating. Sounds awesome, right?" According to the spa Smartbrochures, the latest model boasted pressurized air nodules that allowed guests to experience the weightlessness of space while they slept.

"Naps are for babies!" Benjie flipped his wrist and the Ace of Spades in his hand disappeared. "I don't have to take a nap, do I, Mom?"

"No, honey," her mom said. Willow's mom was short, like Willow, like most of the Filipino *titas*, or aunties, in her family. Her black hair was cut in a crisp, angled bob. "I have to work after lunch. But I'll be done before dinner, I promise."

Willow forced herself not to roll her eyes. She had yet to do anything *she* wanted to do, and the damn cruise was more than half over. Guilt pricked her.

Benjie coughed into his arm.

Her mom frowned. "Are you okay? Do you have your inhaler in your backpack?"

"Of course he does. I always make sure." Willow sighed. "Can I borrow your SmartFlex? I want to check in with Rihanna."

"I'm sorry, I let the battery die. But here—take my staff band." Her mom rooted around in her pocket until she pulled out the red wristband. "Unlimited wi-fi at the tech station, one of the perks of the job!"

One of the only perks. But Willow just said, "Thanks."

"That's an administrative key. It can access almost any door on the ship."

Zia's eyes widened. "Wow."

"Don't get any ideas," her mom warned, locking eyes with Willow. "Please be responsible."

"Of course." She stifled a flare of resentment. When was she not responsible?

A service bot brought them virgin margaritas and artisanal chocolate truffles with sides of fresh fruit. Benjie shoved huge chunks of real watermelon into his mouth until his cheeks puffed out like a chipmunk's. Pink juice dribbled down his chin.

Zia giggled. Benjie made a silly face at her and then they both cracked up. Zia's shoulders convulsed. She clapped her hands over her mouth, but it was too late. She did that gasping, donkey-bray laugh she'd perfected as a little kid. Her mom laughed, too.

Willow smiled, but it felt tight, like it didn't fit her face. She was being selfish, she knew that. She loved her family; she just wished she didn't resent them so much.

The cruise director's chirpy voice came over the ship's speakers: "Ladies and gentlemen, I hope you had a wonderful time enjoying Grand Cayman today! A quick note of unfortunate news. Due to unforeseen circumstances, the *Grand Voyager* won't be docking in Belize tomorrow morning as planned."

A collective groan rose from the passengers.

Zia wrinkled her nose again. "What's going on?"

Her mom shrugged. "I think they're trying to avoid that big storm, what's-its-name. It's nothing to worry about."

"I don't care about missing Belize," Zia said. "I'm just glad we're here."

Her mom smiled, her eyes crinkling. "Me too, honey. Me, too." Her mom looked so relaxed as she sipped her margarita. Content and peaceful. Like Willow hadn't seen her for a long time. It made her happy and sad at the same time.

She popped a chocolate raspberry truffle in her mouth and watched the sunlight glimmering across the ocean like burnished steel. It was so beautiful, her heart hurt. Every day that passed made her heart hurt worse.

Pretty soon, this would all be gone. And she'd never get it back again.

10

GABRIEL

The bridge door swung open. One of the Patriots tossed Gabriel a rifle as he rushed in.

He glimpsed the panoramic windows encircling the room. The long, rectangular console featured a bank of digital charts, position readouts, and satmaps hovering over the sleek surface. He'd been in the bridge dozens of times. But never like this.

Time seemed to slow. All sounds faded save for the blood whooshing through his ears. Two bridge officers, a security officer, and the helmsman turned toward them. The captain stood at the center of the console in front of the helm.

"Don't move!" Hollis screamed at the helmsman, a British man who started for the mayday button as soon as he saw the guns. He lunged for the center console, not hesitating for a moment.

Neither did Hollis. She slammed out two shots in quick succession, puncturing the helmsman's chest. He dropped to the floor, red spots spreading like ink stains across his shirt.

The sound ricocheted louder than Gabriel expected. Silencers couldn't suppress all noise from a projectile weapon, not like a pulse gun. But they wouldn't be heard through the steel door and thick walls.

The remaining officers gaped at the fallen body. Gabriel stared with them, fighting down the acid rising in his throat. The rifle hung limply at his side.

Simeon moved swiftly to Captain Johannes Liebenberg and pressed the gun against his head. "No one does anything foolish, and you'll all live. This fight is not with you. Do you understand?"

Hollis swiveled, aiming her pistol at each of the officers until they nodded. The First Officer, an attractive African-American woman with short hair, stood frozen next to the captain.

The Second Officer stood halfway between the console and the exterior door to the portside wing. He trembled, sweat beading his forehead.

"You'll never get away with this," Captain Liebenberg growled.

"Oh, but we already have." Simeon's voice was steady, but Gabriel recognized the rush of his words. Adrenaline must be kicking through him the same way it streaked through his own veins, filling him with frenetic energy. His heart slammed against his ribs.

"This was easier than hijacking a semi-truck." Hollis laughed, her eyes gleaming. "At sea, there's no law enforcement. No surveillance drones. It's like stealing candy from a baby. A rich, gold-gilded baby."

Gabriel turned to the right, where the security monitors mimicked those in the security room—a large transparent screen showing images in quadrants of four, the feed shifting to various hallways and external areas of the ship in ten-second intervals.

Not a thing looked out of place, though fellow freedom fighters were barging into the radio and engine rooms that very second. The screens revealed nothing.

"Everyone against the wall," Simeon ordered. "Davison and Hernandez, tie them up."

"Why are you doing this?" The Second Officer's voice trembled. He was middle-aged, with short blonde hair and a harsh Ukrainian accent tinged with fear. "Are you pirates? Are you with one of the syndicates? Are you—"

Simeon smiled at him. "You read the daily reports from the

Maritime Bureau's Piracy Reporting Center. You tell me—what should you do now?"

The man licked his lips, his chin trembling. "If pirates board your ship, do not resist. They're after money and ransom. Do what they say, they'll leave you alone. Let the company worry about losses."

"Exactly. Now sit down, hold out your hands, and shut up."

"Voyager Enterprises will pay you. They have hostage insurance. Just tell us what—"

"You're no pirate." The captain's voice was laced with barely contained rage. "This isn't the southern Red Sea or the coast of Somalia."

"Sir, I must respectfully ask that you stop talking," Simeon said.

"You're Americans!" Captain Liebenberg glared at Kane and Gabriel, the only two men not wearing ski masks. "You've both served this ship for months, if not years. You're traitors!"

"Shut the hell up!" Kane barked.

"You're terrorists!"

Simeon slammed the butt of his gun against the captain's head. "I said that's enough!"

Liebenberg's head lolled to the side. A trickle of blood dripped down his forehead and thickened in his left eyebrow. "Whatever you want from me, I will not give it to you."

Kane stood splay-legged, monitoring the hostages as Hollis bound their arms behind them with zip-ties. "If he doesn't shut his ugly mouth, I'm gonna do it for him."

The First Officer still stood beside the captain, a grim smile on her face. No one had touched her.

Gabriel started to lift his gun, but Hollis shook her head.

"This is treason! You're murderers." Captain Liebenberg looked straight at Gabriel. "Each and every one of you—murderers and terrorists!"

Gabriel flinched. His free hand curled into a fist at his side.

"I'm warning you!" Kane swung his weapon around to point at the captain.

The captain raised his chin defiantly. "I'll see you get the needle, if it's the last thing I do."

"Nah, man." Kane smiled with a fierce slash of teeth. "This is the last thing you'll do."

And he pressed the trigger.

11

WILLOW

"Hey! Gwyneth!"

Willow spun around, her cheeks heating. It was the boy from earlier in the week, Finn. Her heart gave a little jolt. He waved energetically from the center of the royal promenade, an awkward giant in a sea of elegant dresses and perfect faces scrunched in disapproval. She liked him already.

"Why is that guy calling you Gwyneth?" Zia asked, her nose wrinkling.

"Just go with it," Willow hissed. She was headed for the library with Zia in tow. After lunch, her mom had dropped Benjie off at the Kid Zone on her way to housekeeping. Willow was stuck with Zia yet again.

"Finn Ellington-Fletcher," he said as he strode up to them, as if Willow could have forgotten. He was a giant towering over her short frame, at least 6'6" and big all over. He was around her age, with smooth walnut-brown skin, dimples in his cheeks, and a gap in his slightly crooked teeth.

She tucked her hair behind her ears and attempted a sophisticated smile. "Hey, Finn. Uh, this is my sister … Monique."

Monique? Zia mouthed in horror. Willow pinched her arm. She wasn't going to let her sister ruin this, too.

"So . . . you having fun?" Willow managed. She was terrible with conversation, especially with an elite. Though he didn't act like any elite she'd ever met.

Finn shrugged, rolling his massive shoulders. "What's not to love? Though I gotta say, getting shunned by my more affluent and socially adept peers has its upsides. One gets to know the tomes in the quaint library quite well."

Willow laughed before she could stop herself. Maybe that was rude, but he didn't seem offended. "Why would you be shunned?"

He gestured at himself. "Too big. Too loud. Too much everything. Maybe I'm not refined enough for their tastes?"

"Their loss." She flushed. "Um, we're headed there—to the library, I mean," she blurted before she could stop herself. She cleared her throat, pretending she didn't care either way. "I mean, you're welcome to come if—"

"I'd love to." Finn fell into step beside her. Zia trailed behind them, scowling furiously.

The library was half tech station, half bookshelves filled with old, mostly leather-bound books. She swiped her mom's staff wristband over the sensor integrated into the sleek black desk. The navbar display appeared, hovering in front of her. She stared at the display. No vids from Rihanna. Nothing. Not even text.

Willow: *You there?*

Nothing.

Willow: *Rihanna?*

No response. She frowned. "This isn't working. I can't connect."

"Maybe the satellite is down 'cause of that storm." Finn lumbered over and scanned his wristband across a different desk sensor. Nothing. He checked his SmartFlex, but it remained as still and silent as the computer.

He grinned mischievously. "We'll just have to roll with the old and archaic forms of entertainment. Would you enjoy a rousing game of mini-golf?"

Willow tugged at her dress. "In this?"

"Excuses, excuses."

She flushed again. "Why not?"

Finn smiled wider, revealing the adorable gap between his front teeth. "Not quite a ringing endorsement, but I'll take it."

Zia's face brightened. "Can I come?"

"It's totally fine if she—" Finn started.

"No way." Frustration and resentment boiled inside her. She'd had enough of babysitting. She didn't want Zia around, ruining everything when she'd finally met someone. "Why don't you hang out here? Read an actual book or something. We'll meet up later."

"I'm not supposed to—"

Willow whirled on her. "Enough! You're not a baby. Stop acting like one."

Zia blanched. "But—"

"I'm doing what I want for once! If that's a sucky game of mini-golf, so be it."

"Hey!" Finn said with mock indignation.

Zia slammed her book shut with a scowl, dust puffing from the pages. "Why can't I go with you?"

Willow refused to feel guilty. Zia still acted like a little kid. At her age, Willow had helped her *lola* cook *tapsilog* and *nilagang baka*, scrubbed toilets, did laundry, and still maintained her grades. Zia needed to grow the hell up. "Because I'm stuck with you all the time!"

Zia sank back in the chair. She did that big doe-eyed thing, like she might cry. "But—"

"Just stop! Don't you get it? I don't want you around!"

Willow regretted the words as soon as they'd left her mouth. But it was the truth. Everything was piling up on her—her irritation at her siblings, frustration with her mom, worry over Rihanna, the gut-wrenching disappointment of her whole stupid life.

It was too much. She needed to get away. She needed to have a few moments of fun for herself or her head was going to explode.

She fled the library before she could see the hurt on her sister's face.

———

Willow strode beside Finn, trying not to wobble in her heels. They were Rihanna's, and she wasn't used to wearing them. The straps rubbed painfully against her fresh blisters.

They passed dozens of people staring down at their SmartFlex cuffs, tapping the screen, shaking their wrists, and holding it to their ears, like their volume just wasn't turned up enough. The connection must be severed ship-wide.

"Your sister likes you," Finn said. "That's cool."

She took a deep breath, willing herself to calm down, to relax. This was her time now. "She's a pain in the butt."

"You don't usually get along?"

"It's—complicated. You have any siblings?"

"Only child."

"You're lucky."

"It's actually pretty lonely. I don't recommend it."

They climbed the stairs to the lido deck and passed through the glass doors. Outside, the sky glowered a steely gray. The wind whipped her dress around her thighs and snarled her hair. "You have no idea what I'd give to be left alone—to just *be* without having to think about them all the time."

"I think you might miss it."

She reigned in her frustration. It wasn't Finn's fault. It wasn't even Zia's fault. Her mom was the one always running off to please her boss, abandoning Willow with her siblings. She'd make it up to Zia later. "I know, I know. You're telling me the grass is always greener on the other side."

"You know where the grass is greenest, right?" He waggled his eyebrows at her. "Over a septic tank."

She snorted.

"Let that little pearl of wisdom sink in for a bit."

"I see your point. I don't concede, though. You've never shared a bathroom with my sister." She winced at her mistake. Rich kids had their own bathrooms larger than her apartment. They never shared anything.

But Finn didn't seem to notice. He moved to the glass railing. "There are some little boats out here. Don't they know a massive storm is coming? Come look at these waves!"

"I'll stay back here, thanks."

"What? Why?"

She swallowed. "I have this little thing about heights. That's like fourteen stories straight down. How are those glass railings not a safety hazard? I mean, a strong gust of wind could push you right over."

"Not me." Finn flexed his arms, shooting her a goofy grin. "I'm much too strong and manly."

"I didn't mean you, of course. I would never suggest such a thing." The air seemed lighter up here. She could breathe freely.

She liked the way he was looking at her. Finn saw what she wanted him to see—what she could be, if she ever got the chance.

12

GABRIEL

Gabriel stared at the captain's slumped body, his stomach churning. "You didn't have to do that."

Kane glowered at him. "He irritated the hell out of me. You got a problem?"

"Nobody has a problem," Simeon said coolly. "As long as we stick to the plan."

"That was the plan?" Gabriel gestured at the dead captain, his voice rising. It was difficult to breathe. There wasn't enough oxygen in the room. In all the months he'd imagined this scene, it hadn't gone like this. "He didn't do anything. He's not—"

"Calm down, son. There is collateral damage in every war. Unfortunately, he chose his side long ago."

"Didn't we need him?" Hollis asked.

"Anything you needed from him, I can do." The First Officer wiped in vain at several specks of red on her uniform. She looked up with a grim smile. "Aisha Walsh, at your service."

Kane slung his rifle over his shoulder and dragged the two bodies around the other side of the console. The two remaining hostages huddled against the far wall in silence, their faces drained of color.

Simeon spoke into his walkie-talkie. "Mission completed. No casualties on our side."

"What happens next?" Gabriel asked. "When do the others get here?"

"Didn't I say to trust me, son?" Simeon slapped his shoulder. "Walsh will take command of the ship. We've taken out the secret service and private security agents per the information you provided us earlier. Everything is on schedule."

Hollis set up the portable satellite navigation system, since the ship's communications were still down. She placed two EMMASAT satphones on the console. "We continue as if nothing has happened, at least until our friends arrive."

Simeon grinned. "And we have many friends. More than we can count."

The radar blipped and Walsh turned back to the console. "These are your boys?" She pointed to five small green dots making their way toward the ship.

Simeon jerked his mask off his face. "Captain Cheng and his men, right on time."

"Is he a Patriot?" Gabriel asked.

"Just hired grunts, like I said before."

"Pirates," Hollis said in disgust.

Gabriel rubbed his slick palms against his pant legs. "Pirates?"

Simeon shrugged. "Look, this is a twenty-billion-dollar-a-year business—hijacking, cargo theft, drug running, smuggling. Syndicates go after ships containing high value commodities easy to sell on the black market: diesel fuel, steel, and copper concentrates."

"Captain Cheng is part of the Singapore syndicate," Kane said. "They control the South China Sea and Malacca Strait, with branches in Vietnam, Malaysia, the Philippines, and now Central America. Their connections with officials in the U.S. government and senior officials on mainland China keep their operations well protected."

Gabriel still couldn't breathe properly. The stench of blood stung his nostrils. He could taste it, sour and metallic. He'd known others were involved. He just assumed they would be fellow Patriots, not hired criminals. Not pirates. "Who are these people?"

"Gabriel, my son." Simeon put his hand on his shoulder. "We need them. They're a means to an end. How do you think we infiltrated the ship so easily as crew? The syndicate uses body shops based in radicalized countries—Indonesia, Pakistan, the Philippines. The syndicate pays the agencies to place certain applicants on the rolls, even with zero experience, with screening completely bypassed or fabricated, including retinal and bioscans."

Kane cracked his knuckles, a satisfied smirk on his face. "It's the perfect crime. How would anyone begin to investigate? In which jurisdiction? A ship built in Japan, owned by a corporation in Malta, managed by a company in Cypress, crewed by Filipinos, financed by a British bank, carrying cargo by multinational companies or international passengers. How could you follow such a paper trail? Dirty officials either look the other way or take part in the piracy."

"Money is pouring in, and everyone wants a drink," Simeon said. "Less than ten percent of attacks are even reported."

Kane grinned. "Of course, we'll proudly admit to ours. Even then, the government will have a hell of a time nailing any actual evidence to the wall."

Simeon moved to the main console. "These guys know how to take over a ship. They've made a profession of it. They'll do anything for the right price. Offer them twenty grand apiece, they'll massacre the entire ship."

Gabriel tried to keep his expression flat, but the blood drained from his face.

"Calm down, kid," Hollis said. "It's just first-time jitters. You'll be fine."

He didn't feel fine. His stomach roiled. But arguing only made him sound weak. Complaining only deepened Simeon's irritation. Simeon had vouched for him. He had to prove his worth, his value to the cause. He fell silent.

Simeon bent over the GPS holo map, then pointed. "Here."

Walsh raised her eyebrows. "That will take us right through the tropical storm, sir."

"The storm will provide cover. Besides, we only have a small window to meet our extraction point. We've paid our weight in gold, but the syndicate doesn't mess around. We make it, or we're left stranded on the ship. Can we make it, Captain Walsh?"

After a moment's hesitation, she nodded. She swiped the console screen, adjusting their course.

"Gabriel, come with me." Simeon took his arm and led him through the exterior starboard door. The bridge wing looked like the narrow wing of an aircraft. It was a suspended walkway supported by thin corbeled struts extending over the ocean a hundred feet below.

The sea heaved in choppy waves, the silver water crinkling like foil. The wind beat about his face, whipping his uniform. The sky was battleship gray, as if preparing for war.

Gabriel couldn't get the bodies out of his mind. Nausea roiled through him. His stomach heaved, and he vomited over the side. He spat the sour acid out of his mouth and wiped his face with the sleeve of his shirt. Shame swept over him at his failure. "I'm sorry."

"I puked at my first dead body, too. Don't worry."

Silence stretched between them. Even speaking the words felt like a betrayal. "We didn't have to kill them, the captain and the helmsman. They weren't—"

Simeon kept his hand on Gabriel's arm. "The helmsman refused to listen to the warning I offered him. He could have lived. He chose otherwise. The captain wouldn't listen to reason. I wouldn't have chosen for him to die, but it is what it is. We prepared for the possibility. That's why we recruited Walsh. She's a Patriot, and a damn fine one. She'll fulfill the duties of the captain. We must accept this, Gabriel."

He stared down at the water, fighting against the weakness inside him. The body of the captain and his dead eyes shimmered in his vision. He blinked.

"Every good soldier in every war experiences the same thing," Simeon said. "In the Revolutionary War, neighbors fought on opposite sides. In the Civil War, brother killed brother. In World War Two, we dropped atomic bombs on Hiroshima and Nagasaki, killing hundreds of thousands of civilians. That bomb we dropped on North Korea three years ago prevented nuclear war. Why did we do it? Because we fought for a larger cause, a greater good.

"We are fighting for the greater good, Gabriel. You must never forget. Innocent people are killed in war every day, including those sanctioned by our own government. But you seldom hear our government speak of this, unless they're attacking someone else for doing the exact same thing."

Gabriel's hands curled into fists. Simeon spoke the truth. He believed it.

"They will try to get in your head," Simeon said. "They will try to twist your own goodness and use it against you. We must remain strong. Your mother died needlessly because of Declan Black's greed. Your father died of a blight manufactured by corporations right here in this country.

"We've lost more and more of our freedoms even as the government leaves us to starve. And now they want to chip us, too? Track us like like dogs? They'll imprison us in internment camps next. This is what we're fighting against. Yes, we may have to deal with certain . . . undesirables. But it is all for the cause. We are true patriots, fighting for our freedom."

He nodded, clenching his jaw. "We are freedom fighters."

"Yes, we are. And I need you. Now is the time to collect the daughter of Declan Black and get her somewhere safe, until I call for you. Take her by force if you have to, but until the rest of the ship is secured, it would be best to stay under the radar."

Gabriel kept his expression even. He felt nothing for her. Then why did the thought of kidnapping her by force twist his gut in revulsion? Last night, when he'd seen her cowering before her father, he'd longed to smash Declan Black's perfect white teeth down his arrogant throat.

He took a deep breath, forcing out thoughts of the girl, forcing out the images of dead bodies, forcing out his fear and doubt and hesitation. He was a soldier. He couldn't afford misgivings. Not now.

The arrogant, indifferent elite had to pay for their crimes. The suffering people needed a voice. They needed someone who would fight for them.

The New Patriots fought for them. Gabriel fought for them. This was his purpose. This was a cause worth killing for, dying for.

"I'm ready," he said, stronger now. "But my brother. I haven't had a chance to warn him. I know you wanted him to fight for us. But it's not in him." Another pang of regret struck him. He should never have let Micah on the ship.

Simeon held up a hand, his eyes kind. "Your emotions are your weakness. In war, compassion is a flaw, a risk. Don't let your feelings for anyone get in the way. Especially your brother. Do you understand?"

His throat tightened. He wouldn't let Simeon down again. He wouldn't let the cause down. "Yes, sir. But—"

"You attend to your duty, and I will ensure that he's out of harm's way."

"Yes, sir." They turned back toward the bridge. The wind swirled around them. The sky darkened, the horizon deepening like a dark, pulsing bruise.

"Take a moment, son." Triumph thrummed through Simeon's voice. "We have officially taken command of the *Grand Voyager*."

13

AMELIA

Ten minutes into dinner, another headache struck Amelia in the back of her head. The pain pulsed from the base of her neck to her temples.

The holo-stars shimmering above her head dazzled like diamonds. But the light only hurt her eyes. At the captain's table, the captain was conspicuously missing. Declan huddled with one of his advisers just outside the Oasis dining room's main entrance, his expression strained. Senator López hadn't even bothered to show up.

The remaining guests talked in hushed, agitated voices and repeatedly checked their disconnected SmartFlex cuffs. Among the strained whispers, she heard the word Hydra mentioned more than once, whatever that meant.

The passengers were tense—upset over what might or might not be happening back home, irritated over the canceled shore excursion in Belize coupled with losing their net connection, and now this—lousy weather to top it off. The waves were choppy. Some people looked green as the floor rolled beneath them.

She scanned the opulent dining room and caught sight of Gabriel standing outside the starboard side doorway. He lifted his fingers to his lips and mimed a smoke.

Her stomach turned over. She wanted to see him. And her father wasn't there to stop her. "I'm getting some air," she said to her mother. She tucked her clutch under her arm and escaped the Oasis dining room.

She breathed in the scent of brine, the wild and salty sea. The wind whipped her hair across her face. The ozone-tinged air raised goosebumps on her arms. For a moment, she closed her eyes and just listened to the crashing waves and the roar of the wind, willing herself to calm down.

"Did I miss the costume party memo?"

"What?"

Gabriel eyed her dress. "The Greek goddess getup."

She blushed and smoothed her gown. Three crystal-encrusted straps wrapped around her shoulders, with another glittering belt at the bust line. The soft fabric draped around her, the shimmering microfilaments hardly visible. If only she felt the way she looked. "My father picked it out."

He raised an eyebrow. "He picks out all your clothes?"

"Of course not. It's . . . complicated." She didn't feel like trying to explain.

Gabriel peered through the Oasis doorway. "Have you seen my brother? I want to make sure he's okay."

"The waiter, right? The shy, cute one with the glasses?"

"Add a book to that picture, and you've got him pegged." Gabriel glanced over her head at something. His voice was light, but his expression was anxious, a thick line appearing between his brows.

A wave slapped the hull. She shifted against the railing for balance. "Is there something wrong?"

"No, nothing like that." But Gabriel's face tensed, his shoulders hunched as if warding off something. Or preparing for it. "It's just—he and I aren't exactly talking right now."

Amelia thought of Silas, the parting words he'd hurled at her during their fight yesterday on the beach in Ocho Rios. He'd accused her of being just like their mother. Weak and subservient. Pathetic. She winced. "I know the feeling."

"I want to make sure—oh, never mind." He sighed and turned his gaze back to her. "Are you okay?"

"I'm fine. A bit of a headache." Just one more lie to pile on top of all the others. She took a closer look at him. "Are *you* okay?"

A muscle jumped in his cheek, his jaw set. A shadow crossed his face, something in his eyes she couldn't quite read. He shook his head. "A bit of seasickness. No need to worry about me."

"Who says I'm worried?"

He smiled, but it didn't reach his eyes. "Certainly not me."

In the distance, flickers of lightning lit up the menacing black clouds. Her dress lashed at her legs. Electrons singed the air with nervous energy. "Maybe we both need to be worried about that storm."

"That's miles away."

"Looks like we're headed right for it."

"Appearances can be deceiving."

She knew that better than most. "Then why are the outside decks closing?"

"Safety precaution." Gabriel lit a cigarette and handed it to her. "Nothing to worry about."

She hesitated for a moment. Silas's words rang in her ears. *You're just like her.* She needed a distraction. She took the cigarette and inhaled.

Gabriel raised his brows. "Are you sure you're okay? You seem upset."

She kept her gaze on the water crashing below. She couldn't talk about the anxiety roiling in the pit of her stomach, the fights with her brother, how her father's contempt filled her with a dark, writhing shame like a living thing. "I'll be fine. I just need—I need a minute."

"Let me take you down to the officers' deck. It's out of the wind. They've got a gourmet coffee bar, lounge chairs, a hot tub."

Her stomach fluttered against her will. He was so close, she could see the stubble on his jaw, his long, thick lashes. Heat crept into her cheeks. "Aren't you supposed to be working?"

"Aren't you supposed to be in there?" He gestured in the direction of the Oasis dining room. "Come on. Can't you feel it in the air? Something wants to happen."

She arched her brow skeptically.

"What? You don't believe in fate? You don't believe some things are meant to be?"

Her headache was a dull thud against the back of her brain. She remembered that terrible look of disdain on her brother's face. *You're as bad as she is.* The whisper was still there, tormenting her. Was he right?

Helplessness and shame cramped her stomach. She hated it, hated that feeling. Her mother never did anything. Her mother let it happen, over and over. But so did she. Silas was right. She was turning into a younger, meeker version of their mother, doomed to spend the rest of her life crushed beneath their father's iron will.

The thought suffocated the breath from her lungs.

No. The whisper was so deep inside she barely heard it over the roar of the wind and the waves. If she didn't do *something*, if she didn't make some choice for herself, however small, she was sealing her own fate. Her future would snap shut over her head like a steel trap.

She took one last drag of her cigarette. "Yes."

14

WILLOW

"Told you I'd destroy you." Finn grinned wickedly as he hefted his golf club over his shoulder.

Willow glared at him. She planted her feet on the sleek white surface and aimed her club at New York. They'd chosen City Icons as their course, each hole a glimmering holograph of a different city or monument.

She sent the neon-blue digital ball spinning between two glowing skyscrapers and over a little bridge, narrowly dodging the Empire State building. It went straight into the Hudson River.

Finn scored another hole-in-one, his bright yellow ball wobbling into a holo version of Central Park like it had a mind of its own.

She snorted. "You failed to tell me you're some kind of mini-golf prodigy."

"That's the hustle, darling." He checked the leaderboard that automatically tallied their scores and gave her a crooked grin. "Only fifteen shots behind with one hole to go. Remember, you're about to owe me four hundred credits. Don't let the pressure get to you, Gwyneth."

"Save your pity." She shoved her hair out of her face. She hated the prospect of having to admit she didn't have forty credits, let alone four hundred.

Flashes of light threaded through the clouds. Finn rolled his shoulders. His oversized polo flapped against him like a flag snapping in the wind. "Wanna make more excuses for your lame-ass skills?"

She refused to tell him she didn't have time for any games. At home, she juggled classwork with daily shifts as a groundskeeper for a landscaping company to help pay the bills. She trimmed hedges, pulled weeds, hacked errant branches, and lugged forty-pound bags of mulch and fertilizer with the best of them. Metalheads could do the work, but human labor was cheaper, at least in landscaping.

She shook those thoughts out of her head. "I don't spend all my leisure hours playing mini-golf, unlike you."

He grinned. "My parents are kinda weird. We love mini-golf. Get this. Before the divorce, we even had board-game night. Sorry, Candy Land, Monopoly, the whole deal. Mega-lame, right? It's a blast though, once you put aside your pride."

"I guess. My dad liked poker back in the day." She tried not to think of the time before, when her family was whole. Her dad taught Benjie how to shuffle cards, how to use sleight of hand, how to bluff. Back before he had to take on a third shift to keep the bills paid. In his exhaustion, he'd wrapped his ancient, manual car around a tree.

Her heart twinged. She pushed the dark memories out of her head. This was her escape, her time to herself, her moment of fun. Her mom was so worried and stressed all the time, she was miserable.

But not Willow. Not today.

Before she could hit the last ball, a crew member made his way out to them, maneuvering around the massive red and black funnel looming three stories above them. It blocked the entire mid and front of the ship from sight. Behind him, a metalhead directed a hover cart piled high with lounge cushions.

"We're closing the decks due to inclement weather!" he shouted.

"What inclement weather?" Finn shouted back.

"Very funny, sir," the guy said. "My job is to clear the decks of all potential debris. I'll go ahead and take those."

They handed him their clubs. After he left, Finn turned to her. "I guess it *is* colder than Jack Frost's balls out here."

She wrapped her arms around herself to keep from shivering. "That's one way to put it. Let's get out of here."

She took several steps before she realized Finn was no longer beside her. She turned around, the wind a dull roar in her ears. Finn leaned over the railing, shielding his eyes with his hand. He didn't speak, only pointed. She edged a few feet closer and looked.

The dark sea heaved far below them. Her stomach lurched, her head spinning. She was about to leap back from the edge when something caught her eye.

Boats. Four—no, five—of them, speedboats traveling fast, coming up along the starboard side of the *Grand Voyager*. The boats looked almost like toys, if not for the cluster of men on each boat. They wore dark clothes and carried little sticks in their hands.

Her stomach dropped to her toes. "What—who is that?"

Finn turned to her. The whites of his eyes were huge. "I'm no expert, but I believe those are pirates."

"What?" She imagined cartoon peg-legs, feathered hats, patches over eyes. She'd heard of pirates taking boats, but cargo ships and oil rigs over in Indonesia and Malaysia and South Africa, countries and continents she'd never been to and never would. Back in the Philippines, she had a second cousin who'd been arrested for piracy a few years ago. But she never imagined anything like this.

They stood, frozen in shock, unable to do a thing but watch in growing horror as the boats closed in. Something small and dark flew through the air and caught on the lowest deck. A rope with a grappling hook on one end. Then another and another. The pirates climbed the ropes, hand over hand like scrabbling spiders.

"Oh, hell," she breathed.

A half-dozen security officers burst onto Deck Four, gesturing wildly, guns in their hands. They aimed at the pirates. A few pirates slipped and fell into the snarling sea.

There were too many of them. Another crawled up to replace the one they lost. Past the ship's lights, the boats swerved, skimming like shadows.

Further down the lido deck, two other officers raced to a large, dark shape. They uncovered an object that looked like a small satellite.

"What are they doing?" Willow asked.

"That's an LRAD, a sonic cannon," Finn yelled in her ear.

The security officers aimed the sonic cannon at one of the boats. The boat jerked and parried, then spun a few times and sped away.

The men appeared to be falling to their knees. One fell out of the boat, arms pinwheeling. Undeterred, the four other boats sped closer and drew parallel to the *Voyager*.

"Look out!" Finn grabbed her arm and shoved her down. She stumbled and fell, scraping her elbows and knees on the deck. She lifted her head in time to see a bright orange ball carve a graceful arc toward the ship.

A firebomb exploded on the lido deck. The world flashed orange beneath her eyelids.

After several moments, she climbed to her hands and knees. The hover cart from earlier was tipped on its side. The metalhead lay next to it. Its scorched silicone skin had peeled away, revealing the metal, wires, and nanotubes of its insides.

Further down the deck, both security officers manning the sonic cannon had fallen, their bodies unmoving. The LRAD was broken off its base and riddled with gunshot holes.

"We've got to get out of here!" She tried to move, but her legs were weak and sloshy as water. Terror pulsed in every cell of her being.

"Crawl around the other side of the funnel. I think they're only on the starboard side." Finn started to crawl, shimmying on his belly.

She still couldn't move. She kept seeing the bodies of the security officers, their white uniforms blooming red.

"Gwyneth, come on!"

The use of the name she'd given him—her lie so much more

grotesque now that they had to flee for their lives—jolted her out of her fugue.

Before she turned and crawled after Finn, she saw them. On Deck Four, a dozen shadows leapt over the railing.

15

AMELIA

Lightning shimmered in the distance. The air was heavy with humidity. Damp strands of hair stuck to Amelia's forehead and neck. The officers' deck was deserted and partially shielded on either side by the steel walls of the ship and the deck above it.

"Everybody's either at the crew mess hall, working their shifts, or entertaining high-value guests. We've got this place to ourselves." His walkie-talkie spat noise. A voice started to speak, but he turned it off.

"You don't need that?"

"Nah. Everything's fine." He placed the walkie-talkie on a small patio table outside the doorway and shot her an appraising look. His brow wrinkled in concern. "You look cold. You're welcome to the hot tub."

Her cheeks flushed."I can't."

"Why not?"

Her mind flailed for an excuse before landing on the most obvious one. She fluttered her dress. "I'm a bit overdressed."

"No one's here to judge you."

She'd never been in a hot tub in her life. She couldn't. Too much heat was dangerous. But she was so tired of all the rules, all the don'ts, can'ts, and shouldn'ts governing her life.

"Maybe I can put my feet in." She put her clutch on the table next to his walkie-talkie and kicked off her heels. She settled gingerly on the tiled edge of the hot tub, hiking her dress up past her knees. The water bubbled hot and soothing against her shins.

Gabriel sat down beside her. He tugged off his shiny black shoes and socks and rolled up his pant legs. "Your father seems upset. He's been on his SmartFlex constantly the last couple of days."

"Have you heard what's happening on the mainland?"

Lines bracketed his mouth, his expression taut. "I've heard enough. They're saying the CDC declared a state of emergency. I have a friend in Baltimore who messaged me yesterday. He's sick. He's sick and he stood in line for six hours to get that damn shot. Your father's latest *cure.*"

"That's not his fault," she said automatically. "The bat-flu is just one of a thousand strains. It mutates. By the time they synthesize a vaccine, it might be a completely different bug."

He clicked his tongue between his teeth. "I thought it was for every strain, hence the term universal."

She flushed. "Lots of things can go wrong with vaccines."

"That's not what they advertised. They promised a *miracle.*" His gaze raked over her, his eyes hard, almost angry.

She blinked, breaking eye contact. "You say that like it's someone's *fault.*"

"Maybe it is."

"Disease always spreads in dense, urban areas. It's been that way forever, since the flu epidemic in nineteen eighteen, the bubonic plague before that and all the epidemics since then—the India outbreak, the bat strain that wiped out half of Dublin five years ago. It's how outbreaks work. It's no one's fault. That's ridiculous."

"Is it?"

"You sound like you're blaming my father." Her words felt brittle in her mouth. Hollow. She thought of Silas. Of her mother, always defending her father, no matter what.

"Your father has made a fortune and a career out of the suffering of others. This universal vaccine. His so-called cancer cure."

"It's not a cure." Her father had first gained world-wide fame when BioGen announced they'd discovered a nanoparticle treatment that permanently reduced cancerous tumor growth. But continuous, life-long medication was required, and her father had received intense criticism for its high cost.

"Close enough," Gabriel said bitterly. "Now his Coalition wants to implant microchips in every citizen."

"The VitaliChip will minimize the spread of all these epidemics by alerting health and government officials of infection immediately. It can detect the presence of elevated antibodies in the blood and recognize markers for over thirty diseases. It'll save millions of lives."

"And how many billions will BioGen rake in, huh?"

Her mouth pressed into a thin line. "That's unfair. You think he should bankrupt his companies by giving it away?"

"No. I think its real purpose is to control us all, chipping us like the dogs they think we are—"

"That's not true."

Gabriel's eyes narrowed, his nostrils flaring like he was gearing up for an argument. But then he stopped. He sucked in his breath, his jaw muscle ticking. "Maybe we should change the subject."

She bit back a flare of frustration. "Maybe we should."

The silence lengthened, uncomfortable and tense. This was a mistake. She should leave. She should go back to the Oasis dining room where she belonged. But she wanted to be there even less than she wanted to be here.

The hot, churning water massaged her legs. Warmth seeped into her body. She stared at the tangerine and violet colors flickering across the bubbling water. She didn't want to leave. "Let's try talking about something nice, shall we? I'll start. If you could do anything, what would you do?"

"I'd change the world."

"Seriously?"

"I would rid politics of corruption. Get rid of the corrupt Coalition. Give the power back to the people."

"Sounds like a nice dream."

"It's real. We could fix things. Real change could happen, if people would stand up."

"Stand up against what? The disappearing bees? The droughts? The crop blights? The dying rivers? Are you going to do a dance and bring rain back to the drought-ravaged west?"

"All problems caused by humans who put greed above protecting the next generation."

"Humans didn't kill off the bees or create deadly plagues or call hurricanes from the sky to decimate cities. Those are acts of God."

He laughed, but the sound came out coarse and jagged. "Why would God do anything like that?"

"Because—" she stopped. The words in her head were her father's, not her own. She sighed. "You know what? Never mind."

For a moment, they were quiet. The lights inside the spa glowed turquoise. The steam dampened her dress, heating her legs. Thunder rumbled in the distance.

"What about you?" Gabriel asked. "If you could be anywhere, do anything, what would you do?"

That answer, at least, was easy. She rubbed the marks on the pads of her fingertips, the permanent indentations of the violin strings from years of dedicated practice. At first, she'd played for her father, for that fleeting flash of approval in his eyes. Her father, who didn't value art or music, but who did merit winning and status, anything that reflected honor and prestige back on him.

Her whole life, everything she'd ever done was to please him.

But she played for herself, too. She'd never regretted the sacrifices her music demanded, the rehearsals, auditions, recitals, and competitions—it was all worth it.

"I'd be at Juilliard, practicing six hours a day. Becoming better. Becoming the best. I'd play for the Chicago Symphony Orchestra or the Vienna Philharmonic."

Gabriel leaned back on his hands. "Sounds like a lot of work for a rich girl who could spend the rest of her life doing lunch, country club hopping, and getting massages."

She flushed. "Money doesn't automatically make people lazy."

"Could've fooled me."

Her headache pulsed at the base of her neck. He seemed angry all of a sudden. Tense and irritable. No matter how hard they tried, this conversation seemed to roll back around to the same antagonistic themes. Who had money. Who didn't. And whose fault it was. They were simply too different.

Part of her wanted to leave, to escape, to give up on this whole thing. But something wouldn't let her. "You work on a cruise ship—you only see people when they're relaxing, not the eighty-hour weeks they pulled for the previous six months."

"Wealth is its own drug. It inoculates you from need. From want. From risk." The bitterness in his voice hit her like a slap.

"You think I don't want things?" she asked, incredulous.

"Not like the rest of us. You don't know need. You don't know hunger."

"That's not true."

"And you, especially."

She wiped sweat from her brow. A wave of dizziness swept through her. "What's that supposed to mean?"

He shot her a blistering look. "Don't play coy. You have that coveted mix—insane wealth *and* the kind of beauty no amount of money can buy. You live a life apart from mere mortals."

Anger swelled through her. She was used to such judgments. Usually she didn't let them bother her. But this was different. She didn't know why, but she cared what he thought about her, this boy with the bronze skin, the intense eyes and the unyielding set to his mouth. She swallowed. "You don't know me."

"I don't need to. Wealth and class always come with privilege."

"Look, I don't know your life, obviously. But you don't know mine, either." Her chest tightened. The edges of her fingers tingled. "Maybe this wasn't such a great idea."

Her SmartFlex beeped. "Warning. Your biostats have exceeded healthy parameters. Please cool your temperature immediately—"

"Disengage." The sensors worked without internet access. But she didn't need her SmartFlex to tell her something was wrong. She lifted her legs out of the water and stood on the ledge of the hot tub. She swayed as a wave of dizziness hit her.

"Wait—" Gabriel said.

She stepped off the ledge just as the ship rolled sharply. She stumbled and lurched forward.

Gabriel grabbed her arm and helped her to her feet. "You okay?"

She pushed away from him. "I don't need your help."

"You look pale—paler than normal." The aggression leaked out of his voice, replaced with concern. He pulled out a chair at a patio table with a closed umbrella. "Sit."

She sat down. But the dizziness didn't go away. The headache pulsed against the walls of her skull. Lights danced in front of her vision. *No. Please no. Not now.*

She hated this feeling—this weakness. Her clutch lay on the table where she'd left it. She wouldn't need it. She willed herself not to need it.

She bent her head, breathing hard and rubbing the charms of her bracelet, pressing the point of the violin into the tip of her index finger.

Gabriel stood in front of her, watching warily.

The tingling sensation spread up her arms, flooded her belly. Her thoughts came slow and sluggish.

Her tongue thickened in her mouth. It was hard to breathe, impossible to speak.

Make it stop. Not here. Not now.

But it didn't matter what she wanted. It was coming.

16

MICAH

M icah wiped the sweat from his brow as he pushed through the galley doors, hefting the evening's special meal—hand-cut Charolais steak tartare placed on sterling silver trays with sparklers projecting from each side.

The lights went out, plunging the Oasis dining room into darkness. The crowd gave a collective gasp. They oohed and aahed as the first waiter pushed through the galley swing doors, the sparklers glittering and flashing like jewels.

The string quartet started in on a rousing song. The waiters marched around the tables as the guests clapped in time. They threaded their way through the room until the procession encircled the table of honor, all eyes on them in the dark.

Micah stopped next to Amelia's mother, Elise Black. The captain wasn't the only one missing. So was Amelia. His heart dropped. He wanted to hear her play her violin again.

He balanced the weight of the tray carefully, watchful of the sparklers burning down their wicks, the sparks getting much too close to his white tuxedo sleeve.

Then he felt it. A sudden swift movement behind him.

Several sharp cracks split the air. Multiple panes of glass shattered all at once, crashing to the floor.

The quartet squealed to a halt. Guests froze mid-clap. Someone screamed. A cacophony of angry shouting filled the dining room.

It was hard to see anything in the dark. The sparklers blinded his night vision. He shoved the platter to the table and twisted around.

He glimpsed large shapes moving fast. Shadows erupted into the dining room from the main entryway. They came through the starboard deck entrance like a horde of ants boiling out from a kicked nest.

Micah froze. His body went hot then cold, cold all over, like the cold was in his very cells.

The *Grand Voyager* was under attack.

Guests leapt to their feet, screaming and bumbling in the dark in blind panic. They bumped into each other, struck tables, knocked over chairs. Cutlery and wine glasses smashed to the floor.

Several more shots cracked the air, followed by orange flashes. Men shrieked unintelligible words.

A bullet struck one of the chandeliers, the shattered crystals raining down on Micah's head. The lights flickered on, revealing a scene too horrific to possibly be real.

He couldn't move. The attackers shouted, swinging their weapons, shooting indiscriminately into the crowd. Everyone yelled and screamed. The Oasis dining room fell into chaos.

Two security guards emerged from behind the bar area, shooting at the attackers. They went down fast and easy, as easy as the rest of the wild, screaming throng.

A woman in a zebra-striped mini skirt ran in a crazed zigzag pattern in front of him. A burst of gunfire exploded, and she dropped to the floor.

An older couple in matching white outfits who'd ordered steak and mashed potatoes stood and stared in confusion. Their bodies jittered and they fell, the old man on top of the woman like he was protecting her.

Every person standing was a target. Instinctively, Micah crouched next to the table. He glanced up at Mrs. Black. She sat rigid in her seat, her eyes wide with terror. He tugged her arm. "Get down!"

She didn't move.

"Crawl under the table!"

Mrs. Black slipped out of her seat as if in a daze. Micah lifted the tablecloth draped half-way to the floor, and she crawled beneath it on her hands and knees. Others at the table followed her. Declan Black pushed his way in, along with the other CEOs and senators.

They huddled against each other, cramped in the too-small space. Micah pressed against Mrs. Black. She trembled as she mumbled a prayer. Micah said his own desperate prayers.

"My daughter," Mrs. Black said. "I don't know where she is."

"Shut up," someone hissed. Micah's shoulder bumped against the table leg. There was a rustle of movement. He strained his ears, his heart banging so hard against his ribs he could hardly hear anything at all.

Black boots. An attacker stood next to the table, only two feet from him.

He tried to draw his legs closer to his body, to make himself invisible. Sweat stung his eyes. He bit the inside of his cheeks, trying not to breathe.

"Silence!" a deep male voice shouted. A volley of shots rang out.

The noises quieted. A strange and terrifying hush fell over the room.

"Declan Black, where are you?" The man's voice was strong and commanding. Something about the way he spoke sounded vaguely familiar. "Please reveal yourself from whatever cowardly hole you've crawled into." And then, incredibly, the man laughed.

"Here!" a woman said from among the group huddled beneath the table. "He's right here. Don't shoot! I'm coming out!"

The attacker with the boots moved. With a crash, the table upended, the china dishes and half-full wine glasses spilling to the floor.

"Stand up! Make your entrance!" A man dressed in gray pointed his rifle at the ceiling.

The group stood. Micah blinked in growing horror. More than two dozen men were scattered throughout the dining room. A few wore ship's officer uniforms, a couple others were dressed as wait staff. Most wore dark clothing, strapped in combat gear with masks pulled over their faces.

Each man carried automatic rifles or pulse guns. They almost didn't look human. They could've been robots, or invading aliens.

All over the dining room, tables were upturned, chairs knocked over, broken china and shattered glass everywhere. Steak, potatoes, wine, and various steamed vegetables mashed into the carpet.

And bodies. Arms and legs flopped awkwardly, gowns and tuxedos spattered with red. At least thirty people were dead.

The unharmed guests cowered on the floor. A balding man in his sixties held his wife, who cradled her right arm, blood dribbling between her fingers. Several people lay prostrate, their hands folded over their heads.

A brunette woman whose elaborate bun sagged halfway down her head moaned, holding out her purse beseechingly with both hands, like that was all they wanted, like it could protect her.

Everyone stared at the men with the guns, their faces leached of color, expressions shocked. It was like they were in a trance, a nightmare they all shared together.

A middle-aged woman with a squash-shaped body and a helmet of glossy blonde hair gathered the trail of her dress in one hand and stepped away from the table.

Meredith Jackson-Cooper pointed at the CEO with a shaking finger. "There! That's him. He's the one you want."

"Judas Iscariot," Black muttered, his face darkening.

A man in a waiter's uniform strode up to Black and pressed a gun against his head.

"Ladies and gentlemen, may I have your attention?" A stood on the musicians' platform. Two violins lay at his feet, one broken, its bow shattered. He had a ski mask and a gun but was dressed in a gray suit with a salmon-colored tie.

A passenger. No wonder he'd sounded familiar. Micah had probably served him a dozen times.

"There will be no heroes, not today," the man continued. "We have secured the bridge and the engine room, the radio room, the security department. The lifeboats are guarded. Attempting to escape is futile. Be assured, any attempt at resistance will result in death."

Some of the women started crying. A couple of men, too. The man in the suit ignored them. "You may be wondering who we are and what we want. We are the New Patriots, the sons of a legacy of liberty too long polluted. We are here to claim it back. We hereby declare war on the sham of the corrupt and greedy Unity Coalition—the shadow puppet masters of the former government of this once fine country.

"We declare a civil war upon insatiable greed and we demand—no, we shall have—justice. It is finally time to pay the piper."

Micah stared at the man in horror. The New Patriots? No, he wouldn't believe it. He couldn't.

Three attackers in combat gear guarded the man in the suit. One of them hadn't bothered with a mask. He was Southeast Asian, with a silver scar carved down the right side of his face. He had twitchy eyes and a hard, dangerous smile, like he was born to kill.

The man in the suit turned to the waiter holding a gun on Black. "Take these agents of corruption as hostages and bring them to the bridge. As for the rest—" he spat on the marble floor. "Round them all up. Kill any who resist."

"They'll want Amelia," Mrs. Black said in a low, desperate voice.

Micah turned toward her. Things seemed to be coming from far away. He tried to focus on her face, but everything was jerky, both sharpened and blurry.

Gabriel, he thought over and over. *Gabriel*. He couldn't die yet, with so much anger between him and the only person who mattered. He wasn't ready to die. Not like this. *Please don't let us die. Keep my brother safe.*

"Whatever they want from my husband, he won't give it to them."

Mrs. Black's eyes filled with fear and desperation. "They'll look for his family to use as leverage. Amelia doesn't know."

Micah didn't hesitate. "I'll find her."

She gripped his arm. "God bless you. Thank you."

Several attackers in masks surrounded the group. "You," said a towering bulldozer of a man. The cords in his thick neck bulged, his eyes dark and beady through the slits of the mask.

Micah recognized him. The one Gabriel always complained about for ogling the passengers and harassing the lower level female staff. Kane. The traitor's name was Kane.

Kane gestured at Micah. "Get back to the kitchen where you belong. The rest of you maggots, fall in line."

"Find her," Mrs. Black said.

Kane prodded her in the back with the muzzle of his rifle. "Shut your mouth, you bi—"

"Don't you dare speak to my wife with such impudence!" Declan Black bellowed. Even with a gun to his head, he was self-assured, convinced of his own worth in the world—and sure everyone else knew it, too. "Your sins will find you out!"

The man in the suit strode up to Black. The ski mask made his face featureless and so much more terrifying. "No, my friend. I'm afraid your sins are about to find *you* out."

He smashed the rifle butt into Declan Black's nose. Blood gushed over his lips and dripped onto his tuxedo. The armed men jerked Black to his feet and led the hostages out of the dining room.

Something jolted in Micah's memory. He knew the man in the suit. Knew that walk, that voice. Simeon Pagnini. The leader of Gabriel's New Patriots group.

Dread stuck in his throat like a hook. This couldn't be happening. This couldn't be real. But it was.

Kane elbowed Micah out of the way. He stumbled over an overturned chair and fell, his glasses sliding off his face.

"You!" A brawny man with a huge belly stretching over his belt pointed at Micah. His eyes were dark slits, his mouth full of yellowed, crooked teeth. He jerked Micah up, wrenching his arm. "Back to the kitchen. Make food. Now."

The ship pitched and rolled, and the man took an unsteady step toward him. He rammed the muzzle of his rifle into Micah's stomach. Micah swayed on his feet.

"How many do we have to kill? Or do you *comprende*?"

"We get it," Micah forced out, shoving his glasses back into place with trembling fingers. The attackers marched Micah and the other waiters back into the galley. Two others stood guard over the terrified cook staff.

Think. He had to think. He had to find a way to escape. Then find Amelia for her mother.

But first, he had to find Gabriel. He could not, would not believe Gabriel was involved in this horror. There was an explanation. There had to be. One his muddled, terrified brain was too confused to work out.

He needed to find Gabriel. Then they'd figure out the rest.

He moved to one of the massive stoves on trembling legs, picked up a ladle, and stirred the pot of bubbling blue lobster soup. At least here, he could find weapons. Knives of all shapes and sizes.

He'd get one.

And then? What next?

He had no idea.

17

AMELIA

The pain beat sharp in every cell, in every nerve.

Amelia pried open her clutch with shaking fingers. She gripped one of the auto-injectors, so smooth and sleek, so hard to hold onto when the shaking started, the rattle of the tracks as a train roared closer, seconds from overtaking her.

"Amelia—"

She ignored him. There was no time. She hiked up the fabric of her dress, revealing her bare thigh. She flicked off the cap and jammed the needle hard into her own flesh.

She counted in her mind, the numbers a shimmering, flickering aura. One, two, three, four, five.

If she got to thirty, she would be okay.

Long seconds ticked by. Nothing happened.

The train stopped in its tracks. The darkness didn't come. The seizure didn't grip her body and shake her like a rag doll.

She pulled the needle out of her leg and leaned back in the chair. She sucked in a breath. Her limbs trembled, the muscles weak and watery. But that was the worst of it.

Relief winged through her chest. She tucked her hair behind her ear. "Thirsty."

Gabriel went inside the crew lounge and brought her a bottled water. She drank it greedily. "Thank you."

"What happened?"

She flexed her hands, willed them to stop shaking. "Nothing I can't handle. I'm fine."

He squatted in front of her. "You don't look fine."

She opened her mouth to protest, but she didn't have the strength. Her secret wasn't so secret anymore.

She forced herself to meet his gaze. His expression was concerned, compassionate, the hardness in his eyes gone. She saw no disgust in his gaze, no revulsion.

This moment was a world apart from her normal life. If she didn't speak the truth now, she never would.

"This isn't an EpiPen." She showed him the auto-injector. "It's intramuscular midazolam combined with a few other things. My rescue treatment, for emergencies. For breakthrough seizures."

"Seizures?"

She took a deep breath. Here was the thing she'd never told anyone outside her own family. The secret that lived inside her, that proved her a failure, defective. "I have a form of Dravet Syndrome. Otherwise known as severe myoclonic epilepsy of infancy."

He just watched her, listening.

"The seizures started when I was a baby. Complex febrile seizures, tonic-clonic seizures, partial seizures—I get them all. They cause brain damage. The mortality rate is twenty percent by the age of twenty."

Once she started talking, she couldn't stop. The long-held words poured out of her. "My type of epilepsy is resistant to pharmacotherapy. It's complicated, but I have this protein called P-glycoprotein, which is overexpressed or whatever the medical term is. The anti-seizure medications don't make it through the blood-brain barrier, so they can't reach the part of my brain to stop the seizures."

"But you seem okay."

She smiled in spite of herself. She knew this story by heart. "In a twist of fate—or faith, as my mother would say—she met my father at a hotel bar. He was in town for a medical convention. At the time, he was working on a new treatment for epileptic seizures.

"He used nanotechnology to develop these biodegradable nanoparticles small enough to penetrate cell membranes. They acted as nanocarriers that delivered the anti-seizure medications through the blood-brain barrier directly to the specific targeted areas of my brain."

She didn't tell him the FDA never approved the drug. It didn't make it past the phase II human trials. In certain patients, the nanoparticles became . . . reactive. They induced unforeseen chemical reactions, causing mitochondrial damage and transforming normal cells into cancerous ones.

But Declan had believed a child's brain was more plastic and would be receptive to the nanoparticles. He'd given the drug to her in secret, smuggling the medication out of his lab, defying the FDA, defying the law.

It had worked.

Her mother had told her the stories so many times, how she'd kept Amelia next to her bed, not trusting the sensors her father had placed in the crib mattress.

How she'd spent Amelia's first two years only half-dozing at night, waking repeatedly to read the monitors, to check her daughter's breathing and study the rise and fall of her tiny chest, the pallor of her pale skin. "My mother had to watch me like a hawk."

His lip curled. "That explains a lot."

"What's that supposed to mean?"

He held up his hands in a gesture of supplication. "I'm just saying she still looks at you like that. Like you're made of glass."

"It's that obvious, huh?" She took another gulp of water. "But the medication works. I haven't had a tonic-clonic seizure in years, other than a close call last year when my dosage was off.

"I get migraines, though. Bad ones. But I can handle them. I don't have permanent brain damage, that's the important thing. I'm still me. I just need to be careful of certain things, like heat and fevers, high stress, and photosensitivity stuff."

"That's why no hot tubs."

"Right. No hot tubs."

"Now I know for next time." He smiled, the smile reaching his eyes for the first time that evening. He acted like a normal human being, not like every conversation was a battlefield to be won or lost.

She grinned back at him, some smoldering thing igniting in her belly that had nothing to do with the temperature.

The PA system crackled. "All passengers are required to go to their assigned muster stations immediately. All passengers and crew, please make your way to your assigned muster station."

"What's going on?" she asked.

"The storm must be bigger than we thought. This captain's over-cautious."

"We should go."

"You need to rest."

She glanced at the used auto-injector on the table. "I don't know . . . mustering is for safety reasons, right?"

"You're safe with me." He was attentive, eager, almost giddy. His eyes brightened. "When will you ever have an entire ship to yourself? When will you ever have a night like tonight?"

She looked out at the dark, frothing sea. The deck pitched uneasily beneath her. Thunder crashed.

"I want to show you something." His voice went husky. "The *Grand Voyager* is building a new attraction, the first of its kind. It isn't open yet. It's so quiet and beautiful, I think you'll love it."

She should go to the muster station. She should find her family. Her entire life, she'd done everything she was supposed to, when she was supposed to.

She'd kept her epilepsy and her medication a secret for her father. And because it filled her with shame. But Gabriel didn't judge her or despise her. He hadn't even blinked.

He didn't care that she was fragile, some part of her deeply broken. He didn't care that she wasn't perfect.

He moved closer. She inhaled the deep, musky scent of him, like something wild. Her heartbeat trembled against her ribs.

So many things she should do. She didn't have to do any of them. Not right now. Not yet. "Take me there."

He leaned toward her. His eyes were huge and dark and beautiful. Emotions she couldn't read filled his gaze, like shadows cast behind his eyes.

He reached up and stroked her cheek with his thumb, his touch trailing wisps of fire. Her whole body came alive. Her heartbeat tried to push its way out of her chest.

He pulled her to him. Heat burned through her. Her skin sparked, her belly alight with fireflies.

He kissed her.

His mouth was hard and hungry, filled with longing. Or maybe the longing was her own.

She'd kissed boys before, rich heirs and bored aristocratic playboys. None of them had touched her like this. None of them had made her feel so alive.

His kiss deepened, urgent, drinking her in. His lips tasted like rain.

Electricity sizzled through her veins, sharp as the electrons singeing the air. He pressed against her, his hands strong and firm on her waist, her back, then tangling in her hair.

It felt like falling.

When she kissed him back, lightning lit up the sky.

18

WILLOW

"We have to go to our muster stations," Finn said. "They just made an announcement."

"What if it's a trap?" They crouched in the stairwell of Deck Eleven. Willow peered around the corner. Nothing moved.

An eerie silence descended over the hallway and balcony, the bar empty of everyone. A service bot sat silent and unmoving in one corner. No one, human or bot, manned the photography stations or the latte stand.

It took them forever to crawl across the length of the lido deck, past the infinity pool and the lagoon hot tub and the raised center stage. The explosion had knocked down half of the transparent tube slide.

A massive chunk of plexiglass smoked and sizzled as they crawled around it. Their hands and knees slipped on the slick deck, the rain pelting them, wind whipping at their clothes.

They'd managed to make it inside and creep down several flights of stairs. Now they huddled in the stairwell, both trembling and panting, terrified and unsure of their next move.

Willow couldn't breathe properly. Her heart was about to explode inside her chest.

Finn wiped beads of sweat off his forehead. His face looked ashen, a sheen of gray filming his brown skin. "Maybe it's just the fear talking, but I think we should follow orders."

"It's your fear talking. We need to find somewhere safe to hide out until the cavalry rides in. Or flies in. Or sails in. Whatever." But even as she spoke the words, she knew she couldn't do it.

She couldn't hole up somewhere when she had Benjie. And her mom. And Zia. Zia must be terrified. And Willow was the one who deserted her. "Oh, hell."

"Your family. And my dad."

"Okay." She took a deep breath. It could still be a trap. But she couldn't just abandon her family. Guilt speared her. She already had. Zia had to be okay. She had to be. "We need to check the library. We—I —left my sister there."

Finn shook his head. "She heard the announcement, too. She'll be at your muster station. Which one is yours?"

"The Galaxy Lounge, I think. Deck Four. I remember staring up at all the holographic stars on the ceiling during the boring safety speeches."

"Not so boring now, are they? I'm in the Trident Theater. Deck Six."

Her stomach dropped. "That's on the other side of the ship."

"We're staying together. We'll go to Deck Six first, get my dad, then head to Four and find your family."

She took a deep breath. It sounded so simple, so easy. "What could possibly go wrong?"

They heard the voices at the same time. One female, one male.

She stiffened, raised one finger to her lips.

She placed her hand on the wall to steady herself, and leaned around the corner. Finn jerked frantically on her arm. But she needed to see what was happening.

Two attackers dressed in black with automatic rifles slung over their shoulders stood behind the counter of the bar. One was tall and bearded, the other younger, with black hair pulled back in a knot and a red bandana tied around her neck.

The service bot beeped at them, starting to speak, but Bandana whirled and shot it in the center of its humanoid chest. It made a mechanical groaning sound and slumped to the floor, sputtering. Bandana laughed.

She grabbed one of the beer bottles off the glass shelving behind the bar and threw it on the ground. The bearded guy joined her. They took swigs from amber bottles, laughing as they smashed the rest, glass shattering into thousands of pieces.

Willow leaned back on her heels, her heart galloping against her ribs. "We need to go now, while they're loud and distracted."

Finn's eyes widened. "They could catch us."

Every muscle in her body screamed at her to stay put. But her brain shot off warning flares like bright streaks behind her eyes. "We're sitting ducks. As soon as they're finished, they'll march this way and blow our brains out."

Finn shook his head furiously. He breathed in shallow gulps, his entire body trembling. Sweat beaded his upper lip, his nostrils flaring as panic gripped him.

She grabbed his clammy hand. "On three. One. Two—"

Several bottles crashed to the ground simultaneously. She yanked Finn to his feet. He was heavy, but she was strong. She pulled him down the last two stairs and around the corner of the landing.

She caught a glimpse of movement out of the corner of her eye and ran faster. *Move!*

She dashed down the next several sets of stairs, nearly stumbling, her heels hitting hard and awkward. At the landing to Deck Eight, the ship pitched.

Her ankle twisted. Pain shot up her leg.

Finn toppled into her, almost knocking her over. "Sorry, Gwyneth."

She leaned against the wall, straining to hear over her own ragged breath. Nothing but distant thunder from the storm. They weren't being followed.

"Are we safe?"

"I think so. For the moment." She took a deep breath and let it out, willing herself to calm down and *think*. "Are you okay?"

Finn leaned against the wall, his head back, his eyes closed. He pressed both hands against his chest. "I'm about to puke violently, Gwyneth. And you?"

At least he was breathing. And he had his sense of humor back. "The same. And it's Willow."

"Huh?"

She wanted him to know her real name, her real self. In case they didn't make it out of here. "I lied to you, before. It was stupid. My name is Willow."

He opened his eyes and stared at her, startled.

She bent down and unstrapped her useless heels. She should've tossed them from the beginning. Panic had muddled her mind. She rubbed the fresh blisters on her heels. "And I'm not rich. My mom won our tickets. And since I'm being brutally honest, this isn't my dress. I don't even like it. Also, I absolutely despise these shoes."

He breathed deeply for a minute. She pretended she didn't care what he thought or whether he liked her. How could it matter when terrorists hunted them? But it did.

He managed a crooked grin and thrust out his massive hand. "It's nice to meet you, Willow."

"You don't hate me?"

"How can I be mad at the girl who just saved my ass?"

She shook his hand, surprised at the relief flooding through her. "Those maniacs upstairs might come down any second. We've got to go."

They hurried down the next two flights. Gunfire blasted on Deck Nine and Eight. The horrific sounds of screaming, shouting, and breaking glass following them down the stairwell.

Finn stopped at the landing to Deck Six. "This is me."

They crept out of the middeck stairwell and into the elevator foyer. To their left was the boardwalk with the Xtreme Worlds virtual reality center, the low-grav arena, and the handmade sweets shop with bioluminescent lollipops bigger than Benjie's head. To the right were the designer shops, a sports bar, and the Trident Theater at the end.

Before they could move, the elevator across from them dinged. The doors opened and a dozen terrorists poured out. "You! Stop!" one said, pointing at her.

Willow lunged for the stairs, launching herself off the landing and taking them two and three at a time. She heard shouting, gun shots, and Finn pounding down the stairs behind her.

Her heart pummeled her chest, her breath tearing from her lungs in ragged gasps. Her ankle jolted with pain, but she managed to stay on her feet.

She rounded the corner of Deck Four. Empty open space, the casino ahead, the bulbs of the huge Galaxy Lounge sign blinking beyond it. Maybe she could find somewhere to hide.

Another burst of gunfire above her. She ducked out of the stairwell and turned to Finn.

But Finn wasn't there.

Something sharp jabbed into her back. Her heart froze.

"Move, girl." A guttural voice spoke from behind her. "In there."

Her knees locked. Cold sweat broke out on her skin. The pounding steps behind her hadn't been Finn. Finn was still up there, with the gunshots and the shouting.

The sharp thing—a gun barrel—prodded her again.

"Move. Or die." Her attacker spoke the words with such indifference that Willow didn't doubt whether he cared either way. He'd shoot her in a hot second.

She moved.

19

AMELIA

Gabriel kissed Amelia again. Dizziness flushed through her. Her stomach fluttered with a thousand whispery wings. It was terrifying and wonderful at the same time.

She pulled away to take a breath. "Wow."

"I thought the same thing." He stroked her cheek with his thumb, sending sparks shooting through her entire body. "And here I was afraid you hated me."

She laughed. "It's hard to explain." And it was. She wasn't sure she had the words for what it was like when people changed around you, acted differently because of how you looked or who your father was.

Gabriel didn't act like she was anything special—or at least, not special because of her wealth, prestige, or lineage. And she liked that.

They kissed again.

Thunder crashed. The wind whipped around them. The rain started, splatting against the deck in fat droplets. Goosebumps pimpled her skin. She shivered.

He pulled away. "It's cold. And you're freezing. Let me take you to the place I told you about. Something even the Coalition chairman's daughter hasn't seen."

An easy calm descended over her. "Okay, big shot. Show me."

He stood and hooked his walkie-talkie to his belt. She took her clutch with the two remaining auto-injectors, and they went back inside, Gabriel's arm draped protectively across her shoulders.

He took her back through the narrow crew passageways, down several flights of rickety metal stairs and past the crew and staff mess and rec areas. They didn't see a single person.

"This is the crew entrance, since the main entrances are currently blocked by construction equipment. Close your eyes."

Her stomach tightened, but she closed her eyes and allowed him to lead her. The air changed, grew colder. She sensed space on either side and above her. Gabriel guided her up two steps.

"Stay here, but don't look. I'll be right back."

Curiosity plucked at her, but she obeyed, rubbing her charm bracelet as she waited.

A minute later, his footsteps returned. He took her hand. Sparks shot through her. His fingers were warm, strong, and calloused. She wasn't used to touching such rough skin. It wasn't a bad thing. "Can I look?"

"Open your eyes."

She gasped. She stood on a small carpeted platform in front of several massive underwater viewing windows built into the ship's hull. The water on the other side of the windows roiled, black and seething. The rest of the room was a theater with seating for at least five hundred people.

"Look up."

The domed ceiling twinkled with a soft blue glow. Beautiful lifelike holographic creatures swam through the air above them—thousands of fish in various colors and sizes, different species of sharks, whales, and dolphins.

It felt like standing at the bottom of the ocean and looking up, up, up through leagues of water brimming with sea life.

"The owner of the *Grand Voyager*, Kevin Murdock, planned this for years. He modeled it after a planetarium, but he calls it the Oceanarium. It'll be ready for its grand opening in a few months. For now, it's empty until the painter returns to finish the murals. Metalheads aren't so great at works of art. Go figure."

He patted the ladder behind him, a splattered paint can on the bottom step. Behind the seating area, ladders, canvas tarps, boxes, and tools leaned against the walls.

A sea turtle drifted by a few feet in front of her, flapping its flippers lazily. The outline of its body glowed a faint electric-blue. "This is spectacular," she breathed.

"Watch this." He reached toward a school of angel fish. The holographic creatures sensed his hand and darted away in a flash of glittering scales.

She followed Gabriel's lead and waved at a bottlenose dolphin gliding toward her. The dolphin waved its flipper. She laughed.

"You can feel them, too. The projections use plasma. The haptics mimic the sensation of touch."

She watched two manta rays sail through the air. "Do they respond to music?"

He grinned. "They do. I'll bring you back here later, and you can play. We'll see which music they like better—classical or good ol' rock 'n' roll."

She couldn't keep a matching grin off her face. She would absolutely love that.

And then Gabriel was beside her again, his hands in her hair. He tilted her head toward him and kissed her. For one wonderful moment, she forgot how she was supposed to act and just let herself *be*. She let herself feel everything—his fingers brushing the curve of her ear. The fizzing in her belly. The rush filling her entire body.

His eyes were dark and fathomless as he gazed into her own. Like he really saw her.

Something crashed somewhere above them. "What's that?" she asked against his lips.

"Just thunder." He kissed her deeper, harder. Her feet might leave the floor. She could float like the incandescent sea creatures swirling around them, blue and sparkling.

The sound came again. A boom, different than thunder. Amelia forced herself to break the kiss. "That was weird."

Thunder rumbled.

"Just the storm." He bent toward her, digging his hands into her hair. She pulled away. "No, it was—"

A rat-a-tat sound. Like firecrackers. Or something worse. She swallowed. "We should probably go."

"Nonsense. Everything's fine."

But the moment was broken, the anxiety of the real world creeping back in. The sound came again from somewhere above them, somewhere on the ship. She wiped her palms on her dress. "If everybody else is at their muster station and I'm not there, my mom will flip out. I should find her and let her know I'm okay."

"I think you should stay."

"I'll come back, I promise." She flashed him a smile as she moved toward the edge of the platform. "Or I'll message you my SmartFlex code and we can meet back here—"

"Amelia."

The way he said her name made her stop. She turned around.

He faced her, his shape framed against the black water in the viewing window behind him. His jaw was set, his face rigid, all the softness gone.

Her gaze lowered, focusing on the object in his hand.

He held a pulse gun. He pointed it at her.

She blinked, trying to erase the image in front of her. But it refused to disappear. Her heart wormed its way into her throat. "What—what are you doing?"

"I'm sorry, Amelia. But I can't let you leave."

Her gaze slid across his face, unable to gain traction. His expression was closed, unreadable. He looked like a stranger, like someone she'd never seen before, let alone kissed. Her confusion gave way to a low, pulsing dread. "Why not?"

"Something is happening, something bigger than both of us. You're gonna have to trust me."

Panic bloomed in her chest. Her frantic heartbeat thrummed in her teeth. "Are you—are you kidnapping me?"

He laughed, but the sound was cold and hard, an imitation of a laugh. The gun didn't move, the barrel still trained on her. "Keeping you out of harm's way is more like it. But we may need you to do a few things for us."

She thought of her mother, her brother. "What harm? Who are you?"

He jutted his chin. "I am the New Patriots."

"What are you talking about?"

"We are taking back our country from the greedy and the corrupt elites and returning it to the people. We're destroying the rotten-to-the-core Unity Coalition, starting with its head."

Understanding dawned slow and ugly. The New Patriots. She'd seen them in the news. The ones always marching and ranting. The ones suspected of bombing several government buildings and monuments over the last few years. "You're . . . a terrorist?"

"No! I am a freedom fighter. Like the Sons of Liberty when this country first fought for its freedom and prevailed. We'll do it again."

She stared at him, barely able to hear his words. The wind howled in her head, a great whooshing sound drowning everything out.

He gestured with the gun. "Now sit down."

She sat. Shock and terror locked her limbs. She couldn't move, couldn't think, couldn't breathe. She'd been manipulated and trapped, as easily as capturing a firefly in a jar.

Her fear came down over everything, snapping shut like a lid.

She'd been used. Again.

20

MICAH

M icah stirred the soup for what seemed like hours, the air in the galley stifling. The armed attackers swung their rifles, alternatively pointing and shouting. Some spoke perfect English. Some didn't speak English at all.

Who were these people? And what did they want, other than death and destruction?

"I need him," Chef Jokumsen said in his Danish accent, gesturing at Micah. He stood at the long food prep table with a handful of waiters and the service bot galley staff, assembling dozens of turkey sandwiches for the terrorists.

"What did you say?" Kane demanded, a menacing gleam in his eyes. He leaned over Su Su, a Burmese girl flipping buffalo burgers at the grill a few feet from Micah.

"You want food? I need more hands. And I need her, too. The burgers are ready."

Kane's gaze slid up and down Su Su's trembling body. "They don't look ready."

"You want to eat today?" The head chef sounded furious, not afraid.

Kane nodded grudgingly. He bent and sniffed Su Su's hair. "Go. For now."

"Boy, turn up the soup before you come over," Chef Jokumsen ordered Micah.

Micah turned the heat to the highest setting. Su Su scooped the burgers onto a platter, her hands shaking so badly she dropped a burger on the floor.

"Pick that up nice and slow," Kane drawled, winking at Micah.

Su Su obeyed, then scurried to the prep table with the burgers. Micah followed behind her. He bit the inside of his cheeks in anger at his own helplessness. Kane had no right to treat another human being that way.

He stood on the other side of the prep table, opposite the head chef. The terrorists leaned against the wall of stoves, watching them. Kane grinned maliciously, his eyes lasered on Su Su.

"Slice these onions." Chef Jokumsen shoved a cutting board, a bowl of onions, and a gleaming butcher knife at them.

Su Su held the knife over the cutting board, tears spilling down her cheeks.

"It'll be okay." Micah wanted to reach out and comfort her, but touching her now seemed like the wrong move. He grabbed a knife and chopped an onion clean in two, slamming the blade with the force of his anger and fear.

"Save your energy, boy," Chef Jokumsen said under his breath. "Your brother is security, yes?"

"Yes," Micah said, not trusting his own voice.

"Do you know how to use a weapon?"

"Enough," he lied. He knew nothing about knives or guns or fighting. He hadn't needed to; Gabriel always protected him.

"These other cooks can only braise lamb. They don't know crap." Chef Jokemsen slapped finely sliced turkey between two slabs of pumpernickel bread. "The lifeboats have satellite beacons. Remember your emergency training."

"How am I supposed to get there?"

"That's your problem. I get you out of here, then you're on your own. You can go around the fresh foods side, to the elevator. Nobody's over there. I checked a few minutes ago. The scumbags supposedly guarding the elevator are in the pastries section, gorging themselves on Devil's Food cake. I create the distraction; you go. No hesitation. Yes?"

Fear raised every sense to high alert. Micah slipped a small knife in his pants pocket. Hopefully he wouldn't accidentally stab himself when he ran.

"Come with me," he said to Su Su.

But she just stared at him with wild eyes, frozen in fear.

"No good," Chef Jokumsen murmured. "I'll watch her. You go now."

Micah nodded.

"Sirs!" Chef Jokumsen said. "The soup behind you is overflowing. If it touches your skin, I'm afraid it will burn."

Both guards turned toward the unsupervised soup spilling over the sides of the pot in a boiling hiss of steam.

Micah said a prayer under his breath. Then he ran. A crash sounded behind him as he dashed around the corner of the wall of ovens.

"I'm so sorry, sirs," Chef Jokumsen hollered. "I'm clumsy today! I've no idea why."

Micah sprinted through the fresh foods section, past the prep tables spread with onions, olives, and dozens of heads of lettuce. He hit the elevator button, his heart slamming. An eternity passed in the seconds it took to open.

Chef Jokumsen bellowed something, arguing with one of the other chefs about nothing, creating more noise to mask Micah's own.

He scrambled into the service elevator and waited for it to lower to the provisions area. The elevator only traveled between the main provisions area and the galley, bypassing all the passenger areas. Hopefully, the terrorists hadn't made it down there yet.

Either way, he had to take the risk.

A voice not the cruise director's normally chipper tenor came over the PA system: "All passengers and crew report to your emergency muster stations immediately."

The elevator doors slid open. Micah rushed out into the cavernous provisions area filled with towering rows of pallets stacked with boxes and bags of goods like cleaning supplies, paper towels, and soap.

He maneuvered around a driverless forklift and passed two workers unloading a pallet of toilet paper.

"Terrorists boarded the ship," he said breathlessly. "Don't go to muster. It's a trap. Go to your cabins and lock and bar the doors with anything you can."

They stared at him, wide-eyed. "You're joking."

"I'm telling the truth." Down here with the loud engine drowning everything out, they hadn't heard the suppressed gunshots or the screams. And he had no time to convince them.

He left them behind, racing through the provisions area to the crew quarters, quickly checking Gabriel's cabin, the mess hall, the crew lounge and bar. Nothing. Gabriel wasn't down here.

Doubt crept in again, and Micah shoved it out of his head. Simeon Pagnini was a terrorist. That didn't mean Gabriel was. It didn't mean his brother was involved.

There had to be some explanation. Gabriel would explain it all, as soon as Micah found him.

Think. Micah had to *think.* Where would Gabriel go? He was probably with a girl. Maybe Teresa, the one he'd been seeing the last few weeks. Or Amelia Black. She wasn't in the dining room.

If Gabriel was with a girl, he'd take her somewhere to impress her, to show off. Somewhere without people, because he'd want to make a move on her.

The Oceanarium. He and Gabriel had joked about its aphrodisiac qualities. A few passenger entrances were still under construction, with a crew entrance on the starboard side. Micah didn't have to pass through any passenger areas to reach it.

He raced along the narrow corridors until he came to a set of metal doors shielded by a sheet of construction plastic. He tore it away and heaved open the door.

He straightened his glasses, blinking to adjust his eyes to the dim light of the Oceanarium. His uniform dampened with sweat, though the air was chilly. He walked down the aisle on legs still trembling with adrenaline.

He took in the vast Plexiglas viewing area, the floating hologram sea creatures, the stadium seating, the two people standing on the raised dais. The Oceanarium wasn't empty.

Amelia stood on one side of the platform in front of the viewing window, resplendent in her white Grecian gown, pale hair glowing silver-blue in the shadowy light. Gabriel stood on the other side of the platform, about ten feet from her.

Micah's brain refused to take in the signals it received. There must be some mistake. This couldn't be real.

His brother held a gun. It was leveled at Amelia.

Micah stumbled, his leg bumping against one of the stadium seats.

Gabriel swung toward him. The gun swung with him. "Welcome to the party, brother."

21

WILLOW

Willow's legs and lower back cramped. Her eyes burned. The Galaxy Lounge didn't have windows. She had no idea what time it was. The lights blared on, minute after minute, hour after hour.

Hundreds of people sagged in the round sofas and tufted arm chairs or slumped on the ground, using the seats as backrests.

Six armed attackers patrolled the perimeter of the room with two more on the stage, the purple curtains closed behind them. Three were women, their expressions hard, their eyes cold as ice.

They used walkie-talkies to communicate, many of them speaking in languages she didn't recognize, other than a few passing phrases in Tagalog, Chinese, Spanish, and English. At least one of them spoke with a Boston accent.

She couldn't stop shaking, her mind shredded. *Calm down. You need to calm down.* She couldn't make her eyes follow the gold geometric patterns in the carpet.

Zia was in here, somewhere. She was still alive. She had to be. But she must be out of her mind with terror. She was just a kid, all alone in a sea of chaos and fear. Her sister was alone because Willow deserted her.

Now she couldn't think of the reason why, couldn't figure out how it had ever seemed important. Guilt ate at her, the words she'd hurled at Zia echoing in her head. *I don't want you around!*

People murmured in low voices on either side of her. Some of them called the attackers terrorists; others used the term pirates. She didn't care. They were the enemy. They were killers.

Through shouts and gestures, the attackers made it known they wanted purses, earrings, bracelets, wedding rings, SmartFlexes—whatever they could get their hands on. They carried pillow cases among the rows, demanding everything.

People pleaded, whimpered, tried to argue and reason. Someone offered the men six hundred million dollars each to let him and his wife go free.

"You have the money now, yeah?" The attacker laughed, struck the man in the face with the butt of his rifle, and moved on.

The attackers kept shouting, waving their guns in people's faces. A few babies wailed. Men and women wept.

"Don't move. Don't speak," the woman next to her had said after the terrorist dragged Willow in and slammed her down at the end of one of the middle rows. The woman clutched a squirming, wiggling little girl in her lap.

The girl wore a lemon-yellow bathrobe, and her inky hair stuck to her scalp in damp strands like she'd just gotten out of the bathtub.

"Don't scream." The woman gripped her daughter's hand so tightly her fingernails dug into the little girl's skin. "Don't scream, don't scream."

Passengers tried to rush the terrorists three different times. Once someone had a pocket knife, another time two security officers had tasers. Three times they failed, the bodies left where they dropped. A middle-aged brunette lady started a terrible keening wail that wouldn't stop. An armed man stomped up to her, shouting. He thrust his rifle in her face.

Everyone watched in mute horror. Willow wanted to look away but couldn't, her mind screaming, *stop, stop, stop.*

But the crazed woman kept wailing. The terrorist pulled the trigger.

Two shots slammed into her. The woman's body jittered, then slumped over.

The little girl in the yellow bathrobe moaned deep in her throat and went still in her mother's lap. After that, no one screamed anymore. Once the screaming ceased, the terrorists stopped shouting. An eerie calm descended over the room.

Willow listened to the strangled whimpers and hushed crying, the gurgle and spit of walkie-talkies, and the constant thud of black boots. And every few minutes, the distant chatter of gunfire. With it came screams so muted they could've been any other low sound, like muffled shrieks at a party.

Willow shivered uncontrollably, tried to close her eyes but couldn't. All the dead bodies wafted in front of her vision like those light bursts when she pressed her fingers against her closed eyelids.

She wanted to cover her ears, curl into a ball, and push out every horrible sound and image. She longed to be back home, where at least she had her own bed and her own comforter.

Where at least she and her family were safe, where she still had her mom and Benjie and Zia.

Find Zia.

She sat up straighter, pushing down the horror and the shock. Somehow, someway, she had to find Zia. Her mom would know what to do. She'd know how to find Zia and rescue Benjie. She'd know the best places to hide. She knew this ship.

But her mom wasn't here. There was only Willow.

She was *Ate*, the eldest, the one in charge of her siblings. She was supposed to keep them safe. *They're your responsibility. Take care of them.* She hadn't. But she could make up for that now.

She had to act, had to do something. She needed to find Zia first— Zia was the one she'd abandoned. Then she'd go from there.

She took a deep breath. She turned to the woman next to her. The woman's name was Ji-Yun. She was Korean, in her mid-thirties, with her hair cut in a bob like Willow's mom. "Have you seen a tiny Filipino girl?" Willow asked.

Ji-Yun stroked her daughter's hair. The little girl, Mi-Na, still wasn't moving. "I saw a girl with short turquoise hair. I remember wondering where she came from. She was on the far-right side, near the front." Her expression darkened. "But when the terrorists first rushed in, there was so much shooting . . . It was chaos."

"Was she hurt?"

"I'm not sure. But—" The woman hesitated. "A lot of people died. They shot into those first rows, and those people had no protection . . ."

The iron knot in her stomach tightened. "But you didn't see for sure—"

"Be quiet!" The man on her other side hunched in one of the orange loveseats, his hands splayed on the coffee table in front of him. He was a big white guy, his gut bulging against his tuxedo.

"Calm down, Marx," said an older Latino man with white hair. "They can't hear us unless they're close. Don't tick them off or draw attention. There won't be any second chances." He rubbed his jaw. "I'm Enrique López. This is Bradley Marx."

None of them mentioned their fancy titles or positions. None of it mattered any more. Everyone just wanted to stay alive.

"They're going to kill us." Marx's eyes were pinched and desperate.

"We don't know that," Willow said.

"Hell yes, that's their plan." Marx paused while two armed men passed by the center aisle, turned, and marched back the other way. "They're breaking us, just for fun. They're going to line us up against the wall and blow our heads off."

López tilted his head. "If they wanted everyone dead, they would've kept shooting. Those are high-powered automatic rifles. There are enough bullets for every person in this room. They have a plan."

Ji-Yun rubbed Mi-Na's back, her face a mask of fear. Mi-Na stared at Willow with dull, unfocussed eyes. Mi-Na had gone somewhere else inside her head. Maybe it was for the best.

Tears stung her eyes, but she fought them back. She would not cry. The terror rearing up inside her was harder to restrain. "What do we do?"

"They're pirates, not terrorists," López said. "Look. They're taking people one by one. They're collecting money and jewelry. They need our biometrics to access the safes. When they get what they want, they'll leave. All we have to do is sit here."

Two armed men flanked an old man in an expensive-looking tuxedo and led him out the side entrance to the left of the stage. López was right about the stealing, at least.

"No way, man," Marx spat. "I'm not sitting here like bait."

"Keep your voice down," López said. "We do what they ask. We trust the system, and we wait for Navy SEALs to come for us. Don't be stupid. Stupid gets people killed."

"Who the hell are these people?" asked a skinny white guy with a goatee next to López. "North Korean? East Asian? Or is it another home-grown terrorist group?"

"Which one?" Marx gestured wildly, his voice rising. "The National Pride Defense League, Soldiers of God, the crazy Earth Liberation Army? If they can take down a luxury cruise liner—no one's safe!"

"Keep your voice down!" López glanced warily toward the stage. Two guards watched them with impassive expressions.

One slung his rifle over his shoulder and headed their way.

Ji-Yun pulled her daughter to her chest. The girl moaned.

"You got something to say?" the guard said in perfect English, with no hint of an accent. In the holes of his mask, his eyes glinted dark brown.

"You're the same terrorist scum we should've strung up thirty years ago!" Marx spat, half-rising from his seat. He never got a chance to stand.

The shot blast was so close it thrummed in her teeth. She pressed her hands over her mouth, somehow managing to keep the scream inside. It echoed in every cell of her body, shattering her bones.

22

MICAH

"You don't have to do this," Micah said.

Gabriel only grunted, tightening the straps around Micah's wrists. He bound Amelia's and Micah's hands behind their backs. They sat against the bottom row of seats, facing the platform and the massive viewing window.

Beside him, Amelia didn't say a word. She didn't move, her shoulders slumped, her head down. Shimmering blue whales and manta rays drifted on windless currents above them. The dark, angry sea lashed the windows.

"Please." A thousand thoughts crashed against his skull. How was this happening? Where was his brother, the guy he'd grown up with? Who'd cared for him, teased him, protected him? Who was this grim-faced stranger? "Are you—are you one of them?"

Gabriel stood and wiped his hands on his pants. "I am a Patriot. We're taking back our country. A new revolutionary war begins today."

"I don't understand. This is *political*?"

"No!" His mouth twisted. "This is *life*. Innocent people's lives. And innocent people's deaths. Hundreds of thousands, millions of lives. All dead or suffering because of a callous, corrupted government which no longer serves the *people*."

"No." Disbelief choked Micah's throat.

"The people have been groaning under oppression for decades." Gabriel paced the narrow platform. "Everyone knows we're sick with all sorts of cancers because of the toxins these corrupt politicians release into our dwindling water supplies. Everyone knows you get less and less food for more and more money. The planet is poisoned. Everybody *knows*, everybody *talks*, but no one *acts*."

"The drugs." An awful blaze of clarity struck him. "You used the drugs to—"

"We smuggled the guns in beneath the drugs. That's why we needed them. I told you it was for a good cause. The drug ring has been set up for years. It was simple to sneak the guns in. We'd already paid the right people off. They never looked too closely. They never considered they might be letting in something worse than drugs."

Micah could've done something. He should've stopped this. Would have, if he'd reported the drugs to the captain. The investigation would've revealed the guns, too. If the bridge had been alerted to a possible internal attack six days ago, none of this would have happened.

Guilt and grief strangled him. He'd turned against his own conscience. He let his brother off the hook. And in doing so, he'd doomed dozens, if not hundreds, of people to death.

The images of the sprawled and broken dead in the Oasis dining room ripped through his mind. "They're killing people."

A shadow passed over Gabriel's face. His mouth tightened. "All wars have casualties."

"This isn't war! This is terrorism."

Gabriel shook his head. "The loyalists called the Sons of Liberty terrorists in the seventeen-hundreds. Now we call them our forefathers."

"I understand. I do. But violence isn't the way—"

"You've never understood, Micah. You've never tried to understand."

"That's not fair."

Gabriel squatted in front of him. "This is why I couldn't tell you before. But Micah, we're making a difference here. We're going to change everything. This is the beginning of a rebellion that will be heard around the world. The people will stand up. Don't you see?

"The Unity Coalition is strangling our people to death. They already stalk us with their surveillance drones and cameras. Now they want to chip us, monitor our every movement, trap us in poverty-stricken ghettos under the guise of quarantine, all in the name of our own health and well-being? No. We will not allow it. We're taking back our country."

"But why here? Why now?"

"It's *symbolic*. We take down the shining symbol of the elite's waste and excess. While the country is starving, they're eating caviar! It's Declan Black and his Unity Coalition behind all this. His cancer cures and flu vaccines are just a cover for their power grab.

"We destroy him and we destroy the head of the Unity Coalition and all they stand for—greed, corruption, hubris. The people will see that we *can* win. We can fight back. They will rise up behind us. And a true revolution will begin."

"What about the rest of the ship? Did you plan to kill everyone?"

"Of course not. We're taking the ship hostage, making ransom demands, raking in billions for the cause. Only a few will die."

'But that's not happening! You didn't see Oasis. You didn't see the dead."

Gabriel's mouth contorted. "If this is the price for freedom, true freedom, then I'm willing to pay it."

"And who else will pay with you?"

Gabriel reached out and touched Micah's face. "You don't know how much I wish you were here beside me."

Micah flinched. "What would Mom think if she saw you like this?"

"If not for these people and their greed, she would still be here. I'm doing this for her. And for everybody else like her. Those elitist asshats don't get to decide who lives or dies. Not now, not ever."

"Mom would never approve of this and you know it. She taught us to turn the other cheek."

"Her faith made her weak."

"No." Micah shook his head fiercely. "Never say that. Her faith gave her strength. She died with dignity."

Gabriel clenched his jaw, a muscle jumping in his cheek. "She *died* needlessly, pointlessly, her life not even valued above an animal's. That's not *dignity*."

Micah tried a different tack. "And Dad?"

"Dad would've been a part of this."

"How can you say that?"

"Why do you think he was such good friends with Simeon? He joined the New Patriots when it was just a political protest group. You were too young to remember. He was angry, too—until Mom died. Then he just gave up. But I'm not Dad. I'm not giving up."

A dull roar filled Micah's ears. His dad would never be part of something like this, no matter how angry he was.

Gabriel believed whatever he wanted to believe. The truth didn't matter. Who knew what lies Simeon had filled his head with all these years? "Gabriel, please. You can still stop this."

Gabriel shook his head. "Not this time." The walkie-talkie strapped to his waist spat static. He turned and strode up the center aisle, out of earshot.

Micah jerked his arms, trying to pull free. The straps dug into the skin over his wrists. He adjusted his weight, a sharp pain jabbing his thigh. The knife. Gabriel hadn't bothered to frisk him.

Amelia remained silent. Her legs stretched out in front of her, the silken fabric of her dress bunched around her knees. She hung her head, unmoving.

"Miss Black," he whispered. "Amelia."

But she didn't answer.

He fought down a burst of panic. He had to think. He had to be smart. His brother wouldn't hurt him. But the other terrorists would.

Gabriel had always been naïve like that. If someone else shared his ideology, he didn't bother to look any closer. He didn't know what these people were capable of. But Micah had seen it. They intended more death and destruction.

"I saw your mother in the Oasis dining room," he said, soft and urgent. Gabriel would only be out of earshot for so long. "Terrorists attacked. They took your parents hostage."

Her head moved slightly.

"They're taking over the ship. That's why all the communication went down earlier. But there are still ways we can call for help. The lifeboats have GPS distress signals we can activate, if we can reach them. And the emergency mayday signal locations. But we need to get out of here. I need your help."

"We're prisoners," Amelia said dully.

A holographic dolphin swam in the air above their heads. The ocean outside the windows hurled itself against the hull like a huge, powerful beast desperate to claw its way inside.

The boat rolled and pitched, knocking Micah's shoulder against hers. She was trembling.

"I have a knife in my pants pocket. If you scoot over, I think you can pull it out and cut the straps."

She lifted her head, blinking as if coming out of a daze. "You want me to help you escape."

"Both of us."

"I heard him on the walkie-talkie," she said slowly. "Talking about me."

"They want something from your father. Do you know what it is?"

"No."

"Gabriel isn't a bad guy." But suddenly he wasn't so sure. How could Gabriel stand by and watch people die? How could he possibly think killing civilians would solve the nation's problems?

A line from *Heart of Darkness* ran through Micah's head: *The mind of man is capable of anything.* No. No matter how much darkness surrounded him, Gabriel wasn't evil. Micah wouldn't believe that. He couldn't. Not about his brother. "These are bad people. But Gabriel—he wants to change the world. He's a true believer."

Her mouth contorted. "And this is how he does it?"

"I didn't say I agree with him. I don't. But he still has goodness in him."

"Not from where I'm sitting." She took a deep breath. "How bad is it up there?"

"They stormed the ship and came barreling into the Oasis dining room. They had people on the inside. One of the waiters. Some security. My brother. Who knows how many others."

"Is anyone hurt?"

He considered lying, softening the blow, but she was looking at him now, her steady gaze searching his.

"I asked because I want to know," she said.

He remembered how she played the violin in the Oasis dining room that first day. He'd been mesmerized as she drew the bow across the strings, the exquisite notes flowing over him, around him, through him.

The song had been sensuous, dark, soulful. The music evoked the same soaring sensation he felt when he read Thomas, Plath, or Cummings.

He'd watched the tension in her face fade as she played, lost in the concentration of her art, her fingers moving with a beautiful fluidity and grace. Long after she finished, the deep, sonorous notes still vibrated in his bones.

This girl wasn't weak. There was strength written in her face, her determination reflected in her eyes. He took a breath. "They killed at least fifty people in Oasis. They took the captain's table hostage."

She swallowed. "And my brother?"

"I didn't see your brother. I'm sorry."

She nodded to herself, as if deciding something. "Okay."

"The knife. Can you reach it?"

"I'll try." She wriggled closer, twisting her body at an awkward angle to grab the knife handle from his pocket. "Got it."

The blade slid along his hip bone. As the floor moved beneath them, the edge sliced through the thin fabric into his skin. He sucked in his breath.

"Sorry."

"Not your fault. Whatever you do, don't drop the knife."

They scooted around until they sat back to back. Amelia's fingers scrabbled over his hands and wrists, fumbling for the zip-tie strap.

"Don't cut my fingers off."

"Not planning on it. But I can't exactly see what I'm doing."

She sawed into the strap. The knife point jabbed into the tender flesh of his wrist. He bit the insides of his cheeks, wincing.

"Sorry, again." She adjusted her body. "I'm not trying to hurt you."

"I know."

A metal door banged open to their left. Gabriel's voice echoed in the cavernous room.

"Faster." He closed his eyes, tensing for the next cut.

Amelia made a desperate noise in the back of her throat. She pressed harder and faster, slicing the top of his thumb. Pain stabbed through him, warm liquid dripping down his palm. Finally, the strap broke and he was free.

Micah scrambled into a crouch. He untucked his shirt and wiped his throbbing, bloody hand. He peeked over the seats. Gabriel headed up the center aisle.

"He's coming! Hurry!" He gestured for her to follow him. He'd free her hands later.

But she didn't move.

"Let's go!"

She dropped the knife. "Even if I got away, he'd come after me. I'm his mission, remember? You're not. You go. Get help."

He wanted to shout, *I'm not leaving you!* But he didn't. He recognized the truth of her words in the span it took her to speak them. "There is goodness in him. Help him find it."

She stared at him, tendrils of white-blonde hair stuck to her forehead and cheeks. He didn't want to leave her, but he had no choice. Gabriel wouldn't hurt her.

"I'll come back for you, I promise." He slipped the knife into his pocket and sprang to his feet.

He'd sprinted halfway to the side entrance when Gabriel spotted him. "Stop!"

Micah turned around, his hands in the air. Blood dripped down his arm. The stinging pain centered him, kept him focused. He took a step backward. Then another.

"I said stop!" Gabriel stood next to Amelia, legs splayed, gun pointed straight at him. "You aren't going anywhere."

"You going to shoot me, too?" His voice shook. Gabriel wouldn't hurt him. Would never hurt him. And yet, thirty minutes ago, he'd believed Gabriel would never kill anyone, would never be a part of something like this. He wasn't sure of anything anymore. "Is that what your cause means to you?"

"You don't understand. I can keep you safe here."

Micah took another step backward. The metal crash bar pressed into his back. He couldn't choose safety, not at a time like this. His mother's words echoed in his mind. *Be good. Be brave.* His heart was a ball of fire in his chest. "I'm going to help these people. Shoot me if you have to, but I'm going."

"You don't know what you're doing!"

Micah stole one last glance at Amelia. Only the top of her head showed beyond the rows of stadium seats. Had he done the right thing by letting her stay behind? It was more dangerous outside these doors. Gabriel made a bad choice, but he wasn't a killer. Micah had to believe that. "You can stop this, Gabriel."

Micah turned and fled.

He half-expected a bullet in the back. But it never came.

His brother let him go.

23

GABRIEL

Gabriel held the gun with slick, trembling hands, his finger on the trigger. His pulse thundered in his ears. Sweat trickled down his neck.

He sighted his own brother's back as he walked away, headed up the aisle between the stadium seats of the Oceanarium.

Micah's uniform shirt was untucked, hanging lopsided over his belt. Only Gabriel knew what lay beneath the shirt, the scars carved into Micah's right shoulder blade from the hoverboarding accident. His gun wavered, the memory pulsing through him, sharp and painful.

The park had been in a ritzy, upscale neighborhood, one much nicer than theirs. Gabriel and Micah hadn't belonged. They weren't wanted. It was a mistake to go.

A bigger mistake to bring his brother, who at twelve was still thin and gangly. He was too small, too vulnerable. The other boys sniffed hunger and need off them like a wolf pack detecting the weakest prey. The boys left Gabriel alone—at least physically.

Four older, crueler boys had pushed Micah off the top of the cement half-pipe. Gabriel still remembered the agonizing shriek as Micah's small body tumbled against the unforgiving cement, his bare back and right shoulder scraping all the way down.

Gabriel dropped his board and raced to Micah, gathering him in his arms and cradling him like a baby. "You're okay, you're okay."

But there was blood. So much blood, slick and wet on his hands and arms. Micah's chubby cheeks too pale, his breath coming in shallow gasps and whimpers.

"We spray for cockroaches here," taunted the biggest boy at the top of the half-pipe, a white kid with a hooked nose and ugly, hateful eyes. The others laughed and hurled their own insults.

The boys' jeers ignited Gabriel's brain with rage. He wanted to throttle them with his bare hands. To cave their skulls in with a swing of his board, or a baseball bat.

But blood gushed through his fingers. He could see pink muscle beneath Micah's shredded skin. He needed a doctor, though their dad would only be able to afford the corner clinic, and even that would take a month of his salary.

"I'm coming back for you!" He shot the boys one last murderous look, memorizing their faces. Then he took off for home, twelve long blocks away. The merciless sun beat down on them. His brother's weight strained his arms and shoulders, his grip slipping on Micah's bloody skin.

The guilt stabbed him as every jarring, excruciating step caused Micah more pain. The dull, threatening buzz of the neighborhood patrol drone following them down the street. Not because they were victims. Because they were intruders.

Gabriel went back for those boys, just like he'd promised. He'd cased the neighborhood for days, ferreting out the hidden camera and sensor locations, timing the drones, and stalking the lead bully, the insolent fool with the hooked nose.

He knew the consequences if the drones caught his revenge on their surveillance feeds. But he was patient. He waited for his moment.

Every time he returned from school and saw the wounds on Micah's back, his resolve strengthened. His hatred sprouted, entwining with a dark and ugly rage.

When the moment came, he didn't hesitate. He beat the rat-faced bully with his own hoverboard, breaking the boy's jaw in three places.

Scratched and bruised, Gabriel came home that night with bloody knuckles and a loathing in his heart that only grew stronger with each passing year. When Simeon found out, he took Gabriel under his wing, nurturing his hatred, his rage, and his skills.

Until he was ready. Until today.

Gabriel blinked back to the present. It had started with his brother. With protecting Micah.

The side door slammed with a finality that echoed in his ears. He lowered the gun. He couldn't do it. It was his job to protect Micah. He could never hurt his brother. It was his weakness, just as Simeon had warned him.

The five hundred empty, plastic-sheathed seats stretched in front of him, judging him silently. Micah didn't understand. He would never understand why Gabriel and the New Patriots needed to act with violence.

All other avenues had failed repeatedly, for years. It took strength to stand up. Courage to fight to change things. And an iron will.

Micah was soft. It was Gabriel's fault. He'd protected him, had kept him sweet, innocent, and loving. In the process, he'd failed his brother completely.

And now that same weakness permeated him. He'd let love cloud his judgement, allowed Micah to escape into the bowels of the ship. And Micah wouldn't just squirrel away and hide. He was soft, but he was no coward.

Gabriel's chest tightened. Micah would do something stupid and get himself killed. He might snarl up the whole mission. For half a second, Gabriel thought about chasing after him.

Why had he gotten Micah on this ship in the first place? Because Simeon wanted him. Because Simeon believed Micah would join their cause. Only Gabriel had always known, deep down, that his brother was weak. He would never fight. He would never kill.

They're killing people. But there were always casualties in war, just like Simeon said. Gabriel had to be strong. He had to be willing to do whatever it took. Whatever the price.

Just like he did when he protected Micah all those years ago. Just like he did when he worked with the New Patriots to bomb the Illinois capitol, the Boston municipal courthouse, the palatial Unity Coalition headquarters. Though, those buildings had been empty but for sani-bots.

He gritted his teeth as he turned toward his prisoner.

Amelia Black sat on the floor, her beautiful dress rumpled and stained with red.

"Why are you bleeding?"

She stared up at him with those unnerving ice-blue eyes. "It's your brother's blood."

His gut twisted. "Is he hurt? How bad?"

"You just had a gun pointed at him."

"I'm aware of that. Why is he bleeding?"

"He had a knife. I cut him loose. But since I was tied up, I accidentally cut him."

For a long moment, neither of them spoke. Dolphins, whales, and stingrays swam in the watery glow surrounding them. The ocean lashed against the viewing area windows. A tiny holographic fish darted in front of him and flashed away.

He stared at the ocean, his eyes dry and gritty. He'd been longing for this day for months. For years. It wasn't supposed to feel like this. A pain stabbing deep. That horrified look of shock and betrayal in Micah's eyes.

"Why didn't you stop him?" Amelia asked.

"I wouldn't shoot my own brother. I'm not a monster." He shoved the pain, the anxiety, the questions—all of it—out of his mind. Pain was weakness. Emotion was weakness. He couldn't be weak. Not now. "Micah's nothing. He doesn't matter."

"You could've run after him."

"I couldn't leave you," he said darkly. "Simeon made you my mission."

She winced. Satisfaction flashed through him, then guilt. Everything that happened between them was simply that—a mission, a duty. He couldn't acknowledge the feelings stirring in his gut. They weren't real.

What he'd felt when she fell—a stab of fear, concern, compassion— and then later, when she'd first smiled at him after her near-seizure, small and sad and completely vulnerable. It had undone him.

But it wasn't real. It couldn't be.

He made his voice hard, indifferent. "Not that it wasn't an enjoyable mission. It definitely had its perks."

She lifted her chin. Not the reaction he expected. "You aren't the first person to use me. And you can be sure you won't be the last. Trust me, I'm used to the likes of you."

"I doubt it."

"You think you're different from them?" Her mouth twisted in defiance. "Different from the power-hungry game players upstairs? You're playing your own game. And you use whomever you have to in the process."

"I'm nothing like them," he scoffed. "They're corrupt. Soulless. Evil."

"You're keeping me out of the way until your boss decides he needs me. For what? To get my father to spill whatever secrets you want? How do you think he's going to do that? He's going to—" She took a breath. "He's going to torture me."

"No, he's not." But doubt pricked his mind. *They're killing people.* He rubbed the back of his neck, ran his hand over the stubble along his jaw. "Simeon isn't like that. We aren't like that."

"Then why are you down here babysitting me? What other possible end game is there? I'm leverage against my father. He's a hostage because they want something from him. When you drag me to the bridge, they're going to put a gun to my head."

"Simeon would never shoot you."

"Would *you*?"

He wanted to say, *Of course not.* He had the sudden urge to lean in and wrap her in his arms, to kiss the fear off her face. What an idiotic thought. Furious at himself, he scrubbed it from his mind.

The romance was manufactured, and the feelings with it. They'd dispensed with that pretense.

"You said this was a war."

"What of it?"

"All wars require collateral damage."

Saliva filled his mouth. He swallowed hard. "Yes."

"So, you'll kill innocent people?"

"I don't kill innocents."

Her eyes flashed in the bluish light. "Who gets to decide who's innocent? You?"

"Do you know how many thousands—how many millions—have suffered needlessly? Died needlessly? All because of greed and corruption."

"You didn't answer my question. Who gets to decide?"

Her questions irritated him in ways he couldn't explain. Simeon had said no one was innocent. Simeon said collateral damage was always the cost of revolution, of freedom. Gabriel believed that with all his heart. Didn't he?

He couldn't think clearly with her voice in his head. Everything was muddled. He needed to be clear. He needed to be smart. He was a soldier, a warrior.

This was the truth. No one was innocent. Especially not him.

24

MICAH

The sound of breaking glass shattered Micah's concentration. He froze.

He was on his way to the starboard side of Deck Four to reach the lifeboats. He headed for the mid-ship stairwell on Deck Four. He'd passed the Jazz Lounge, the comedy club, and the Blaze disco lounge with the photoluminescent walls.

The eight-thousand square foot Undersea Paradise Casino loomed before him.

More breaking glass. This time from behind him.

He rushed blindly into the casino. He raced past red velvet gaming tables featuring Blackjack, Caribbean Stud Poker, Baccarat, and Roulette. He stumbled over one of the tufted leather chairs, cursing silently as it crashed to the floor.

His heart hammered in his chest, adrenaline spiking through his veins. He was an exposed target.

He eased around a giant holographic spinning prize wheel and dove behind the first set of slot machines. Hundreds of machines bunched in groups of six or ten like a blinking, jangling maze.

Though the casino was empty, the slot machines still glowed, their sleek panels lit up with rotating holos of cherries, dice, stars, and triple sevens. He leaned against one, the metal cooling his back, the holo-screen boasting '3000 Chances to Win!'

He strained to hear over the clanging, spinning sound effects and the frantic banging of his own heart.

Nothing.

He crept deeper into the electronic jungle, scrambling from one bank of slot machines to the next. He stepped over several dead bodies, begging their forgiveness in his mind.

An elderly woman in a beautiful scarlet gown crumpled on her stool, her glassy eyes staring at him, unseeing. He inched around the stool, careful not to disturb her body.

Voices came from the front of the casino.

His breath stilled in his chest. He crouched beside the body, hunching himself into as small a form as possible.

He gripped the knife in both hands. It wouldn't do much against a semi-automatic or a pulse gun. It was all he had. But could he attack another human being, even to defend himself?

He didn't want to die here, bleeding out like an animal. His mom had faced her death with courage. But he wasn't as strong or as brave as her. His faith wasn't as strong.

He was afraid. Terrified. He wasn't ready. There were so many things he'd never done. He'd never gotten a chance to live yet. He'd never fallen in love. He'd never—

Movement on his left. A chill zipped up his spine. He whipped his head around.

One of the terrorists squatted in front of the bank of slot machines to his left. He wore dark clothes with combat gear and a black mask pulled over his face. He cradled a rifle in his arms.

Micah shrank against the stool, his back bumping the woman's still-warm body. Her body toppled from the stool and landed on the carpet with a dull thud. He flinched, fear throbbing through him.

The terrorist still hadn't moved. He waited for something.

"You heard that?" The guttural voice was closer now, only a dozen yards away.

"Nah, man."

"I swear I heard something."

Micah could hear their footsteps over the clattering, clanging slot machines. They were close.

The terrorist across from Micah rose into a crouch, lifting his weapon. Micah flinched.

Two men rounded the corner. They aimed their weapons at Micah, their eyes lit with blood lust. "So many rats on this ship." One of them shoved his gun in Micah's face.

Terror roared in his ears. His veins turned to ice. He couldn't move now even if he'd wanted to.

The gun shots blasted Micah's ear drums, vibrating through his chest. He squeezed his eyes shut, waiting for the explosion of pain. Waiting for death.

But it didn't come.

"Boy."

He didn't breathe. He didn't think. He waited to die.

"You think this is a good time for a nap, boy?"

He forced himself to open his eyes. The two men who'd just had their guns trained on him lay crumpled on the ground, blood staining the carpet beneath them. The third terrorist stood over him, his rifle angled toward the floor.

"W-what just happened?"

The man pulled up his ski mask.

His brown skin gleamed in the light, sweat beading his brow. He rubbed his square, clean-shaven jaw with the back of his hand. "Ed Jericho."

Micah's lungs deflated. He stared up in shock, not quite believing he was still alive. "Declan Black's security guy?"

"You got a name?" Jericho's voice was deep, with the hint of a Nigerian accent.

"M-Micah."

Two figures appeared behind Jericho. The first was a slim, bearded Indian man in his early forties dressed in the same stolen combat gear.

Micah recognized him as Raj Patel, one of the security officers who worked with Gabriel.

The second was a boy a few years younger than Micah. He was tall and wiry, with short dark hair and a sullen, brooding face. The son of Declan Black.

Patel clapped him on the back. "Glad to see you, Rivera. Have you seen your brother?"

Micah bit the inside of his cheeks. He hated to lie, but he couldn't reveal his brother's location, no matter what he'd done. They'd kill Gabriel if they knew. "Um, not lately, sir."

"That's too bad. Hope he's kept himself alive."

"Me too."

Silas stared at him, a sour, suspicious expression on his face, like he could see right through Micah's lies.

"Where is everyone else?" Micah asked, shifting uncomfortably.

Jericho shrugged off his backpack and pulled out a fresh magazine. "Silas and I were in the VR gaming center on Deck Six when we heard the terrorists sweeping the deck above us. These assholes are schizophrenic. Some are taking hostages. Some are shooting anything that moves."

"How many are there?" Micah asked.

"As far as I can tell, there are fifty or sixty hostiles. They've got hostages in the Galaxy Lounge and the Trident Theater. Small groups are still sweeping the ship, but the concentration of hostiles are in those two places."

"Declan Black is being held hostage on the bridge," Micah said.

Jericho nodded. "I suspected as much."

Micah caught a glimpse of a handgun, a couple of sheathed knives, and something metallic and disc-shaped before Jericho rezipped the pack. This guy knew what he was doing. Micah wasn't sure if he should be relieved or frightened.

Jericho slotted the magazine into his rifle and slapped the stock. "Look alive, people. Stay on your toes and follow me."

25

AMELIA

For what seemed like hours, Amelia did not speak. She stared at the black wall of water and the floating projections of sea animals reflected off the glass. Glowing phosphorescent bacteria swirled around her like stars.

What was going on above her? How many innocent people might be dying right this second? What was happening to her father, her mother, her brother? Helplessness and fear tangled in her stomach.

She licked her lips. "I'm thirsty. May I have a drink, please?"

Gabriel retrieved a water bottle from one of the opened boxes leaning against the far wall. He squatted down and tilted the bottle to her mouth.

She gulped it down, shame flooding her belly. She hated accepting this kindness from him, hated needing anything from him at all.

"Thank you." She said it automatically, instantly despising herself. If there was any time to discard social niceties, surely this was it.

Water dripped down her chin. Gabriel untucked the front of his uniform shirt and wiped her face. This time, she didn't say a word.

His walkie-talkie spat a garbled message. He strode back up the center aisle, out of earshot.

Her neck hurt. Her arms ached from being tied so awkwardly

behind her back. She did this to herself. She allowed this to happen. With her arrogance, her stupidity.

No wonder her mother never let her out of sight. No wonder her father only used her for one thing—parading her around like a prize to charm and woo his business partners.

She'd wanted to take control of her life. She made her own decisions for a single pathetic night, and look where it'd gotten her. She was the idiot who fell for a freaking terrorist.

And now here she was. Helpless. Just another pawn on someone else's board. Everything she loathed about how her father treated her, and here she was on the other side, playing a lethal version of the same game.

She shifted, trying to find a more comfortable position. Her ring finger stung. She'd sliced it when she freed Micah. The cut wasn't too deep, no permanent damage that would affect her music. If she ever got to pick up a violin again.

Tears pricked her eyes. She forced them back, focusing on Micah instead. Where was he now? Had he been captured? Killed? Or had he done what he said he would, and found a way to alert the outside world? Was someone coming to rescue them?

There is good in him, Micah said. *Find it.*

Even if the Navy or the Marines came, they'd be too late. Gabriel would take her to the bridge. Whoever was in charge would torture and possibly kill her to get what they needed from her father.

Would they waterboard or shock her? Pull off her fingernails? Chop off her fingers, one by one? Worse?

The panic reared up again and her heart hammered so hard it almost burst through her ribcage. She took shallow breaths, willing herself to calm down.

She was trapped, tied up, with no weapons. She had nothing. Nothing except herself. *Use what you have.* Her mother taught her that.

A memory surfaced, sharp and sudden. It was two years ago, before one of her father's Unity Coalition fundraising galas. Amelia had sat in front of the vanity mirror in her bedroom as her mother wove a trio of fishtail braids down her back.

She remembered her mother's eyes smudged with shadows, her skin tinged sallow. "Are you all right, Mom?"

"I'm fine, honey," her mother had said mildly. "Now, let's go over everything again."

Amelia tried not to roll her eyes. "Tyler Horne. Founder of the nanotech microchip thingy."

"He's young, powerful, and arrogant. He has a weakness for thrills. He's a gambler. Racked up massive debts to the syndicates. He'll want to flirt, but dangerously. Which means—"

"Never be alone with him."

Elise nodded as she wound her fingers expertly through Amelia's hair.

"How do you know all this?"

Her mother shook her head, averting her gaze. "No one is ever what they seem. Everyone has layers, fears and weaknesses and personal demons. Some you learn to avoid, to protect yourself. Others you can use to manipulate to your own purpose."

"Like Father does."

"Sometimes. Learn to pay attention, and you'll be fine."

Amelia stared at herself in the mirror. She'd rather stay home and watch horror movies with Silas or practice Bach's Largo from Sonata no. 3, which she'd been working on for an upcoming competition. "Why does he always make me do this?"

"Your father knows what he's doing. Everyone loves attention, especially from a pretty young girl. It just—it smooths things."

"Sometimes it makes me feel . . . gross."

The light dimmed in her mother's eyes. "We all must use the gifts we've been given. Your beauty is a great gift. The world is a much harsher place without it. Trust me. You must use what you have."

"It takes time away from practicing." Her father wanted her to play, so she played every extra moment she had. He wanted her to be the best. So she wanted to be the best.

Her mother smiled at her in the mirror. "Oh, my darling. So driven, so focused."

"But I still don't see why—"

"This is what your father wants. So this is what we do."

Everything she did was to please her father. Everything. But still. "What about what *we* want?"

Her mother knitted her brow. "We owe an enormous debt to your father. He saved us both. Everything we have comes from him. Remember that."

She studied her mother in the mirror. Her mouth pinched, her gaze strained. She never talked about the time before. Only that she'd been nothing, had nothing, and Declan Black saved her.

He wasn't Amelia's biological father, but he might as well have been. To her mother, he was. She never spoke of the 'genetic donor' who contributed half of Amelia's DNA.

Declan had taken her in when Amelia was a baby. And he was the one who'd engineered the medication that saved her. The meds that kept her alive, kept her brain from turning to mush.

He brought both her mother and Amelia into this life of luxury and glamour. He gave them everything they had, including Amelia's life. For these things, her mother worshiped him. And she expected nothing less of her daughter.

"Much of the country is a cruel, dangerous place. Count your lucky stars every day that you are safe. It's all that matters." She gave Amelia a weary smile. "You're all that matters."

Amelia hadn't asked more questions then. It was no use prying further. Her mother never gave any other answer. She kept her past—and her secrets—hidden somewhere deep inside herself.

Her mother taught her how to read people. But so did her father. She had to read him, to know his moods, to anticipate his wrath. She'd been doing a version of it her whole life.

Use what you have.

She stared at the glass walls, remembering something else her mother had said once. *Glass is beautiful but weak. But it can be strengthened by heat—made strong by fire.*

She needed to be strong now. She just had to think. Be smart.

Use what you have. She could do that. But she couldn't act like she normally did. Flattery and charm wouldn't work on Gabriel, not like it did on fifty-something politicians, public officials, and CEOs blinded by their own bloated egos.

Find the good in him. Maybe his feelings for her hadn't all been an act. Or she was thinking of her own emotions, her own reckless attraction. She bit her lip.

Gabriel advanced up the aisle, the walkie-talkie clipped to his belt, the gun in one hand and two snack-sized bags of chips in the other. "Thought you might be hungry."

"Thank you," she said as sincerely as she could.

In the distance, more gunfire, followed by a rumble of thunder. The ship rolled sharply. She slipped sideways. Gabriel grabbed her shoulders and steadied her. "Sorry."

"It's okay." She swallowed. *Use what you have.* Now or never. She might fail—most certainly would fail—but at least it was something. At least she tried.

She'd spent her whole life too scared to try. She wasn't going to die the same way.

26

WILLOW

Willow was thirsty, her throat parched, her skin hot and sticky. The smell of sweat and blood permeated the air. Bodies crowded the Galaxy Lounge, both living and dead.

López wasn't talking anymore. His gaze locked on some speck on the opposite wall. He rocked against the seat behind him. Thump. Thump. Thump.

Beside her, Ji-Yun wept quietly. Mi-Na lay draped across her lap. Her eyelids fluttered, her breathing ragged.

Blood splattered across their faces, their clothes. It stained Willow, too, tiny droplets like a veil of freckles across her arms. She scrubbed them fiercely with the fabric of her dress.

She couldn't rub off the faint smears of red on her skin. Just like she couldn't erase the screams in her head or the stench of death filling her nostrils.

She tried not to look at the broken body slumped in the orange chair beside her.

Her throat was raw, her tongue thick and swollen. She imagined water droplets shimmering like some precious crystal. She thought about all the blue water filling the pools, flowing in the fountain in the atrium.

Two terrorists clomped down the aisle past her, their black guns so shiny, so close. She imagined grabbing one out of their hands. She'd never killed anyone before, but it must not be that hard, if you were angry enough, scared enough. And right now, she was plenty of both.

She sensed movement toward the front of the Galaxy Lounge. Several voices shouted simultaneously. Bursts of gunfire exploded through the room. She rose to her knees to peer over the seat in front of her.

The purple stage curtains jerked open. A dozen men poured through the gap. They launched themselves at the guards manning the front of the stage.

Several wore security officer's uniforms and aimed handguns. A few others gripped fire axes, the kind affixed to the wall behind protective glass.

The first terrorist dropped to the carpet. The second lifted his gun, but a passenger with an axe reached him first, wedging the blade deep into his chest.

The rest of the terrorists guarding the sides and back of the Galaxy Lounge ran for the stage, rifles blasting. The passengers and officers on the stage dove for cover, but not before sending their own volley of bullets shrieking over the heads of the hostages.

People screamed and threw themselves to the floor.

A terrorist ran down the center aisle next to her. He stumbled and fell. A puddle of red soaked into the carpet beneath his chest.

She stared at his body, unable to move, to breathe. She was close enough to see his eyes, wide and glassy, staring at nothing. His mouth hung open, a gurgling sound coming from somewhere inside him.

"Get his gun!" someone yelled.

Fear gripped her belly. She couldn't move. Every fiber of her being screamed at her to stay where she was, sheltered by the rows of seats in front of her. *Just stay put. Do what you're told. Stay alive.*

She couldn't. *Zia.* That single word, zapping through her.

It was her fault Zia was alone. It was her responsibility to find her sister. Her mom's voice spoke inside her head: *Take care of them.*

If she didn't, how could she face her mom? How could she ever face herself?

She had to do this. She had to be brave. She had to be brave right freaking now.

She scrambled to her hands and knees. A rat-tat-tat of machine gun fire came from her left as she half-crouched, half-ran across the aisle.

She stepped over the terrorist's body as a middle-aged man and a young woman crept forward and grabbed the rifle. A few others leapt from their seats and ran for the back exit.

She dove between a row and scrambled over feet and legs until she reached the furthest aisle along the far-right wall of the lounge. The terrorists guarding this side had gone, part of the fray in the front center of the room.

She tried not to think about what was happening—who was winning or losing the battle raging on the Galaxy's stage.

She moved down the rows, searching the stricken faces for her sister.

"Zia!" she called as loudly as she dared. It was a miracle anyone heard anything over the din of bullets and shouting. "I'm looking for a Filipino girl, short hair dyed turquoise," she said a dozen times to anyone within reach.

"Wait." A silver-haired Indian woman in a sherbet-orange pantsuit waved at her. She hunched between a glass coffee table and the back of the curved sofa in front of her. "Turquoise hair?"

Willow's heart stopped. "She's my sister."

The woman's expression was haggard, her eyes bloodshot. Her right earlobe was torn and crusted with dried blood, as if her earring had been ripped out. "She was right in the front, on this side. But honey, you need to know—"

She didn't hear the rest. She moved, scrabbling down the aisle, headed for the first row. Her pulse roared in her ears. She couldn't swallow, couldn't breathe.

Zia. She had to find Zia.

No one guarded the front right exit. She could escape. Flee this ornate coffin and find some hole to hide in until this was all over. Other passengers had the same idea. They slipped out one or two at a time.

Only a few moments more and they would be brave enough to flee en masse. The stampede would draw the attention of the terrorists.

She reached the front row and crept forward. Zero obstructions stood between her and the battle at the front of the stage. The bodies of terrorists, passengers, and officers littered the floor. Bullet holes riddled the stage curtain.

A few engaged in hand-to-hand combat. Shouting echoed from the balcony above her. Good guys? Or more terrorists coming for reinforcements?

A bullet punched into the stage only a few yards away. She ducked, flattening herself against the carpet. She turned her head, her cheek pressed against the nubby fibers.

And saw her sister. A cold dread filled Willow worse than all the fear and terror that had come before.

Zia sprawled beneath a coffee table, shards of glass scattered across her prone body. She didn't move. Her head was tilted at an awkward angle, blood speckling her mouth and the turquoise spikes of her hair.

Her eyes were open. But they didn't see Willow.

They didn't see anything anymore.

27

AMELIA

Gabriel sat cross-legged in front of Amelia. He fed her several chips in silence. They tasted like salty cardboard in her mouth, but she ate them anyway.

His face was closed, his jaw set. She couldn't read him. But he didn't have to feed her. He didn't have to give her water. That kindness had to mean something. *Use what you have.*

"May I ask you a question?"

He stared out the viewing window and rubbed the back of his neck. He clenched his jaw, his forehead furrowed.

"Was this—us—all just a ploy?"

"Of course." The muscle in his cheek jumped.

"Even out by the hot tub? Even in here?"

His gaze didn't stray from the window. "That's what I just said."

"Okay." Pain jabbed between her ribs. "But why? Why are you doing this?"

"You should stop talking." His voice hardened.

"You don't think I deserve to know?"

For a long minute, he didn't speak. Maybe she'd misjudged him. Or misjudged her play, making a mistake before she'd started.

"I'm sorry I had to deceive you. I wouldn't have—I wish things were different."

She kept her face blank, hiding the relief rushing through her. "I want to understand. I thought—I thought you were a good person."

Something flickered across his face. "I am."

"You've got a gun and a hostage. That doesn't exactly make sense."

"Sometimes we have to do things we'd rather not. Justice requires sacrifice."

"What justice are you fighting for?"

His eyes flashed. "Justice in everything. Justice for all. For the people."

"For what people?"

"For everyone, except for you in your glass towers or ivory palaces or whatever." He spat the words. "All you elites with your private jets and cancer cures and age regeneration procedures—what do you think pays for that? It's ours—bought with our blood, sweat, and tears."

"That's not true—"

"Do you have any idea what it's like for the average person out there? Inflation spiking so high we can't afford fresh vegetables anymore—if they're even for sale. They feed us lab-made prefab slop while your people take whatever's left of the real food not destroyed by that fungal rot epidemic.

"And jobs? No one can afford college anymore. You need a paper degree just to get a crappy manager's position overseeing metalheads at McDonalds. Jobs are a joke."

Her fingers twitched, itching for her charm bracelet. Was it truly that bad? The newsfeed headlines popping up on her SmartFlex always screamed death and disaster.

Critical water shortages. Epic storms. Droughts and famines. Riots in Chicago and Atlanta. Terrorist attacks. But no one she knew really talked about it except as a problem to clean up, a scourge to get rid of. "You sound angry."

He jumped to his feet and started pacing. "Yeah, we're angry. People are angry. Worse, people are sick. And dying. And no one does a damn thing to help. There is no justice. Not in this country. Not anymore."

"How can I help? My father has power and influence. I can talk to him. I could—"

He gave a sharp jerk of his head. "The time for talking is over."

She licked her lips. "What are you going to do?"

"Going to do? We're doing it now."

"But what happens next? What do you get?"

This brought a tight smile that didn't reach his eyes. "We infiltrate and destroy this bastion of luxury, this symbol of reprehensible waste and excess, then we bring the whole bloated, corrupted system to its knees.

"The president, Congress, the Unity Coalition—everyone will know. A second revolutionary war has begun."

He was too agitated, his eyes bright and furious, the gun swinging wildly in his hand. She didn't know him well, but this didn't sound like him. It didn't sound like his words.

This was the wrong tactic. She had to calm him down, not rile him up.

She had to make him *see* her—really see her, not his preconceived, distorted view twisting her into the enemy. To him, she represented everything he hated: excess, greed, corruption, vanity.

She had to show him she was human.

There was a moment when his guard dropped. When she fell. When her vision wavered, another vicious seizure thundering down on her.

She'd been weak—a weakness she loathed, but it reached him. She'd seen real concern in his eyes. Compassion. And when he'd kissed her—that was real.

She knew it.

She still felt it. In spite of herself, in spite of everything. That dizzy rush when he looked at her, that fluttering in her gut. Part of her cursed her own traitorous heart. She shouldn't feel a thing for him but hate and fear and disgust.

But she did. She did and she couldn't stop it.

He was so different from everything she'd known her whole life, the endemic indifference, everything so shiny and fake and false. He was full of passion and intensity and desperate desire.

Being near him made her heart beat wild inside her own chest, made her want to be different, too. Made her want to be more. To be someone he could respect.

It was her weakness—one of many—but she was sure it was also his. She had to find it again, find it within him and push on it, wedge her fingers in the tiny gap and force her way in. "Your life sounds difficult."

"Everyone's life is difficult." His face filled with more than anger. Pain shadowed his eyes. "It's not a secret. It's all over the vlogs and newsfeeds—well, their own twisted version. But you don't care. None of you care."

"That's not true." But it was, and she knew it.

"Do you read the newsfeeds and pings on your SmartFlex? Or do you flick it off because it depresses you? Because you can't deal with all the negativity?"

Amelia opened her mouth but found she couldn't speak. She thought of the day a few years before when she'd come home from orchestra practice to find her mother crumpled in front of the holoscreen, sobbing.

Amelia had dropped her bag on the kitchen counter and rushed into the living room. "What's wrong?" Someone important must have died, Mema or—

Her mother had looked up, tears staining her face, her makeup still perfectly applied. "No more elephants."

"What?" Amelia stood there, staring.

Her mother gestured at the holoscreen. "The last elephant just died at the Namibia Wildlife Sanctuary in Africa. Elephants are officially extinct."

"But we just saw one at the zoo."

She waved her hand dismissively. "Those aren't—they're not real elephants. They're modded. Genetically engineered."

"But why are you crying?" Amelia was perplexed, but also anxious and a bit alarmed, like she'd missed some important puzzle piece. But she didn't know which piece it was or what shape.

Her mother always got upset at stuff like this, as if the three-toed sloths, black rhinos, and polar bears were these precious family pets she knew and loved, not pictures on a holoscreen or shambling creatures they visited on school trips to the zoo once a year.

The elephants and rhinos and other animals at the zoo seemed real enough. You could ride them for a fee.

That same disconcerting anxiety flitted through her now. She started to see a fuzzy outline of the missing piece. It always seemed so far away—extinct animals on other continents, the children starving in Arizona, the rioting in Tampa and Chicago, the drowning cities in New Orleans.

Only, here Gabriel stood right in front of her, pain etched across his face. "I'm sorry."

"If I didn't have the right connection, a loyal friend to help me out, I would have nothing. No security, no job with benefits, no way to put a roof over me and my brother's head."

He paused in his pacing, leaned against the ladder, and swallowed a swig of water. "Some American dream."

"What about your parents?"

His expression softened. "They tried their best. My dad worked in construction before most things got automated. After working all day, he'd come home and cook dinner for us. Ma hated cooking, but Dad enjoyed it. He made *arroz con habichuelas,* simple rice and beans, but he could make them taste amazing.

"On Micah's tenth birthday, Ma decided to make his favorite *tostones,* fried plantains, but she got distracted reading one of her books. Next thing, the fire alarm's blaring, the plantains are blackened, and Ma's beating at the billowing smoke with her paperback."

"That's a wonderful memory."

"I tell you this because she was *real*—a real person with real feelings, not a statistic, not a number, not a cost-benefit analysis sheet. Ma got sick when I was fourteen. She'd be asleep when we got home from school. Then her hair started falling out.

"Insurance wouldn't touch any of the drugs that might have fixed her—like your dad's cure. Too damn expensive. Do you have any idea what it's like to know a cure exists, but no one will give it to you?"

His voice snagged. He took another swig of water and capped the bottle, his hands trembling. "My dad, he just . . . he lost it. He gave up. We used to work on this train set down in the basement. He'd whittle the houses and these little wooden trains for Micah and me to play with.

"But after . . . He started taking Silk to cope, to get through the day. He stopped doing things little by little. Cooking, cleaning, whittling, working. Even eating, at the end. You ever watch a man starve himself to death? That's what Silk does. Micah and I watched them both die."

Every word was a hot poker piercing her gut. Her worries over her violinist career and pleasing her implacable father so inconsequential they seemed obscene. "Gabriel, I'm sorry."

He stared at her, shadows haunting his face, so many dark emotions swirling in his gaze. "What would you know? You don't know anything."

It was true. She didn't know. Whatever problems she had, her privilege and her wealth spared her from the worst of it. She'd been selfish, consumed with her own world. "I really am sorry."

Anything else she'd planned to say—to appear pathetic, to garner his sympathies, to manipulate him—turned to ash on her tongue.

28

WILLOW

A low moan escaped Willow's lips.

Zia stared off at nothing, her eyes glassy and unseeing.

She tried to reach beneath the shattered coffee table to administer CPR on her sister's body, even as her brain told her, *she's dead,* and her heart screamed, *I'm sorry! Don't leave me!*

She inched forward, her hands and bare knees scraping against needles of broken glass buried in the carpet. She didn't care. She didn't feel any pain. Her pulse throbbed in her fingertips, her belly, her throat.

She held her sister's arm and pulled herself closer, until they lay face to face. She touched Zia's clammy skin, rubbery like some unreal thing, like the stupid robot skin that gave her a shivery rush of revulsion if she looked too closely. Humanlike, a proximity, an imitation—but not human.

Not alive. Not anymore.

I don't want you around. The last words she ever spoke to her sister, so angry and ugly. Words she didn't mean.

Zia didn't know how sorry she was. Would never know. She would give everything she had to take it back, to get Zia back.

Great shudders ripped through her body, wave after wave of grief rolling over her. Zia with her weird donkey laugh and obsession with turquoise, her loud, exuberant voice filling up every room.

Optimistic, sweet, and silly Zia. Zia who only wanted Willow to pay attention to her.

She rested her forehead against her sister's, the way they used to when they were kids, when Zia had a nightmare and crawled into Willow's bed, nestling her tiny body against Willow's. When all she had to do was say, "It'll be okay," and it was.

She lay like that, gripping her sister's cold hand, staring into eyes that weren't Zia's eyes anymore and never would be again.

The silent scream inside her would not stop. Would never stop. Would go on forever, and ever, and ever.

29

MICAH

"We're ghosts here," Patel said. They crouched behind a line of six slot machines at the back of the casino. "No security cameras can catch this angle, only the internal casino surveillance cameras. We don't need to worry about those."

"Where are we going?" Micah asked.

Jericho grabbed the fallen men's radios and clipped them to his own belt. "First, the CSO's office to get a few more weapons from the safe."

"How are you going to get access?" Micah asked.

Patel grimaced. "The CSO and several other officers are hiding there. I couldn't bear to cower and do nothing, so I left to look for help."

"And you found it," Jericho said. "As soon as we get more weapons and more men, we take the bridge. I need to secure Declan Black."

"What about the rest of the passengers and crew?" Micah still couldn't breathe properly, couldn't suck in enough oxygen to ease the tight, drowning feeling in his chest. He kept seeing that shadow falling over him. Kept reliving the gut-wrenching rush of fear as his own death closed in.

"We're outnumbered." Jericho ran a hand across his close-cropped black hair. "We'll be slaughtered if we try to retake one of the muster stations. My primary objective is to get Declan Black and his family off this ship. You just got damned lucky."

"But all those people—"

"Are likely already dead."

Micah shook his head. "We have to at least try."

Jericho rose to his feet. "No, we don't. Every minute we delay increases the probability of detection."

"He's right," Silas said. "A small group has a better chance of survival. This is no time to play the hero."

Anger zapped through Micah like an electrical current. "This is exactly the time to be a hero!" But no one listened to him.

Jericho pointed at the bodies of the terrorists. "Put on their clothes. You can move through the ship without worrying about the cameras."

Silas's face twisted. "They're covered in blood."

"Not much. Do it quickly. I'll cover you."

Silas and Micah stripped the combat gear and dark clothing off the bodies. Micah fought waves of nausea as he moved dead limbs still soft and pliable. It was like changing a giant doll. Except the doll had been alive five minutes ago.

This man had his own dreams, disappointments, regrets. His own family. People he loved.

Micah peeled off the ski mask and sucked in his breath. The man was young, pimples still dotting his forehead, Gabriel's age.

"You aren't going soft, are you?" Silas smirked as he strapped on a bullet-proof vest.

Micah ignored him, concentrating on removing his own clothes and redressing. The terrorist's shirt had two small holes in the shoulder, the spatters of blood still wet. He gagged again, turning away to keep Silas from noticing.

But his stomach roiled from more than the blood. He thought of Su Su, Chef Jokumsen, and all the other innocent people trapped in the muster stations by those monsters with guns. And Amelia, held against her will in the Oceanarium.

He should tell Jericho about Amelia. Where she was, who held her captive. But the words jammed in his throat. To Jericho, Gabriel was nothing but a terrorist. Jericho would shoot him without a second thought.

Micah couldn't risk his brother's death, not when he knew Gabriel would never hurt Amelia. He was mixed up in something awful, but he wasn't a killer. She was probably safer down there with him than up here.

"What about a distress signal?" Micah asked instead. "The lifeboats each have one. We can activate the emergency beacon so the Coast Guard can rescue us."

"No time. Our priority is the bridge."

"We have to at least do something!"

"Keep your voice down." Jericho cracked his knuckles. "We move out in one minute."

Chef Jokumsen had risked his own life so Micah could do something. He had to act. He couldn't stand by and do nothing. "Then I'll go myself."

Silas snorted. "You'll get yourself killed."

The ship pitched. Micah stumbled, then straightened. He shoved his glasses up the bridge of his nose. "That's a risk I'll take."

"Suit yourself," Silas said.

Patel scratched his beard. "It would help to see how well-guarded the lifeboats are. And we don't know how long it'll take to regain the bridge. Successfully deploying an emergency call seems worth the time —and the risk."

Jericho narrowed his eyes, studying the map. He sighed. "We'll head to the CSO's office and the bridge after the lifeboats. But it will be dangerous. I can't promise we won't walk into a death trap."

"Thank you, sir." Micah sagged with relief. "You won't regret this."

"We'll see." Jericho handed him a wicked-looking rifle. "Don't use this unless you absolutely have to. You respect it. And whatever you do, don't panic and shoot your own team in the back. You understand?"

He nodded. Jericho rechecked the ship map on his wristband, then gave him rapid-fire instructions on how to use his new weapon and what to do if—when—they came under enemy fire.

Run in a zigzag pattern. Find cover, but don't stay there too long. Be aware of tunnel vision. Don't spray and pray. Accurate fire wins the fight. The first shot will usually miss; it's the second and third shot that kills as the shooter adjusts his aim.

"This is a baptism by fire," Jericho said. "You ready for it?"

Micah tightened his grip on the gun, trying to keep his hands from shaking. The cuts on his fingers reopened, leaving fresh red smears on the black metal. He could barely hear Jericho over the roaring in his ears.

Finally, Jericho seemed satisfied. He motioned for them to move. Micah followed him, a little behind and to the left. Silas flanked him on the right, and Patel brought up the rear.

The rifle was bulky and unwieldy and heavier than he'd thought. He held it with the butt pressed against his armpit, the muzzle pointed off to the right of his right foot, the way Jericho showed him. He could lift, aim, and shoot in one fluid movement.

His stomach churned at the thought of shooting someone. A terrorist was still a human being, no matter how wicked.

They went up a flight of stairs to Deck Five and crept warily along the edges of the Royal Promenade, working their way toward the starboard side. They passed the Pink Reef Café, the brick patio scattered with overturned tables and chairs.

The terrorists had broken the glass windows of every designer shop, smashed the display cases, and stolen the jewelry, purses, and designer SmartFlexes. They'd upturned racks of jewel-toned smartwear dresses, the merchandise strewn across the floor.

His feet crunched shards of shattered glass, china, and crystal from the shot-up chandeliers. Jagged pieces of ornate bronze panels had fallen from the ceiling high above them.

But the worst thing was the dead. So many bodies. The terrorists hadn't given them a chance to make it to the muster stations. Hundreds of passengers were mowed down where they stood.

Micah forced himself to look at the dead, whispering a prayer for each one. Some were dressed in beautiful gowns and tuxedos, others in shorts and flip flops. Every face frozen in a rictus of terror. None of them expected to die today.

He passed by a boy with curly blonde hair, no older than ten.

Micah's finger trembled next to the trigger. How could God allow this?

No, not God. How did Yeat's poem go? *Man has created death.* Men did this. Gabriel did this. Gabriel and his radicalized New Patriots. Gabriel hadn't planned this violence, but it had fallen upon them anyway.

Violence begot violence. Death begot death. This was where it ended. Not with one side winning, but with grief and suffering on both sides. With dead children.

How many more would die before this was all over?

30

WILLOW

The world was ending all around her, but for Willow, the world had ended *right here*.

The world was over for Zia. It should be over for Willow. Death would be a release, a relief, a just punishment for letting her own sister die—

Benjie.

The thought drilled through the shock and the heart-wrenching grief cascading over her. She groaned, closing her eyes. But her mind wouldn't let her. *Move!* It shrieked at her.

Move!

Half of her wanted to give up, to curl next to Zia and let the wave of blood and violence take her like it took everything else. But the other half of her longed to live. She couldn't die now. She still had Benjie. He needed her.

Her brain registered the sound of bullets and the shouting, lessened now. The battle was waning. She had to move now.

She longed to wrap her arms around her sister and never let go. Leaving her here like this, her body just lying there, like trash—it was a betrayal. A desecration.

"I'm sorry." Her voice clogged with sorrow and regret and grief. "I'm so sorry."

Every muscle in her body ached as she pulled herself to her hands and knees. Her palms burned from a dozen tiny cuts. Her knees left a swath of blood across the carpet.

She had to focus on escape now. She had to save Benjie.

She glanced toward the stage. Four men knelt in the carnage. One terrorist guarded either side, two others faced the hostages, screaming at them, thrusting the end of their rifles in the hostages' faces.

Most of the passengers remained seated, too terrified to flee, shocked rigid at the scene unfolding in front of them.

She glanced back toward the right front exit. The doorway was only a half-dozen yards away. The exit sign blinked red above the door, one of the letters shorted out.

A gunshot blasted. The first hostage went down, falling over backward like a sack of flour.

Willow crouched, legs like coiled springs. She ignored the screaming in her brain, the agony of the glass still stuck in her palms and kneecaps, the roar of her pulse so loud it drowned out the rest of the world—

She leapt to her feet and ran.

Five feet. Ten. Tears stung her eyes, everything around her a blur.

She cleared the doorway. No shots fired. No shouts directed her way.

She fled down the hallway, searching frantically for the nearest stairwell. She raced up two flights of stairs before pausing on the landing, gasping.

Muffled screams filtered from the Galaxy Lounge below. Think. She had to *think*.

What should she do? Where should she hide? She touched her mother's wristband. She could get into any room.

She should get below, into the crew quarters, and find a lowly cabin to hide in until the Navy SEALs or whoever came to save them. The pirates had no reason to go down there. The crew had nothing worth scavenging.

Benjie. The thought shot through her as loud as if someone had shouted in her ear.

She couldn't hide. Not yet. She had to find the remaining parts of her family. Benjie first. Her mom would want her to go after Benjie. *They're your responsibility.*

Once she found them, they'd lie low until rescue arrived, like López said. Someone would come for them. Every passenger on this damn ship was as rich as Midas. The whole U.S. Army would ride in and save them.

She started to head up the stairs on tiptoe, as if that would make a difference.

A sound.

She craned her head, searching above and below, to the left and right. It came again. From below her. Footsteps. Someone coming up the stairs. At least one, possibly more.

She couldn't tell how many flights below they were, and she couldn't risk peering over the railing. But they headed closer. A male voice muttered something and another laughed.

Adrenaline spiked through her veins. She ran out of the stairwell, desperately hoping she wasn't fleeing from the frying pan into the fire. She rounded the corner and pressed herself against a brick façade wall.

A dozen small tables and bar stools bunched beneath a trellis strung with bioluminescent lights in a hundred different colors. She had the impression of wide open space all around and above her. Everything was dim and hard to see.

She blinked, trying to get her eyes to adjust as she followed the wall to an alcove with a tall fronded plant. She crouched behind it, squeezing herself between the wall and the huge ceramic planter, adjusting the fronds to hide herself.

It sucked as a hiding spot, but it would have to do. She forced herself to take several deep, steadying breaths as she peeked between the leaves.

The ship's suite balconies rose up on either side of the four-story atrium. A mosaic tile pathway wound past the café into a stand of manicured trees and bushes, all lit from below with flickering lights that gradually changed colors from blue to red to pink to magenta. She'd reached the Coral Gardens.

Far above her, the rain pounded against the transparent ceiling. No overhead lights lit her way; there was only the dim atmospheric lighting to allow for stargazing on clear nights. This was not one of them.

She was on the stern—the backside—of Deck Eight. What else was on Eight? She tapped her wristband twice and the hologram of the ship appeared.

A bunch of cafes, high-end designer shops, and the digital art gallery circled the Coral Gardens—a huge park area with tile pathways, artfully placed waterfalls and streams, and little bridges winding through tropical trees, topiary bushes and plants shaped like a coral reef.

She'd avoided this deck until now because it lacked teen or kid activities. The decks above her held the bars and theaters, the casino, the snow room and low-grav center, and the sundecks, where anyone with a gun would see her a mile off.

Once she reached the mid-stairwell, she could go all the way up to Deck Fourteen.

The voices drew closer. She shrank against the wall. Two terrorists with their huge guns flanked a svelte silver-haired woman in a silk gown and a mink shrug.

They passed by only a half-dozen feet away. Her heart punched into her throat. If the men looked to their left, they would see her through the fronds. *Don't breathe.*

The woman wept as she stumbled on the cobblestones in her four-inch heels. One of the men grabbed her elbow and yanked her up. The other man carried a half-full pillowcase bulging with jewelry.

"You don't have to do this," the woman begged. "I can wire you any amount you want. Please, don't hurt us."

The man with the pillowcase spat something in Tagalog. Willow didn't speak Tagalog at home, but her *lola* did sometimes. At home, the Filipino Channel was always on in the background.

She recognized a few words. *Shut your mouth, pig.*

They marched past and disappeared into the shrubbery.

She let the air out of her lungs. The ship rolled and her stomach rolled with it, making her queasy. Thunder crashed overhead.

Time to go. She should head back to the closest stairs. Her legs ached from crouching. She pushed herself to her feet.

And froze. More sounds from the stairwell.

Her hiding spot was too flimsy to keep working. She'd gotten lucky last time. She had to move, and she had to move now.

She edged around the planter and pushed herself off the wall. Using the path was a recipe for disaster, but she could go through the park itself. Most of the foliage would provide good cover.

She pushed through the café tables and chairs, careful not to bump into anything that might make a noise, and crept between a boxwood shaped like a giant brain coral and a laurel shrub formed into a purple fan.

Mulch, twigs and fallen pine needles dug into her bare feet. She inhaled the scent of flowers and holly, craning her ears to listen over the sounds of birdsong piped into the speakers.

She pushed aside two chest-high plants formed into pumpkin-orange pillars. A thorn snagged her dress and she jerked it free. The garden burst with color—yellow sea anemones and blue elkhorn, pink and green dragon-eyed something, and a host of others she couldn't name.

For a moment, she could almost forget. For half a second, she could—

Pain shot through the center of her heart. She could never forget, would never forget, not for one moment, that her sister was gone, that she'd died a horrible death.

Worse, she had died scared and alone. And it was Willow's fault.

Willow leaned against the trunk of a Japanese maple, red leaves like tiny hands fluttering all around her. A strangled sob escaped her lips. She slapped both hands over her mouth, shoulders shaking.

She couldn't freak out. Not here. She couldn't grieve. Not now. Not if she wanted to survive. She squeezed her eyes shut, willing the pain back, shoving the grief and sorrow and despair into a tiny box in a corner of her soul.

When she opened her eyes, a bolt of lightning lit up the atrium. Three dark shapes moved amongst all the motionless ones. Only a few dozen yards ahead of her, they glided along the path like silent shadows.

Thunder crashed. Above the birdsong chirping in the branch next to her, she heard other sounds. Footsteps and voices. Behind her.

She froze, her heart a pellet of ice.

She was trapped.

31

GABRIEL

"We haven't known each other that long," Amelia said haltingly. "But I felt something."

Gabriel stared at her. The blue glow from the holograms glimmered across her face. She was so breathtakingly beautiful. A tiny chasm opened inside his heart.

"I felt something. You think you can judge me, but you can't. I don't have the time or the—I don't have close relationships. The girls my age are all daughters of politicians or CEOs or celebrities. They want to get close to my father's power. Or they want to be written up in the latest celebrity gossip vlog, pictures of themselves with their arms slung around me plastered all over the internet."

He curled his lip. "Cry me a river."

"I know. I *know*, okay? That's nothing compared to actual suffering. But—what I'm trying to say is, before you, I've never—"

She cleared her throat, a blush spreading from her neck. "We're so different. But I saw something, something in your eyes. I can be myself around you. You aren't impressed by my father's influence and power, my wealth and status."

He snorted.

"See? That's what everyone else *wants*. With you, they're barriers. I've never met anyone like that before."

"You're socializing in the wrong circles."

"Yeah, I'm starting to get that."

He almost smiled. "You'd be surprised by how human we can be."

She met his gaze, steady and unblinking. "I am surprised. I admit it. You surprised me."

A shard of guilt punctured his lungs. He looked down at the weapon in his hands.

"What I felt was real." Her voice cracked. He glanced at her. Her face looked crumpled, like she was fighting back tears. "It kills me to say this —to admit it. But I felt it. And I know you did, too."

The ship pitched. Nausea swirled in his stomach. He hardened his voice. "It was an act. I told you."

"Is it so hard to admit?" A phantom of a smile crossed her lips, her chin quivering.

She was the daughter of Declan Black, billionaire CEO, corrupt chairman of the Unity Coalition, the man who kept the BioGen cancer cure from every person not born with a silver spoon in their mouth, including Gabriel's mom. He'd watched his mom die because of her father.

This girl was the enemy.

Then why had his heart just split wide open?

"It's always hard to be vulnerable," she said. "No matter who we are."

"Vulnerability is nothing but weakness where I come from."

"I don't believe that. You love your brother. I saw that clear as day."

He didn't answer her. Too many tangled emotions snarled in his gut. Too many things he didn't want to feel, wasn't supposed to feel. Couldn't feel.

The memory of their kiss flushed through him—the soft, open expression on her face, so different from the cool reserve she showed the rest of the world.

She was getting under his skin. And he hated it.

He leapt to his feet. "I'm getting a drink."

He slung the rifle over his shoulder and stalked up the darkened center aisle to the stack of water bottles against the back wall. His walkie-talkie spat static, and Simeon's voice came on the line. "Gabriel."

"Yes, sir?"

"I'm checking in. The muster stations are quiet. There haven't been any major attempts to escape. We're headed to our extraction point. Everything is on target, except for Black. He's quite . . . difficult. How is the girl?"

"Everything's fine."

"Be ready to bring her to the bridge."

Gabriel glanced toward the front of the Oceanarium. Amelia stared back at him. His heartbeat stuttered. "Simeon—"

"What?"

But he couldn't ask the question. "I'll be ready."

He clipped the walkie-talkie and pulled two water bottles out of the box. He returned to the dais, knelt, and offered her a drink.

"Can I ask you a favor?" she asked. "The bindings on my wrists. They're so tight, I can't feel my fingers. Nerve damage could affect my playing. Please."

Her eyes filled with anxiety and fear. He'd seen her with a violin. He knew how much she loved it, how skilled she was. It wouldn't hurt anything to free her for a few minutes.

He pulled his knife from its sheath at his waist and a new zip-tie from his pocket. She bent forward, and he slid the knife between her hands and cut the strap.

"May I rub my fingers?"

He nodded.

She brought her hands in front of her and sucked in her breath. Her fingers were purplish and swollen. An ugly red mark encircled each wrist.

His mouth went dry. "I'm sorry."

"See? You don't have hatred in you."

"Yes, I do."

"How could you, when you show such kindness?"

"I have both hatred and love in me. That's what we get wrong. We think it's one or the other, but it isn't. And love and hate don't have much to do with justice, do they?"

"We still have our feelings. What about yours?" Her gaze pinned him. "Do you hate me?"

"No," he answered honestly. He couldn't help himself. He was supposed to hate her. Everything in him wanted to, needed to—but he couldn't. He looked into her eyes and saw sadness and fear, but below that, strength. And courage. "I thought I did, at first. But I don't."

"Then choose something else. Choose love."

"It's not that easy." Shame and remorse skewered him. His heart ripped in pieces. Everything inside him sharp and jagged, like broken glass. "This is bigger than me. I can't choose my own selfish desires when people are starving and sick and dying. That's not justice. I must be willing to sacrifice."

She rubbed her swollen fingers. "Maybe you're sacrificing the wrong things."

He couldn't help it. He reached for her hand.

She looked up at him. Their faces were inches apart. He counted every pale eyelash, traced the faintest spray of pimples along her hairline.

He saw everything in the deep wells of her eyes—his own pain and turmoil reflected back at him.

She interlocked her fingers with his. "Gabriel."

He should pull his hand away. He should tie her up. He should get as far away from this girl as he could.

But he didn't. He couldn't. She had a warmth to her, a glow that lit her up from the inside.

He wanted to be near her.

Amelia leaned forward. Her breath quickened, so close he felt it on his cheek.

Her lips grazed his. His blood buzzed at her touch, his skin hot and tingling.

His heart thudded against his ribs.

She kissed him.

She kissed him hard and deep. He opened his mouth, letting her kiss him, letting her in.

She buried her fingers in his hair and drew him to her. Dark and fierce emotions burst inside him.

He groaned. Everything rose to the surface at once. All the things he hadn't allowed himself to feel—his doubt, his fear, his overwhelming loneliness.

He kissed her. Heaven help him, he was kissing her back. He dropped the knife and grabbed her by the waist and pulled her onto his lap.

She stroked his scalp, her hands on either side of his head.

He kissed her, hard and urgent and desperate, filled with a longing he couldn't name. For this moment, here with her, the darkness within him receded like a great black wave.

He took in her warmth, her nearness, her scent like lilacs in an open field. She felt safe. She felt like coming home.

She pulled away. He opened his eyes and took a ragged breath.

She placed her hand on his chest, over his heart. Her gaze bored into him with her intense, ice-blue eyes. "This is real. Do you feel it now?"

"Yes." His voice was hoarse, his throat raw.

"And I'm real. I'm a real person. I feel fear and pain and love, just like you."

"I know." He reached for her again, but she slid off his lap.

"I'm not bad. I've made mistakes, but I'm not evil. Being born into a rich family doesn't make me a bad person. Being poor doesn't make you bad. It's our actions that count. Our—our choices."

"Come here."

She came back to him. He wrapped his arms around her, sinking into her softness, her warmth. His skin was on fire. His bones were melting.

She kissed him again, long and slow.

Something cold and razor-sharp slid across his throat.

Amelia pressed the knife against his Adam's apple.

Stupid! How could he be so stupid! Rage crackled through him. Sparks flew behind his eyes, red against black canvas. He should've known she was just like the rest of them. "How could you—!"

"I talk," she said. "You listen."

All this time he'd thought he manipulated her, but she'd used him and manipulated him right back. And now he'd screwed up so badly Simeon would never forgive him.

He'd betrayed the cause. Betrayed his own heart. He'd die a coward, a traitor, his life utterly meaningless.

"Are you listening?"

He clenched his fists, furious at her, furious at himself. But she had him. He was helpless.

"I could kill you right now," she said. "I'll run out of here and some other terrorist will shoot me or torture me or—it doesn't matter. But whatever happens next, I know what I should do. I'm supposed to kill you."

A sharp bitterness welled on his tongue. "Just do it."

She pressed the blade deeper.

32

WILLOW

W illow was trapped.

Three figures advanced down the path toward her. At least two headed her way from behind. The Japanese maple wouldn't provide enough coverage. She was exposed.

A bridge. Ten feet ahead. It was the closest thing. The only thing. She dropped on all fours and crept toward it, hoping the storm and the ambient noise would hide her movements.

She shoved through several manicured bushes she didn't know the names of. Thorns and sharp twigs poked her face, scratching her arms.

She broke through and slid down the pebbled bank into the water, careful to keep from splashing. The water was cold and three feet deep. She crouched low, the waterline at her neck, and swam beneath the bridge.

The bridge arched above her, about six feet wide. Beneath it, the shadows lurked dark and heavy. As long as she wasn't spotted slipping into the water, she should be—

She bumped into something. Something bumped back.

She stifled a screamed.

Something wet and warm gripped her arm. "Shhh!"

She blinked, her heart thumping, every nerve and cell in her body on high alert. Her eyes adjusted to the shadows.

A girl her age stared back at her, the whites of her eyes glimmering.

Willow recognized her as one of the richies who sauntered around the ship like she owned it—a tall, African-American girl with a cloud of coppery coils forming a halo around her face. Her features were perfect, with her full lips and sculpted cheekbones. Even in her fear, she looked like a creature from another planet.

She blew out a breath.

The girl dug her long, manicured fingernails into Willow's forearm. She raised one finger to her lips.

Willow nodded. Both girls lifted their heads toward the bridge above them and listened.

Heavy footsteps clomped over the bridge. The voices came from both sides. "Status report."

"Found about ten hiding out in the ice rink. They had a few fire axes and one had a gun. We lost Cruz and Sampson. Took 'em all out, though."

"Keep going. I want every corner of this ship cleared. No more surprises."

"Got it."

Willow's heart thundered louder, banging against her ribs. Surely, they would hear it. They would find them and then—

"Get to it, then, you stinkin' rat."

Two sets of boots stomped off the bridge toward the aft of the ship.

"It's almost over," a second voice said in a soothing tone. Female. An accent Willow couldn't place. "We've got two more. Then the whole thing's ready to blow."

"I'm shootin' that little maggot myself."

"I'm sure you will. We've got a deadline to meet, first."

The second group strode off in the opposite direction, toward the stern.

Willow counted the seconds in her head. They waited a full minute before either of them dared to move or breathe.

The girl started to cry, tears leaking down her cheeks. "I was with my girlfriend, Kendyll, in the casino. We heard the stupid muster call, but we were on a lucky slot machine and she was up six thousand bucks. And now—now she's dead."

She took a gasping breath. "They just stormed in, like this solid black wall . . . they killed so many people. Just—just shot them, as if they were *nothing*."

"I know." A chill spiked up Willow's spine. Her brain couldn't focus. It kept dragging her back to the conversation they'd overheard. She repeated the sentences over and over in her head.

"I ran—I just . . . What was I supposed to do?"

"I know. It's okay. I'm Willow. What's your name?"

"Celeste Kingsley-Yates. What do we do now?"

She lifted her wrist out of the water, exposing her wristband. "My first thought was to head to the crew quarters to hide out in a cabin until the Navy or whoever comes to rescue us. But I need to—"

"You can open the staterooms?"

"It's my mom's. She has access. But I'm not going—"

But Celeste moved away from her. They swam out from beneath the bridge, checked their surroundings, and climbed out.

Water dripped down Willow's arms and legs. Her dress stuck to her wet skin, drenched. She pulled at the fabric, rolled it into a ball, and squeezed.

Celeste stumbled on the path, twisting her ankle.

"Take off your shoes," Willow said. "It's a miracle you haven't broken something."

Celeste straightened with a scowl, but she obeyed. She tossed her heels into the stream, stiffening at the sound of the splash. But no one else was near enough to hear. Even drenched from head to foot, Celeste oozed sophistication and class. She'd been born with it. "What are you waiting for? Let's go."

But Willow couldn't move. Her muscles refused to work. "Something's wrong."

Celeste fisted her hands on her hips. "Hello? That's the understatement of the century."

"Those pirates or terrorists or whatever they are. What they said—"

"Who cares? Let's just go!"

Dread scrabbled up her spine. "They were talking about bombs."

Celeste's eyes widened. "What?"

"They're wiring the ship with explosives."

"No . . ."

"Yes. They're gonna blow up the ship."

"Then what do we do?" Celeste cried, her voice tinged with hysteria.

"Be quiet!" Willow's gaze flicked up and down the mosaic path. Still nothing. "Maybe the lifeboats. But those are probably guarded to keep anyone from escaping. But that's not where I'm going."

"What are you talking about?"

"I can't hide or go for the lifeboats. I have to get my brother first."

"The only thing to do is to save yourself. Everything else is stupidity. You'll just get yourself killed!"

Every word Celeste spoke was truth. Willow longed to flee with her, to get the hell out while she still could. Every second she delayed risked her own life. But she had to find Benjie. She couldn't leave him, even with the ship about to go down in flames.

Her mom was an adult. She would take care of herself. But Benjie needed her more than ever.

She had to save him. She had to at least try. It was the least she could do after—but she refused to let her mind go there. "I'm sorry. I can't."

Celeste pursed her lips. "You're being utterly ridiculous."

It would be so easy. Just one step. Take one step toward Celeste and the decision would be made. *Think of yourself. Save yourself.*

Instead, images of Zia's broken body flooded her mind. She couldn't. What good would her life be if she couldn't bear to look at herself in the mirror?

She had to do this. She had no choice. "Look, you can come with me. But I'm not hiding. And I'm not going to the lifeboats without my brother."

"You're insane!"

"I have to do this."

"Just give me the wristband!" Celeste's eyes burned bright and fever-ish. "I'll find a stateroom to hide in. I'll wait for you."

Willow looked at her. She took a step back. "That doesn't make sense. And I can't give you the key. I'm sorry, but I might need it."

"I'll wait for you. I just said that, didn't I?"

"Look, it's nothing personal."

Something passed over Celeste's face in the dim magenta lighting. The light changed to yellow, flickering in the shadows beneath Celeste's eyes like a ghoulish flashlight. The skin around her eyes and mouth tightened, masklike.

Her gaze flicked to Willow's wrist.

She lunged for Willow at the same time Willow jumped backward. Celeste pushed her, and they both stumbled.

Celeste grabbed her ankle. She kicked hard, connecting with soft tissue.

Celeste squealed, but it was low, stifled.

Willow clambered to her feet on the path, the mosaic tiles undulat-ing, shifting from palest pink to sherbet orange to pulsing violet. She was out in the open, exposed. Any terrorist might see them from one of the balconies above. She moved back toward the coral-shaped bushes.

"Look what you did!" Celeste rubbed her nose and wiped her hand on her dress, leaving a swath of red. Blood dribbled down her lip.

"You started it." The words barely left her mouth before Celeste attacked again.

Celeste ran at her but stumbled. Her soaking wet dress clung to her thighs, restricting her movement. Willow danced out of her reach.

The ship rocked. Celeste tripped on a jutting tile. She dropped to her hands and knees, breathing hard.

"I'm faster than you are," Willow said.

Celeste's shoulders slumped, her face crumpling. She stared at Willow, her eyes huge with terror. "I'm sorry, okay? Don't leave me. Please."

Pity sprouted in her heart. Underneath her posh clothes and her bluster, Celeste was as scared as everybody else. They were all just humans now, made equal by fear and a desperate desire to survive.

"Then come with me. But I told you, I'm not hiding. I'm going to Deck Fourteen to rescue my brother."

"That's suicide."

"Maybe. But I'm going. Are you coming?"

Celeste went rigid. "No way. I can't."

"Then I can't help you."

"What am I supposed to do?"

Willow sighed. "Try to reach the lifeboats, or hide nearby. Be careful."

Celeste just stared at her, confusion and terror warring across her face. "You're really going up there?"

She took a breath. "I am."

She left Celeste kneeling in the pathway. She didn't like the thought of being alone any more than Celeste did. But she had no choice. Benjie was her priority.

She slipped through the bushes, advancing as quickly as she could without moving the foliage too much. The hairs on her arms and the back of her neck prickled. Was someone on one of the balconies above her, watching her through their scope, about to pull the trigger?

Her legs trembled. Weakness overtook her, her muscles about to give out. She forced herself to move one foot in front of the other. She couldn't give up. She wouldn't.

The rain hammered the transparent roof. Thunder boomed. The ship tilted and rolled. She stumbled, her ankle groaning in agony.

She only knew one thing for certain.

She had to save her brother.

33

AMELIA

"I should kill you." Amelia pressed the blade against Gabriel's throat.

He knelt in front of her, his dark eyes furious.

She won. For once in her life, she'd won. She'd manipulated him into falling for her, into dropping his guard. Now it was her turn. She was supposed to strike without mercy. To save herself.

But still, she hesitated.

Behind the rage and betrayal in Gabriel's eyes, she saw the pain. The confusion, hurt, and helplessness wrapped in cords of rage.

Part of her mind screamed at her to stab the knife into his neck. She had every right. He was a terrorist. A kidnapper. A murderer.

And yet.

"I'm supposed to kill you before you kill me. That's all we do, isn't it? Both sides—every side—we hate each other and fight each other, and when we get the chance, we go for the jugular. And all our talk is just jockeying for position, hunting for weakness. It's not really listening to each other. It's not trying to understand or make things better."

Blood trickled down his neck. They were so close. Dark stubble smudged his jawline like charcoal. His breath warmed her cheek. The glow of the holographic creatures tinged his skin blue.

"Just do it."

"I'm not done." She was about to unravel, thin threads of herself rippling off and floating away. "I—I don't want to kill you. I don't want to. Your brother said you were good. He said there was goodness in you. He told me to find it. I think I did."

Gabriel wasn't evil. She didn't believe that. She couldn't. She'd read people her entire life, her father especially.

Gabriel was nothing like her father. Compassion existed inside him. Empathy, mercy, kindness. She'd seen it.

Gabriel was flawed. His actions were wrong, but his cause wasn't. His willingness to sacrifice and die for something larger than himself, to take charge of his own future and fight to change it for the better—she respected that, envied it, wanted it for her own.

She couldn't live in the tiny box her father had built for her, thinking his thoughts, believing his beliefs, doing only what he wanted, playing the part perfectly but never really living, never making her own choices.

Choice required risk. And sacrifice.

She held the words carefully on her tongue, like they might break apart in her mouth. "Everything I said before, I meant. Every word of it. I'm asking you to take a huge risk. I'm asking you to change. But I can't ask that of you if I'm not willing to do the same, can I?"

He stared at her dully.

She took the knife away from his neck. She folded the blade into the handle and held it out to him on her open palm. "This is me, taking that risk. This is me finding the good in you."

———

Amelia leaned against the viewing window, facing away from the black water lashing the glass. Gabriel sat beside her, his head back, his eyes closed. For this moment, at least, the strain in his face had relaxed.

His eyelashes fluttered against his cheeks, his lips parted. He looked beautiful in the dim light—both strong and fragile at the same time.

She rubbed her red, swollen fingers and breathed deeply, storing up each second of quiet calm. It wasn't safety—they certainly weren't safe, not yet.

What still faced them was too terrifying to think about. But for this moment, at least, they had peace.

Her thoughts turned toward her family. Where was her mother? Her father? Her brother? Were they safe? Were they in pain, terrified and suffering?

Fear and dread curdled her stomach. What was Silas doing now? Was he still alive, or—

She refused to let herself think those thoughts. The last words they'd spoken to each other were spiteful and angry. She couldn't bear the idea that she'd never get a chance to make it right.

Her mind drifted back to the last conversation she'd had with her brother. Two days ago, the day before the Prosperity Summit, she and Silas had lounged on beach chairs beneath a cabana, sipping margaritas and gazing at the white sand and glittering turquoise waters of the private beach in Ocho Rios.

Sweat had trickled down the base of her neck. All around her, people chatted, dozed, or enjoyed massages in their cabanas. Service bots hovered between the lounge chairs, offering guests chilled fruit kabobs and frozen drinks. Little kids frolicked at the shoreline, splashing in the gentle waves. But she couldn't focus on the paradise in front of her.

"Can we talk?" she asked. "It feels like you've been avoiding me all week."

He slouched deeper in his chair. "That's because I have been avoiding you all week."

She hated this separation, like a wall stood between them instead of less than a foot of empty space. "Don't be like that. Silas, please."

"What do you want?"

I want my brother back. Silas's harsh words from earlier in the week echoed in her head. They used to be so close. They barely had to exchange words to know what the other was thinking.

Amelia grabbed the waterproof case her mother put her meds in and wrapped the strap around her wrist. She stood and held out her hand. "Will you go on a walk with me?"

"Whatever." Silas hauled himself to his feet. "Hurry it up. That lounge chair is calling my name."

She followed him to the shoreline. "Can I ask you something?"

He raised his eyebrows in that sarcastic, flippant way of his. "You're already asking."

The soft white sand squished between her toes. A mile of pristine beach stretched before them, palm trees and jungle undergrowth on one side, a gentle turquoise sea on the other.

She could live the rest of her life in a place like this. So peaceful, with no expectations or demands, free of the stress and anxiety always twisting her stomach. "Why did you quit hover-hockey?"

"Because I wanted to. You should try it sometime."

"But what about Father?"

Silas scowled. "What about him?"

"He's upset."

"I don't care."

"How can you say that?" Her chest tightened. The way her father looked at Silas, with such scorn and contempt in his gaze, if he bothered to look at him at all. "He's treating you like you don't exist."

"Good."

"You don't mean that."

He quieted for a moment. The sounds of laughing children and screeching seagulls filled the air. "I'm done, Amelia. And you should be, too."

"With what?"

He made an irritated sound in his throat. "Don't be obtuse. It's unbecoming."

"Please don't be like that."

"Just stop. Stop being weak and subservient, just like Mother. It's pathetic. Stop hanging your happiness on his every word."

The waves lapped her feet. The clear water glimmered like glass. She should be angry at him, but instead of anger, fear washed over her, sucking at her like an undertow. "That's not fair."

He stopped walking and turned to face her, one fist shoved into his shorts' pocket, the other swinging his wine bottle. "He's not a god, like everyone thinks he is. One of these days, he's going to topple and fall down his own mountain."

"Why do you hate him so much?"

"Why don't you hate him enough?" Silas shot back.

She opened her mouth, but nothing came out. Because how could she explain it? How do you hate the man who saved your life? How do you hate the person you've spent so much of your life desperately trying to please? To make yourself worthy of his sacrifice? Of his love?

He had never hit her. Never raised his voice or yelled at her. How could she hate him?

Her feelings for her father were a dark, complicated knot. She couldn't separate the tangled strands of love, resentment, respect, and fear. "You don't understand."

Silas reared back as if she'd slapped him, his face contorting. "I don't understand? Are you serious? Oh, that's right. How could I forget? You think you're special, the only broken one."

He whirled away from her and stalked back down the beach.

"I didn't mean it! Silas!" The wind took her words and flung them over the water.

But he didn't turn around.

Something shriveled inside her. Beads of sweat formed at her hairline, heat beating down on her head and shoulders. The sun hung suspended in the sky like a burning heart.

She closed her eyes. The bright light burned through her closed lids, through her eyeballs and struck the center of her brain, like a harsh, blazing sun inside her own skull.

Amelia could still see that sun burning behind her eyes when she closed her eyes and thought of her brother.

She took a breath to steady herself, to choke back the tears threatening to bubble up out of nowhere. She couldn't let herself feel it, not now.

She had to find a way back to him, so she could tell him how sorry she was. Silas had to live. She had to live. With Gabriel by her side, she'd make it. She had hope.

Beside her, Gabriel stirred. He rubbed his eyes with the back of his arm and groaned.

"Did you sleep?" she asked softly.

"I was thinking." He stared at her with red-rimmed eyes, his expression tense, exhausted. By freeing her, by choosing her, he betrayed his own people. It looked like it was tearing him apart.

"What happens next?"

"I'm working on a plan. But we have time. We're safe here. You're safe."

She did feel safe with him. Even in the midst of all this chaos, she felt safe. She rubbed her swollen fingers.

He glanced at her hands and made a noise deep in his throat.

"They'll heal," she said.

"Here." His voice was hoarse, guilt-stricken. "Please, let me."

Gabriel took both of her hands in his and gently ran the pads of his thumbs over the lines of her palms. He stroked her fingers. Her skin tingled, sparking at his touch.

"Are you sure they're okay? It won't affect your playing?"

She watched his strong fingers massaging her own, the dirt beneath his nails. "I can feel everything and move everything. I'm okay."

"Good."

"You know, I don't know your favorite color."

"I guess we skipped over some of those pleasantries, didn't we?" He glanced up, meeting her gaze. "It's blue."

Warmth filled her. "Mine, too. See, we agree on something."

He smiled at her, that dimple forming in his left cheek.

They sat there for a long time, Gabriel tenderly rubbing her fingers back to life. When he looked at her, his eyes were haunted. "I didn't mean to hurt you."

She heard everything he couldn't say. "I know."

34

WILLOW

Voices and footsteps came from further down the corridor, just around the corner. Willow crouched and lunged for the closest hiding spot—a dessert bar with shattered display cases of cakes, pastries, and pies.

She scooted around the counter and searched frantically for some kind of weapon. She picked up a large glass shard and wrapped a handful of her dress around the lower half, making a pathetic handle.

The voices grew louder. A guttural male voice laughed.

She jerked open a cabinet door, wincing as the hinges squeaked. It was full of junk. The second one was the same. The third cabinet beneath the sink held only an industrial gallon of soap, a bottle of all-purpose cleaner, and a package of sponges. She just might be short enough.

She shoved aside the supplies with trembling fingers and scooted inside the cabinet. She ducked her head beneath the pipes and the bowl of the sink and squeezed in.

The door wouldn't close all the way.

Damn her father's big-boned genes. Her muscles ached in protest as she contorted herself into the smallest shape possible. Inside the cabinet, the air smelled dank and stale. She blinked to adjust her eyes to the darkness. Two inches of open space still gaped between the cabinet edge and the door.

Heavy footsteps stomped around the side of the dessert bar, heading straight toward her.

Sweat trickled down her neck. Her hand tightened on the shard of glass, pain biting into the flesh between her thumb and forefinger.

A shadow fell across the narrow sliver of opened door. She glimpsed dark cargo pants, a walkie talkie clipped to a belt, and the hard muzzle of a pulse gun.

The sink over her head turned on. Water rushed through the pipe pressed against her cheek. She did not move. She did not breathe.

"Did you hear something?" the guttural male voice asked.

The moment stretched, every second excruciating. *He knows.* He knew she was there, huddled in the cabinet. He was aiming his rifle now, a second from ripping open the door—

Every muscle in her body tensed. She couldn't die here. Not like this, cowering like an animal. She hadn't found her family. She hadn't rescued her brother. She hadn't made up for her sins.

She steadied her trembling hands, blinking sweat out of her eyes. Her lungs burned for air. *Please just go the hell away.*

"Nah, must be the creaking from these damn chandeliers," the second guy said. "Let's go."

Their heavy boots crunched through glass as they left the bar and made their way down the empty corridor. The silence returned, thick and heavy.

She closed her eyes as she gulped in mouthfuls of stale air, so relieved she could have wept. She waited, counting to one hundred twice in her head before she allowed herself to move.

She pushed open the cabinet door and crept out from her hiding spot. She stared at the shattered cake display for a long time, willing her hands to stop trembling. She dropped the glass shard clutched in her fist and wiped her stinging hand on her dress, leaving streaks of scarlet.

She pressed a hand towel against the cuts on her palm to staunch the flow, the way her mom had taught her. She swallowed hard, her throat dry and scratchy as sandpaper.

She tried not to imagine what might be happening to her mom right now. If she was still alive.

Willow opened the mini fridge beneath the counter. It was half-full of soda, orange juice, and water bottles. She grabbed a bottle and guzzled the whole thing down, water dripping off her chin. She swiped her fingers in the mess of frosting and cake, careful to avoid the fragments of glass.

It had been hours since she'd had anything to eat or drink. She had no idea of the time. This nightmare went on forever and ever. There was no way to wake up.

She needed a better weapon. The next time she was trapped, she needed to at least try to fight back. She glanced around.

Where there was cake, there must be a cake knife. Somewhere. She slid open several drawers. Gloves, straws, strainers, napkins, forks and spoons. Nestled next to a packet of hair nets were two of the most beautiful knives she'd ever seen.

She grabbed the largest one, took a deep breath, and headed back out.

She considered the crew corridors, but they were narrow with long stretches of absolutely nowhere to run or hide. The passenger areas were marginally safer. But not by much.

She forced herself to keep moving. She had a mission. Rescue her brother. Find her family. Stay alive. She couldn't fail now. She stepped out into the corridor, heading toward the stairwell leading to Deck Fourteen and the Kid Zone.

Somehow, being alone made everything a thousand times worse. Her heart crashed against her ribs. Her ragged breathing roared in her ears. Adrenaline flushed through her, icing her veins.

Her bare feet on the marble floor echoed like slaps in the awful silence. Every step she took could be her last.

Blood smeared the floor, mingling with shattered glass. Bodies lay everywhere.

She looked at each of the fallen, trying to memorize their faces and their hair and clothes in case she was asked who she'd seen.

If she ever made it off this ship alive.

If anybody did.

35

MICAH

Micah followed the group as Jericho edged toward a hallway on the right between the Champagne Bar and the OnAir Comedy Club. Jericho peered around the corner, then looked back at them, holding up one hand. They stopped.

Jericho motioned for Silas and Micah to stay back. Silas swung his rifle up, ready to shoot at anything that moved. Micah did the same. His heart jerked, bucking against his ribs.

Patel and Jericho slipped around the corner, silent as ghosts.

He went rigid, not daring to breathe. The hairs prickled on his neck, his arms. Even sullen, unflappable Silas looked anxious.

A minute passed, each second ticking in his brain. Patel appeared and gestured for them to follow him into the hallway, a space twenty feet by twenty feet. Bathrooms on one side, elevators on the other. The closed doors to the deck directly in front of them, the storm lashing the glass.

Two bodies lay crumpled on the floor. One with a knife blade sticking out of his back. The other lay in a rapidly growing pool of blood. Jericho knelt over him and retrieved a thin wire dripping red. His arms were slick with it.

"You used a garrote," Silas said, awe in his voice.

"Where silence is necessary, it is an excellent weapon." Jericho wiped off the wire and stuffed it in his backpack. "Albeit messy."

"Teach me that," Silas said.

Jericho gave a sharp shake of his head. "You know how to shoot a gun. That's enough."

Acid rose in Micah's throat. He retched, narrowly avoiding spraying chunks all over his own gun.

Violence was everywhere. Jericho cleaned fresh, hot blood off his arms like it was nothing, like that blood hadn't been inside a living man not sixty seconds ago. Both Jericho and Silas spoke of the murder like they'd discuss which steak to order for dinner.

These were the good guys, he told himself over and over. He knew that. Then why did this feel so wrong?

Micah looked down at the bodies again, bile churning in his gut. It could have been Gabriel lying there, killed without mercy or a second of remorse.

He said a quick prayer over their bodies. His mom would want him to. Even the wicked deserved someone to mark their passing.

Patel retrieved both terrorists' walkie-talkies and clipped them to his belt. "We may only have a few minutes before they're supposed to check in. And who knows if we triggered any cameras."

Jericho went to the glass doors. "They're guarding the lifeboats from the inside because of the storm. We got lucky with these guys. They were both half-drunk. Also, the view is limited from inside. I can only see the next lifeboat from here. Normally I'd want to take out the next few sets of guards, but we don't have time."

"Because of the bridge," Silas said.

Jericho nodded. "They'll track us the second we open these doors and go for the lifeboats. I didn't notice any cameras in this alcove, but you never know. Hostiles could be on the starboard wing, waiting for us. Up there, they've got the high ground."

"Great." Micah moved toward the doors. "Let's go."

Silas followed him.

"Hold up, Silas," Jericho said. "My job is to keep you alive."

Silas's face contorted. "You're the one who taught me to shoot. You know I can handle myself."

"I can't let you go out there."

"So you're making me stay behind like a yellow-bellied pansy?" Silas sneered. "You've got to be joking. I can do anything this asshat can."

Jericho gripped his shoulder. "I've no doubt. But I need you to provide cover. You're a good shot."

"That's a load of bull—"

"I'm expendable." Micah struggled to keep his voice even. "That's why I need to go." For half a second, shame flushed through him, then a flash of Gabriel's anger.

Micah wasn't rich. He wasn't powerful or important in any way.

He was just a poor, overworked Puerto Rican waiter on a cruise ship. About as expendable as one could get, if you valued life based on wealth and prestige. If the money in your bank account made you somehow worthier.

Silas's gaze flashed to Jericho. Jericho nodded grimly.

Micah handed his weapon to Patel. Already, he felt naked without it. Exposed. He'd be more exposed out on the deck.

But if they didn't send out a distress signal, no one would know their location. No one would rescue them.

Expendable or not, he had to do this. Expendable or not, he could still be brave. He—not these people—decided who he was.

If he had to die here, he could at least make sure it meant something. "Cowards die many times before their deaths," he whispered. "The valiant never taste death but once."

"What?" Silas squinted at him.

"Shakespeare." Jericho tapped the side of his head. "Reading sharpens the mind. You ready?"

Micah nodded. He said a quick prayer in his mind, opened the doors, and stepped through.

The wind buffeted him, nearly knocking him off his feet. Rain pummeled his head and face, blurring his glasses and drenching him instantly. Above him, the storm roared. Several lightning bolts shattered the sky simultaneously.

He'd witnessed dozens of intense, destructive storms like this, but always safely inside a building. Never outside, unprotected, suspended above a pitching, boiling sea.

The ferocity of it was astonishing; it thrummed inside his chest, vibrating in his bones, his teeth. For a second, he froze in fear and awe.

Jericho pushed him from behind. "Stay on your toes. Now go!"

Micah slid across the deck and hit the glass railing stomach-first. It was like a punch to the gut. The orange-bottomed, plexiglass lifeboat swayed next to him, strapped to its cradle. He stared at it.

The canvas cover flapped in the wind, slit down the middle, the hatch slid open. Every boat was the same, all the way down the line.

Jericho grabbed his arm. "We're too late!"

No, no, no! The terrorists had gotten to the emergency beacons and ripped them out or destroyed them. All of them.

Thunder exploded overhead. Something whizzed by him. A crack distinctively *not* thunder. The wind so loud, he couldn't hear much of anything or pinpoint where the sound had come from.

Further along the deck? From behind them? Or from up on the bridge wing? He could hardly see anything through the fog of his glasses.

Jericho yanked him back. Micah stumbled on the slick deck. Lightning flashed bright as daylight. The wind thrashed at him, threatening to pull him right over the edge.

He hunched his shoulders, ducking his head against the wrath of the storm, and slammed through the glass doors.

"They'll come for us now." Jericho wiped the rain from his face with the back of his arm.

Micah stood there, cold water slaking off him, his clothes soaked and clinging to his body. He shivered uncontrollably, despair flooding through him. "We're all alone out here. No one's coming—"

Jericho got right in his face. "Get it together, boy. Are you going to stand there and blubber like a baby, or are you gonna do something?"

Jericho was right. Micah couldn't panic, not now. "Do something," he forced out between chattering teeth.

Jericho nodded. "All right, then. Let's get the hell out of here."

36

GABRIEL

G abriel's walkie-talkie burst with static. "Do you read me?"

"I'm here."

"It's time," Simeon said. "It is as I feared. Black is resistant to all persuasion. He is unaffected by the wife. Bring the girl to the bridge."

Gabriel's tongue thickened in his mouth. He couldn't speak.

"Gabriel." Simeon's voice darkened. "Are you having second thoughts?"

His silence said everything.

"We spoke of this. The girl is manipulating you."

Gabriel glanced across the room. Amelia sat on the floor, leaning against the ladder. Her eyes were closed. Her hands clasped together in her lap. She looked exhausted.

His heart swelled with compassion. "I don't think so."

"Think, Gabriel! Her father and his people are the kings of manipulation, propaganda, and twisting the truth to their own aims. He's raising her to be a replica of himself. She lies as often as she breathes."

Amelia *had* lied and manipulated. But so had Gabriel. She did it to survive. She had a chance to kill him, and she'd trusted him instead. Her words echoed in his mind. "You're planning to torture her in front of her father."

Simeon didn't speak for a long moment. Staticky thunder rumbled in the background. "I have kept certain things from you to try to spare your conscience. You're sensitive. I understand that. But everything has changed. Everything."

"You told me we would only kill our specific targets. Only the guilty."

Simeon sighed. "Listen to me. Cheng and his men have gone off-script. Cheng is . . . difficult to contain. All the more reason to take what we need from Black and get to our extraction point. Do you understand?"

"How many innocent people have died?"

"Cheng is the one killing people. I had nothing to do with this, I swear to you. But Gabriel, none of them are innocent. Not one."

Acid burned the back of his throat. He wanted to tell Simeon to go to hell, but the words wouldn't come. Simeon was his mentor, his friend. Gabriel still feared disappointing him. "This—this isn't what I signed up for."

"You aren't listening. Everything has changed. This epidemic is the worst we've ever seen. What's happening out there—what the virus does to people—"

The ship surged beneath Gabriel's feet. He stumbled, then righted himself, gripping the back of a stadium seat for balance. "What does that have to do with anything?"

"Black has the vaccine. The true vaccine. Whatever issues your conscience is having, put them to rest. Right now."

Dizziness washed over him. Everything tilted, suddenly unstable. The foundation of his life shifted, breaking apart beneath his feet. "What's going on?"

"I'll explain later. But Gabriel, you are a Patriot. You have a duty to the people—your people. If we fail now, the death toll will be staggering."

"But the girl. She's innocent."

"We don't have time for this!" Simeon's voice rose sharply. "You know this. Every war has casualties! Every revolution is built on the deaths of innocents. This is the only way."

His mouth filled of nails. He didn't speak. He couldn't.

"Are you going to throw away everything you believe in because of some rich slut you've suddenly developed *feelings* for?"

He closed his eyes. He did have feelings for her. He'd fought against it for as long as he could. But she'd gotten to him. Her dignity, her vulnerability, her honesty, her strange ability to be both weak and strong at the same time. How her skin crinkled around her eyes when she smiled a real smile, how it lit up her whole face. "She's not like that."

"Would you sacrifice your own life to save thousands—millions of lives, Gabriel?"

"Of course."

"Sometimes it is not our own life we must sacrifice. Do you understand?"

His throat constricted. "I—"

"You have always been loyal. You've been my most faithful recruit. I believe in you. Since you were fourteen years old and you showed your unflinching strength and courage against those thugs, I've believed in you. Don't let me down now, son."

"I won't." The *but* hung in the air between them.

Simeon sighed. "I give you my word, Gabriel. I will not harm her. But millions of innocent lives are on the line. I need you to think of them."

Gabriel let out his breath. His shoulders slumped. "I understand, sir."

"We're on the brink of a great victory, son. Bring her to the bridge."

Gabriel clipped his walkie-talkie to his belt. He walked back to the platform on legs like concrete blocks. Everything he'd longed for, worked for, fought and bled for. A great victory for the New Patriots and the country. A great defeat against the Unity Coalition and the greedy, corrupt elite.

But at what cost?

She would never forgive him. For one stupid moment, he'd allowed himself to believe their little bubble would go on indefinitely, unburst by the outside world. But that was impossible.

It didn't matter how strong their feelings were for each other. It didn't matter if they loved each other, or could love each other someday, if given the chance.

They were on opposite sides in a hidden war waging for decades, for centuries.

If he didn't bring her to the bridge, it would be treason. Simeon and the New Patriots would disown him, or worse. They were his brothers. His family.

Simeon, who was like a father to him, who'd taken him under his wing and trained him and given him his dignity, his life. Simeon gave him meaning after the meaningless death of his parents. Simeon gave him a purpose, a duty.

He could never betray Simeon. He could never betray the cause. It would be betraying himself.

Innocent people were dying. The stakes had been raised exponentially. Whatever was happening on the mainland with the epidemic, Simeon believed Black had the true vaccine. He must be withholding it for his own kind.

Gabriel could do something. Must do something. He must help save thousands, possibly millions of lives. This was what he'd longed for, worked for, fought for.

He closed his eyes against the dread coursing through him, the pain like a physical ache in his chest. Simeon was right, as always. He must act.

This was his duty. This was his chance to make a real and lasting difference for his people. His own peace—his own happiness—was inconsequential.

His hands curled into fists at his sides. She would hate him. And he would deserve her hatred. After the risk she had taken for him, refusing to hurt him or escape when she had the chance—she would hate him, and he would have to live with that.

He had argued for her life. It was all he could give her. It would have to be enough. "Amelia."

Her eyelids fluttered open. She gazed up at him, smiling, her face open and trusting.

It was like boiling water pouring into his chest. "Amelia. I need you to come with me."

"Where?"

"The bridge."

A gap opened in the startled silence.

He pulled his gun out of his holster. He couldn't let his guard down. Not again.

Her smile flickered. Her gaze shifted from his face to the gun hanging loose at his side, a terrible understanding dawning in her eyes.

He expected her to beg, to cry, to try to convince him to change his mind again. But she didn't. She just stared at him, aghast. "Why?"

"You know why." His voice sounded hollow and distant in his own ears.

"I thought you were good."

"I am good! But sometimes goodness demands sacrifice."

"And I'm it? I'm your sacrifice?"

"This is so much bigger than you and me. That's what you'll never understand."

"I could have killed you. But I didn't. I could have run. I didn't. I chose *you*."

The words were barbed wire on his tongue. "You chose wrong." He gestured with the gun. "Now move."

A thousand emotions flitted across her face simultaneously. She raised her chin. "And if I don't?"

He hated every word he spoke. He hardened his voice, hardened his heart. "I'll knock you unconscious with the butt of my gun and carry you there."

She remained still.

"Move!"

"May I bring my clutch?" It lay on the floor next to her feet.

"Of course."

"Thank you." Her voice came out cold and emotionless. The same as his own.

She picked up her clutch and rose to her feet. She walked in front of him, her back straight, her shoulders squared, her posture perfect. She looked regal, dignified as a queen.

He longed to say *I'm sorry*, a thousand times *I'm sorry*.

The words died in his throat.

37

WILLOW

A bullet struck the wall less than a foot from Willow's head. A sudden shout came above her. She sprinted down the nearest hallway, her knife gripped in one hand.

It had taken her the better part of an hour to escape Deck Ten and make her way up to Fourteen. Like Eleven and Twelve, it consisted of staterooms, but the bow of Fourteen contained the Kid Zone.

The corridor in front of her was long and narrow, the stateroom doors all on the left side. Each doorway offered only a shallow alcove.

There was nowhere to hide.

More shouting behind her. A flurry of gunshots. Bullets peppered the wall above her head. They didn't bother with the ruse of hostages. They shot to kill. If she wasn't so short, she'd be dead.

She cut to the left, then the right. Screw it. It was only slowing her down. She lunged left and slammed into a stateroom door, thrusting her mom's wristband at the sensors. The door released with a hiss.

She fell into the room just as another bullet whizzed over her head, so close it stirred the hairs on her head. She leapt up and hurled herself at the door, locking it with shaking fingers.

"Welcome, Guest!" the room AI said in an irritatingly calm voice. "Your stress indicators are elevated."

"Nothing gets past you, Sherlock." Willow scanned the stateroom. The former occupants had switched on the outer space option, and brilliantly colored constellations, nebulas, and shooting stars swirled across the polymer walls.

There were two large, egg-shaped sleep pods, an ornate settee, a mirrored vanity and massive holoscreen, and a gold-gilded bathroom. The exact same furnishings as her own room, only larger and fancier.

Hiding was futile. There was nowhere to go. Nowhere to escape.

"May I suggest a relaxing rejuvenation facial to lower your biostats to a comfortable and pleasant level? A personal beautician can be delivered to your room in—"

"Just shut the hell up!" she hissed.

Someone banged on the wood door. Angry male voices hurled curses. She had only a few moments before they shot or rammed their way in. A strong breeze tousled her hair. Rain spat through the open glass door.

She ran for the veranda.

The rain hit her like a slap in the face. Lightning stitched the sky. She was drenched instantly, her dress sodden, her hair plastered to her scalp.

Her heart in her throat, she inched across the veranda and forced herself to lean over the glass railing. Vertigo rushed through her. The sea seethed well over a hundred feet below. From up here, the waves lashed the hull like heaving mountains.

Her heart stopped beating. Her legs turned to lead. She gripped the railing with whitened knuckles. *No, no, no. Don't look down.*

More shouting.

She was out of time. It was either jump, climb, or die.

Willow chose to climb.

She moved to the left side of the veranda on wobbly legs. A thin metal wall separated the balconies. The wall didn't protrude any further than the railing itself. She felt along the edge. It was slick, but several large two-inch bolts stuck out on either side.

"Oh, hell." The wind snatched her words before they'd left her mouth and hurled them down, down, down. Into the abyss. Her stomach lurched. Don't look. *Don't look.*

She took a deep, shuddering breath.

She had to move fast. No hesitation. And no mistakes.

She grabbed a patio chair and wedged it against the side wall and the railing. She slipped the knife inside her bra and hiked her (stupid, ridiculous) dress over her hips, tucking it into her underwear.

She imagined Zia laughing at her, doing that weird shoulder-hunch donkey-laugh thing she always did. The pain struck her between the ribs—sharp, almost unbearable.

She couldn't think about that now. First, she had to survive.

Willow stepped on the chair and grabbed the inside bolt on the wall with her left hand and the outside bolt with her right. She swung her leg over the glass railing, past the wall, and over the railing on the next veranda.

There was no chair on that side to rest her weight on. She pressed her body against the wall, bending her knees to wrap her legs around the top of the railing. She clung to the bolts with all her strength.

Vertigo surged, pulsing through her in swooping, dizzying waves. Her terror grew talons and fangs and wings.

The wind lashed her, whipping thick strands of hair into her eyes. Rain pelted her like stones. Thunder crashed like a supernova exploding inside her chest, trembling every cell in her body.

The ship rolled. Her right hand slipped and her body started to sway. She shifted, sliding backward. She clutched frantically at empty air. Her arms flailed, her fingernails scraping the slick, wet metal.

Time slowed. The chair slid across the veranda, struck the opposite wall, and tipped over. She was going to fall. She slipped, falling, about to plunge over the side—

Her fingers found purchase. She gripped the bolt so tightly that a few of her fingernails cracked.

At her back only infinite space, like a black hole waiting to swallow her up. *Don't look down.*

She didn't want to die. Not now. Not like this.

Her fear beat at her with frantic, savage wings. If she moved, she would fall. She was certain of it.

She wasn't sure God existed, but she prayed anyway. To God, to Buddha, to Poseidon, to any deity who might listen. *Don't let me die.* She breathed through gritted teeth, every muscle quivering.

She had to move. She had to move *now*.

The ship pitched again, but she was ready this time and moved with it. She scooted her butt on the railing as far as she could to the side while still gripping both bolts. She rocked herself to the right, pushing hard against the glass panel of the railing with her left foot to give herself momentum.

She launched herself to the next veranda.

She landed hard on her side, smacking her right hip, forearm, and shoulder against the floor. Her head hit the patio table leg, but she welcomed the stab of pain.

She lay on her side, trembling and weak, gasping in great gulps of sweet, beautiful air. Stinging rain struck her skin.

She made it. She made it and she was alive. Short, chubby Willow Bahaghari was a badass, after all. She wanted to whoop and holler and shout in triumph.

The voices came from the other side of the wall. From the veranda she just came from. She leapt to her feet and shoved herself flat against the wall. She pressed her hands over her chest to still her frantic heart, afraid to move, afraid to breathe.

The rain fell in gusting sheets. Thunder crashed, and the ship rolled so deeply the patio table and chairs scraped across the floor and tumbled against the railing.

"She ain't here!" one of the terrorists said. "Must've jumped!"

The other one said something in another language, too quiet for her to make out in the storm.

"Too bad!" the first one said, and laughed.

Finally, they left. She was alone. Rain ran in rivulets down her cheeks, dripping off the tip of her nose.

Lightning shattered the sky. And hundreds of feet below her, the sea writhed, still ravenous.

Not today. *You won't get me today.*

She untucked her dress and pushed it down around her thighs with trembling fingers. Goosebumps peppered her flesh. All the black hairs on her legs she always missed while shaving stood on end. Her nails were ragged and torn, the muscles in her hands throbbing.

She hugged herself to keep from shivering. It was useless. The wet chill leeched into her bones. She'd be cold for the rest of her life.

But she was alive.

And she had an idea. She crept back to the glass railing and leaned over the edge, squinting through the pouring rain. The Kid Zone deck was to her right. Only three verandas from her own.

The thought of climbing the exterior of a storm-tossed cruise ship—again—stole the breath from her lungs. But this was the best way. Possibly, the only way.

For Benjie, she would do anything.

Something took shape inside her, alive and winged and fearless.

38

AMELIA

Amelia blinked, adjusting to the gloom of the bridge. She remembered the captain explaining how the bridge remained dim at night to aid with navigation. Only the soft florescent glow beneath the control panel and the low lights along the floor illuminated the room. Everyone had spoken in hushed, subdued voices, almost like it was a cathedral, a sacred place.

Except it wasn't a sacred place any longer. Blotches stained the gold carpet like someone had knocked over crimson paint cans.

A dozen terrorists ringed the console, their huge guns dominating the room. Most were dressed in dark clothes and combat gear. The rest wore crew uniforms—security, officers, wait staff.

The bridge smelled sour, like body odor and sweat and fear, but also like something freshly rotting. It smelled like death.

Eight hostages sat along the far wall below the security monitors. Their hands were bound behind their backs. She recognized a few of them from the captain's table. Four were dead, their bodies crumpled on the floor. Four more were battered and bloody, alive but unconscious.

Her mother slumped on the end nearest the bridge door, her head resting against the shoulder of Senator Omar Ferguson. Bruises and cuts marred her face. Dark smears stained her arms, her cheeks, and the front of her dress.

"Mother!" But her mother didn't look up. Amelia lunged toward her.

A man grabbed her arm and yanked her back. He didn't look like much, at first glance.

The second glance revealed the truth—the slow-blinking but intelligent, crafty eyes, the red slash of a mouth. "Not yet, my dear. I assure you, she is alive, though unconscious at the moment. But we have more important matters to consider."

"What do you want?" But she had a good idea.

The man pressed the muzzle of a pulse gun against her side.

"Simeon—" Gabriel said from behind her.

"Leave her alone." Declan Black sat in the captain's chair, his suit jacket draped over the back. His coiffed hair was mussed, his crisp white shirt dirtied and torn. Deep shadows were smudged beneath his eyes. Angry purple bruises marred the left side of his face and forehead. His bottom lip was split.

Fresh terror gripped her. Her father ruled his world with an iron fist, always in utmost control. Seeing him like this—helpless, impotent, at the mercy of thugs—terrified her more than she could say.

And yet, some tiny part of her whispered, *now you know how it feels.*

"Let's get on with this." A man in an officer's uniform stood a little behind and to the right of the captain's chair, his rifle pointed at her father's head.

He was huge and muscular, his neck as thick as his head. He looked at her with glittering, rattlesnake eyes. He grinned, teeth bristling.

Her heart constricted. The awful man from the ballroom.

"Soon, Kane. I promise." Simeon turned toward Amelia, smiling at her like an honored guest. "We've calmly explained to your father that we will exchange the vaccine and the cure for his life and the lives of his family members. However, he appears too obstinate to cooperate with us, even for his own good."

"Go to hell," Declan growled.

"What are you talking about?" She willed her voice to remain calm. Her throat was dry as sandpaper. "The vaccine was administered to millions of people for National Health Day. The week before last. It was all over the newsfeeds."

"Oh, yes, my dear." Simeon's lip curled in disdain. "The so-called vaccine BioGen unleashed on the poor American shmucks hasn't exactly performed as promised, has it?"

A headache pulsed at the back of her skull. She stared at him, uncomprehending.

"Do you know they have a name for it now? The Hydra Virus. Fitting, yes? The many-headed beast whose poisonous blood was so virulent even its breath could kill you. Cut off a head and two grow back. Death coming at you from so many directions at once. Virtually impossible to destroy."

"I don't understand what—"

"Enough!" barked one of the terrorists in combat gear. He didn't wear a ski mask. He was east Asian, with malevolent, raven-dark eyes and a scar striping one side of his face. He stood with his feet spread, shoulders taut, pulse gun at the ready.

Simeon removed the gun from her side and placed it against her temple, the metal cold against her skin.

"We've gone through this whole rigmarole so many times already." Simeon sighed. "Cheng's tired of this. I'm tired of this. Are you tired of this, Kane?"

Kane grunted. "How about we gut her and see how she squeals?"

"Too messy." Simeon nodded at Kane.

In one smooth movement, Kane pointed his pulse gun at the group of hostages against the wall and fired twice.

She couldn't tell at first who Kane shot. Someone wept. A woman. Her mother lifted her head, awake now.

The man next to her slumped against the wall, a hole in his chest, the shirt around the wound disintegrated. The laser pulse vaporized his flesh. A foul, charred stench filled the air.

Relief mingled with guilt flooded her. Her mother was still alive, but Omar Ferguson wasn't. Not anymore.

A second man groaned. Beside Ferguson, Tyler Horne's stylishly blonde hair was matted against his skull. He clutched his tattered right arm, smoke wisping from a scalded wound in his forearm.

"You monster!" her mother cried.

"I was aiming for you." Kane spoke to her mother, but he looked at Amelia, his lips peeled back like a dog baring its teeth.

"I also have poor aim." Simeon could've been discussing tomorrow's tee time. The cold barrel of the gun pressed harder against her temple. "Unless, of course, I'm close enough to the target."

Her mother shrank back against the wall. "Don't hurt her, please! Take me instead. I'm begging you!"

"Sorry, lady," Simeon said. "We tried that. And if you don't shut up, I'm going to have to let Kane shoot you, too."

"Hostiles on Deck Four." The terrorist next to the security monitors pointed at one of the screens. "They're wearing our gear. And they just took out two of our guys."

Cheng's walkie-talkie hissed static. A deep male voice sputtered something. Cheng's face darkened. "They're headed for the lifeboats. Go."

Two of his men sprinted to the starboard bridge wing. Muzzles flashed in the darkness.

Cheng's scowl deepened. His scar bulged like an angry worm. "Enough with this foolishness."

"We're almost finished." Simeon grabbed her shoulder and shoved her into a kneeling position. "Now, where were we? Gabriel?"

"The cure." The sound of Gabriel's voice twisted like a knife in her gut.

"Ah, yes. We need the cure now or everyone dies, starting with your daughter."

"What cure?" she asked hoarsely.

"And I keep hearing how clever you are," Simeon said. "What do *you* think happened?"

Something sprouted to life, some small niggling thought in the back of her pulsing, aching brain. It was hard to focus, to clear her jumbled thoughts. "There was a mistake, an error. The vaccine doesn't work like it's supposed to."

Simeon grabbed her hair with his free hand and wound it into his fist, his mouth an inch from her ear. "Wrong answer."

39

WILLOW

Willow crossed the last wall between the verandas, pushed off the glass railing, and threw herself to the deck of the Kid Zone. She was drenched and trembling, her heart slamming in her chest.

But she made it. She was alive.

The exterior wall of the Kid Zone wasn't all glass like some areas of the ship, but there were several windows and two sliding glass doors. She crawled along the slick deck on her hands and knees, crouching beneath the windows until she reached the first set of glass doors.

She peeked inside, glimpsing tables full of tablets, a robot-building center, a small VR gaming station, and bins of luminescent building blocks.

Several staff members slumped against a wall swirling with garishly bright colors. Their hands were tied behind their backs.

Only one terrorist guarded the room. He lounged on a pumpkin-orange floating chair, his rifle resting harmlessly across his knees. Most importantly, he faced the only entrance, his back to the deck.

Out here, the storm raged black and fierce. But inside it was still. Quiet. The lights were dimmed, the children scattered around the room, curled up on circular cushions on the floor.

Dead? Her heart constricted.

But no. A curly-haired boy stretched and pulled his blanket over his head. They weren't dead. They were sleeping.

There couldn't be more than ten of them. When the terrorists boarded the ship, most of the parents had already signed their kids out for dinner.

There was no blood. And no bodies.

Whatever had happened on the lido deck, in the Galaxy Lounge, the Royal Promenade, and everywhere else hadn't happened here. Not yet. She scanned the room, searching for her brother.

There he was. Benjie had fallen asleep on his stomach on the mat next to the building blocks, surrounded by the hovercars and space-ships he loved to build. He still wore his raggedy Star Wars backpack.

She let out a trembling breath. Something inside her released like an unclenched fist. Her brother was alive. Now she just had to save him.

She pushed herself into a crouch and tried to open the door. It didn't budge. The deck doors were locked for safety reasons, to make sure the kids didn't wander in and out unsupervised.

She tugged the knife from her bra and gripped the handle, her heartbeat throbbing against her palm. She waited for the crash of thunder to hide the beep, then she swiped her mom's wristband over the door sensor.

Everything seemed to fall away. The blood rushed in her ears. Her vision focused.

She slid the door open just enough and slipped inside. She crept through the Kid Zone, silent as a ghost on her bare feet.

Five steps. Ten. Fifteen. She was almost on him.

He wore a wrinkled waiter's uniform, the collar folded awkwardly. He had reddish-blonde hair, unkempt and a little too long in the back. A constellation of freckles dotted the back of his neck.

The terrorist slouched in his chair, probably dozing. He was strong, but not like this. Not when she stood behind him. She had the power, the momentum, and the element of surprise.

Willow tensed as the floor bucked beneath her. In one swift movement, she reached around and pressed the knife to his throat. "Don't move, asshole."

He jolted awake and stiffened as she pressed the blade against his skin.

"Put the gun down and kick it away."

He obeyed. The gun slid across the floor, bumping against the feet of the childcare workers. All three of the women stared at her, fear etched in their faces.

She kept the knife pressed to his throat and moved until she faced him. She adjusted the blade so the point pricked against his Adam's apple.

"My sister is—she's dead," she choked out. "You people killed her." Rage welled and for a moment she couldn't speak. It filled her whole body until she was shaking, her eyes glazed and burning with grief.

Her fingers tightened around the handle of the knife.

He started to shake his head, then froze as the blade scraped his skin. A trickle of blood dripped on his shirt collar. He swallowed. "I didn't. I've never killed anybody."

His voice was clear and smooth. He might have been a singer in another life. He was younger than she'd thought. Acne sprinkled his oily forehead. He had shaggy hair, chapped lips, crooked teeth.

He looked like an average kid fresh out of high school. He didn't look evil.

Her heart constricted. Evil didn't look any special way. It could be beautiful. It could come at you with a smile, a dagger in its teeth. "Shut up."

"I swear." He raised his hands slowly, his gaze darting around the room. "I haven't hurt a single hair on their heads! I fed them, let them play. I'm keeping them safe until we leave."

"He speaks the truth," one of the hostages said, a Middle-Eastern girl in her early twenties, wearing a hijab. "He hasn't harmed us."

"You can just leave—" he started.

"There is no 'leaving'. Your friends brought explosives along with their weapons. They're gonna blow the whole ship and watch it sink in flames."

He paused for a moment as that fact sank in. "Take the kids to the lifeboats. I won't stop you. You don't believe me? I have zip-ties in my pocket. You can tie me up and leave me here."

She licked her dry lips. It was as good a plan as any. "Okay, asshole. Take out those zip-ties, nice and slow, and hand them to me."

She bound his hands behind his back and freed the hostages.

"If we leave him tied up, we're condemning him to die," the Middle-Eastern girl said gently. She was pretty, with a strong nose, thick eyebrows, and a soft, oval-shaped face. "I'm Nadira."

"Nice to meet you, Nadira," she said. "Maybe he should die. He made his bed."

"This is not our choice to make."

Willow glanced at her. "I think it is."

"If the ship is burning, then we should untie him—or at least make it possible for him to escape. Otherwise, we become murderers."

She looked back at her prisoner. It wasn't how she thought it'd be. The monster was just a boy, with a face like hers. He wasn't the one who killed her sister.

This wouldn't be vengeance. It would be murder. She was many things, but a cold-blooded killer wasn't one of them.

Her anger leaked out of her, leaving an ache like a hot stone in the pit of her stomach.

"Oh, hell." She placed the cake knife on the floor behind his bound hands. "If you touch this knife before we leave, I'll gouge your eyes out."

He met her gaze, grateful relief written all over his face. "Thank you."

"Keep an eye on him," she said to Nadira. She picked up the terrorist's rifle to use as protection. She had no clue how to shoot it, but she could use it as club if worse came to worse.

"*Ate!*" Benjie sat up and rubbed his eyes. His hair stuck up all over his head. She knelt beside him, plastic blocks digging into her knees, and gathered him into her arms.

The cuts on her palms throbbed, still seeping blood, but she didn't care. Benjie's warm body sank against her. His heartbeat thumped against her own chest. His hair smelled like green apple shampoo. He smelled like home.

She groaned and hugged him tighter. Alive. He was alive. Her mom would be proud of them, wherever she was.

"Where's Mom?" Benjie asked as if reading her thoughts. He sniffled and rubbed his nose with his arm. "Where's Zia?"

Darkness flashed behind her eyes. Her demons, whispering deep in her soul. *Your fault. Your fault.*

The words clotted in her throat, but she forced them out. "We'll meet them at the lifeboats. We're going on an adventure. But we've got to be brave, okay? And we need to hurry. Let's wake up your friends."

She hoped Benjie would forgive her someday. The lie was the least of her sins.

40

AMELIA

The ship rolled. Simeon stumbled, tightening his grip on Amelia's hair.

"Please stop!" She hated the whimper in her voice. "You're hurting me!"

"Simeon—" Gabriel said from behind her, his voice strained.

"You going to tell her or should I?" Simeon asked her father.

Declan Black's swollen lip curled. "I'll burn in hell before I give a thing to scum like you."

"I guess I'll just have to do it." Simeon jerked her head back, exposing her neck. Her scalp blazed with pain. Several strands of white-blond hair drifted to the carpet. "Declan Black, CEO of BioGen Technologies, has conspired to commit a heinous act of biological warfare upon his own people."

"You're not my people," Declan spat.

"Most people received a harmless, inactive placebo within the BioGen vaccine," Simeon said. "But a carefully selected population received something very different. Their BioGen vaccination contained the DNA of several virus strains recombined into a single, highly virulent genetically-engineered pathogen."

Amelia heard the words but couldn't understand them. They didn't make sense.

Behind her, Simeon shifted. "Certain members of the CDC and the Department of Health and Human Services were paid not to look too closely, under the auspices that the vaccine be rushed to the people who needed it most in a highly-publicized display of good-will, which would bode well for the reputations and vlogger coverage of all involved. In reality, National Health Day was a cover, an effective means to disperse the bioweapon quickly and efficiently to the target demographic."

Cold went through her all the way to her bones. The room pulsed, the oxygen sucked out of the air, out of her lungs. The storm roared outside the bridge windows. Rain hammered the glass in gray, slashing sheets. Lightning split the sky into jagged pieces. "That can't be true."

"The bioweapon was administered to a rigorously pre-selected population. Every single one of them a burden to the government, all refugees or illegals or poverty-stricken families out of work for years due to the above-mentioned government giving all the jobs to the metalheads."

She looked at her father. "Is—is it true? What they're saying?"

His eyes flashed with derision. "Of course not."

She'd spent too much time and energy studying his facial expressions and anticipating his moods to not be able to read him now. The tick beneath his left eye. That extra hitch to the swallow in his throat. "You're lying."

Simeon laughed. "She is her father's daughter, isn't she?"

"How many?" she forced out. "How many died?"

"Well, that's an inexact science, now isn't it? It's an impossible number to pinpoint. However, the most recent models from our sources inside the White House have informed me the engineered virus was deliberately injected into somewhere around one hundred thousand men, women, and children."

Amelia sucked in her breath.

"Now, back to business," Simeon said coolly. "We need the cure, and we need it now."

Her father said nothing, his face carved from stone.

"Remember, you're the one making me do this." Simeon yanked her hair, knocking her off balance. She toppled to the floor. He aimed a savage kick at her stomach.

Sharp pain shot through her ribs. She curled into a fetal position, gasping for air. Tears stung her eyes. *Don't let them see you cry.* She blinked them back fiercely

"Stop!" Gabriel said.

"Hollis, put your gun on him," Simeon ordered.

"Happy to." Hollis moved from the other side of her father and stopped a few feet from Gabriel, her weapon trained on his chest.

"Leave my daughter alone!" Declan said.

"You wish for me to stop? Start telling the truth. Now."

Declan only glared at him.

"Are you just going to sit there and let us hurt your own? First your wife, now your daughter. What kind of man are you?"

"You're the one beating a child," Declan spat, his tone venomous. "I should ask you the same question. But I know what kind of man you are."

Simeon's mouth pressed into a bloodless line. "I'll gladly spare her. That choice is up to you." He bent down, yanked her head up by her hair, and struck her in the face with the butt of his gun. Agony exploded behind her eyes with a flurry of stars.

Kane slid a knife out of a scabbard at his belt. "Maybe we take a finger or two. To start with."

"Don't you dare touch her!" Declan roared.

Dimly, she heard her mother weeping. "Declan, please! Just tell them! Give them whatever they want!"

"If you're going to cry," Simeon said, "cry for the innocent dead and dying souls back home. It's too late for them."

Declan squared his shoulders, his eyes flashing. "They will find peace. Which is more than they had in life. It is a mercy."

Simeon scowled. "A mercy?"

White noise filled Amelia's head. "You did this on purpose?"

"Not alone, I assure you." Her father raised his chin defiantly. "It has been done before and it will be done again. In an age of dwindling agricultural yields and scarcity of resources, with virulent diseases spreading like wildfire and dangerous ideals spreading faster, it is incumbent upon a government to restore order and protect the security of its people. If they refuse to recognize the necessary means, then someone must step in and do what must be done."

"And that way is to murder a hundred thousand innocent people?" Gabriel asked, horror in his voice.

Declan shot him a baleful look. "America thrives on strength. To be weak is to invite the jackals to tear us apart, limb by limb. To protect the chosen, to ensure our national interests and survival—yes, a few were sacrificed to save the many. It was a moral imperative."

Amelia couldn't comprehend his words. All her conflicted emotions knotted up inside her. He was her father and he was a mass murderer. She loved him and hated him like she'd loved and hated him her entire life.

"*Moral?*" Simeon spat. "You're justifying your actions as moral?"

"Aren't you?" Declan's face turned a fierce, ugly red. "The Coalition acted to save millions more. It was a matter of national security. We cannot—will not—let fear control us. If that means tracking citizens to separate the sheep from the wolves and successfully destroy the wolves —then we will do so.

"You people would vote against your own self-interests, letting the world burn around you while you wave your pitiful flag of freedom. If we must sacrifice the chaff to save the wheat—the best and the brightest, those who will work to restore our country and ensure America remains the shining beacon of the world—then that is a choice I readily make."

Hollis grimaced. "You're insane."

"Not insane. Pragmatic." Her father leaned forward, his eyes bright. He spoke with magnetic intensity, like he was convincing his board to take on a promising new acquisition. "The Coalition has the strength and courage to do what the current, ineffective leadership does not."

"You killed all those people . . ." she moaned.

A tic jumped in his cheek. "People die all the time. They were sick and starving and weak. Half of them had already contracted the bat-flu. They would have died anyway. We did it so America could survive."

"So the rich could survive, you mean," Hollis said.

"So the *deserving* could survive!"

"I don't understand," Amelia said. "Why? Why would you do such a thing?"

"Because the Coalition is going to label it a terrorist attack," Hollis said. "They didn't have enough votes to pass their stupid bill. These elite scumbags want to chip and track the rest of us like animals. Just one more way to increase their control. But the people resisted. So, they're going to scare them into voting anything they want in exchange for the illusion of safety."

"It's not an illusion!" her father roared. "Under the Coalition's authority, our country will be transformed. All citizens safe and protected. A new era—"

"Enough!" Cheng spun toward Declan. "The cure. Now."

Thunder crashed, booming through the bridge so loud and close the floor seemed to tremble. Lightning forked the sky, lighting up Declan's hard, defiant face. His mouth twisted. "You want your so-called cure? Get me and my family off this ship."

"We've discussed this," Simeon said. "You provide access to the cure first."

"You think I have it with me? It's stored in an undisclosed, secured facility."

"I'm surprised you left without it."

A shadow passed across Declan's face, so fleeting she couldn't read it. "It was unforeseen. An anomaly."

Amelia spat out the blood pooling in her mouth. Her head throbbed. Her stomach pulsed in agony. There was something else, something she'd missed. Things seemed fuzzy and far away. Everything happened through a red veil of pain.

Simeon swiped something into his satphone with one hand. "Provide me the security codes to the location and identifying characteristics. My contacts will take possession of the cure and ensure its validity. Then we'll discuss getting you off this ship."

"Do you think I'm stupid? I will give you nothing before you provide safe passage for myself and my family."

Simeon swore. "Unacceptable. Give us what we need immediately, or we kill your daughter."

Declan lifted his chin. "I refuse to allow anyone to threaten me into submission. You will not receive the cure in exchange for her life or anyone else's. I will not barter with terrorists."

Simeon kicked her again. "Then we don't need her. Too bad. She's a pretty thing."

"Simeon, no!" Gabriel said.

She tried to sit up, pain throbbing through her ribs. "Father!"

"Such a waste." Simeon pressed the gun to her temple.

Something flickered beneath her father's composed features, an expression she had never seen before. His eyes widened, the whites showing around the irises. And there—a glimmer of anguish.

Hope beat in her heart. He did love her. After all of this, in spite of everything, he loved her. He would do something, somehow, to stop this. To save her.

"Father! Please!" she pleaded.

His face contorted. Remorse flared in his eyes.

"Help me!"

Just as swiftly, it winked out. His gaze dropped to his lap.

"Dad!"

He wouldn't look at her.

In the dim lighting, she barely recognized him. Maybe tears glistening in his eyes. Or maybe they didn't. She couldn't tell.

Either way, he'd abandoned her. Either way, she was dead.

He wasn't going to save her.

He didn't want her. The single thought beat through the haze of terror and pain. He didn't want her. He was her father in everything but DNA. He had raised her. But he hadn't loved her. He couldn't have, after this. Dismissing her suffering—her impending death—without a mote of actual feeling.

After all she had sacrificed for him, spending her life trying to please him, trying to earn his respect, his love. It didn't matter. None of it mattered.

She didn't matter. Not to her father. Not to Gabriel. Not to anyone.

Kane's gaze slithered over her. "Give me the girl."

Fear plunged a dagger into her belly.

"No," Simeon said. "That's not how we do things."

"You owe me!" Kane snarled.

Cheng spoke into his satphone. "Enough!" His scar pulsed purple. He barely raised his voice, but all the attention in the room turned to him. "We're out of time."

Simeon shot him a look, his brows knitted, his jaw set. "What are you talking about?"

"The *Voyager* is wired with explosives. They're set to go off in just under twenty minutes."

Simeon's face blanched. He stared at Cheng with his mouth half-open. "What?"

"The ship sinks."

Simeon's eyes clouded with fury—and wariness. "You can't do that. What about—?"

Cheng's rifle came to rest not quite pointed at Simeon, but very close. "We have our own orders. I'm sure you understand."

"What orders?" Simeon asked. "From who?"

Tension sizzled in the air. Every terrorist stiffened, fingers hovering over the triggers of their weapons. Cheng splayed his legs, his chest out, his nostrils flaring.

The power had shifted, subtly but irrevocably. Simeon and the New Patriots were no longer in charge.

Amelia didn't know what it meant, but she knew it was bad. Things were about to get worse. Much worse.

"Who gave those orders?" Simeon demanded.

The barrel of Cheng's rifle swung up. "We share the same benefactor, I believe."

"And our extraction?" Simeon's voice went hoarse.

Cheng shrugged dismissively. "It will be taken care of. As promised."

"I want the girl," Kane said again.

Cheng nodded, not taking his eyes off Simeon. "Be my guest."

Her breath stilled in her throat. Her bones turned to water.

Gabriel charged forward and grabbed Simeon's arm, his face etched with anguish and outrage. "You swore to me! You can't do this!"

Simeon pivoted, pointing his weapon at Gabriel's chest. "Do not interfere. We all must make sacrifices."

"She's a human being, not a sacrifice!"

Simeon's expression was strained, his voice hoarse. "Sometimes we don't have a choice, son."

Kane grabbed her by the hair and jerked her to her feet. The floor rolled beneath her. She stumbled as he half-shoved, half-dragged her to the bridge door. She managed to hold on to her clutch, grasping it like a lifeline, like it could somehow save her from what would come.

"No!" Her mother cried. "Please! Don't hurt her! Declan, do something!"

Her mother's voice was the last thing Amelia heard before the bridge door slammed behind her.

41

MICAH

Micah stood with Silas, Jericho, and several security personnel in the CSO's office. The walls were a bland white, the desk and shelves industrial steel.

When they'd entered the office a few minutes earlier, they'd found the group Patel had told them about—five men cowering in a small storage closet in the back—including Chief Security Officer Franz Schneider.

"What do you need?" the CSO asked. Schneider, a German national, was a tall man with a proud, arrogant bearing, his graying red hair shorn close to his skull, his eyes watery from decades of smoking cigars. Anger flared in Micah's chest every time he looked at him.

"Weapons and men," Jericho said.

"We do keep a few weapons on board, but not enough." Schneider pressed his hand against the front of a large safe. The sleek surface glowed around his fingers as it read his biometrics. The door clicked open. The interior of the safe contained a half-dozen pistols and rifles.

"Could've used these a few hours ago," Jericho said sourly, grabbing a gun and clipping it to his belt.

Schneider rubbed his neck. "This is established cruise industry protocol and the official recommendation of Voyager Enterprises.

Guns are forbidden in most parts of the world. Most of our international crew wouldn't know how to use one. To avoid undue stress on passengers, ship's officers do not carry weapons."

"Undue stress?" Jericho's eyes bulged. "They're worried about stress? How did Voyager Enterprises plan to protect their investment from hostiles, especially considered the caliber of your guests?"

Schneider shifted uncomfortably. "We have emergency protocols. We have plenty of security. There has never been an attack on a ship such as the *Grand Voyager*."

"You made the erroneous assumption that a hostile attack would only come from the outside," Jericho said.

Schneider blinked. "That is correct. We had no idea we'd been infiltrated by terrorists. No safety protocol can protect against all possibilities—"

"What about the drugs?" Micah was too furious to remain silent any longer. "You're smuggling Silk. You're a terrorist, too."

"Is that true?" Jericho narrowed his eyes. His hand drifted to his holster.

Schneider looked about to deny it, but he sighed instead. "Only the drugs. I had no idea about anything else. We weren't smuggling it into the U.S. We were smuggling it out. There is high demand in certain countries for a substance that calms and subdues its users, rather than inciting violence and gang warfare."

Rage jolted through Micah. He wanted to punch the man in the face. "It subdues the life out of them!"

"We all know what it's like to try and take care of our families." Schneider's voice rose. "No job pays enough. They offered forty grand a shipment. I have two daughters. I could not turn it down."

"And the guns?" Micah asked.

Schneider raised his hands. "I had nothing to do with any guns. I swear."

Micah noticed Silas staring at him out of the corner of his eye, his brows furrowed in scrutiny, like he recognized Micah and was trying to place him. Did Silas know Gabriel was his brother, that he'd turned traitor? Heat crept up Micah's neck, shame filling him. He looked away.

"We don't have time for this," Jericho said. "We have two objectives. Free the hostages from the muster stations and move as many survivors into lifeboats as possible, and infiltrate the bridge. The hostiles are holding high-value hostages as well as controlling the ship."

"The ship can be steered from the engine room," Schneider said.

"The hostiles have the engine room. They gained control through subterfuge. We would not be so lucky. The door is reinforced steel and the windows are plexiglass. We could attempt to break in with sledge-hammers or an acetylene torch, but we'd be sitting ducks in the process."

"What do you recommend?" Schneider asked uneasily. He handed a pistol to each of his men, his eyes darting from the weapons to the men's faces. "A shootout on a ship is a huge risk. This will only escalate the violence."

"While you've been in here cowering like little girls, the violence has been plenty escalated," Silas snapped.

Schneider shook his head. "The golden rule of piracy is give them what they want. Don't resist. They drain financial accounts and steal jewels and SmartFlexes and they leave."

"These aren't just pirates." Jericho's voice hardened. "They're terror-ists. They're out for blood. You're done hiding, do you understand? It's time to fight."

Schneider's nostrils flared. He lifted his hands placatingly. "We weren't hiding! We were enacting safety protocols. In the event of any hostile attack, all personnel should retreat to their cabins. We are not trained in combat. We are given explicit instructions never to engage—"

"Enough." Jericho checked the clip on his semi-automatic rifle. "None of that matters now. We need a plan. To evacuate the passengers, we need a diversion at the muster stations, as well as security to sweep the deck as passengers board the lifeboats. The storm makes things tricky, but it'll be harder for the hostiles as well. We took out two of the scumbags guarding the boats earlier. You may have a clear passage, or you might have to fight through. I need a few of your men to help me take the bridge."

"You have them, including myself. We aren't afraid to fight. We were simply following—"

"Do you have access to the bridge?" Jericho interrupted.

"As Chief Security Officer, my retinal scan will automatically go through, even if they've tried to change the security code. The problem is the security camera. They'll see us coming and shoot us as soon as the door opens."

"That's why we need a distraction." Jericho frowned, cracking his knuckles. "Can you pull up the HVAC system?"

"Yes, I have access. But—"

"How much space in those ducts?"

"Ductwork, wiring, and such take up two feet between decks. The amount of airflow required for the size of the ship ensures most ducts are wide enough for a small, nimble adult—if that's what you're thinking."

"It will do. Micah, Silas, you'll come with me. Micah, you're the only one here small enough. Are you willing to volunteer?"

Micah didn't hesitate. He would do anything to put a stop to this, to end the killing. "Absolutely."

"That's what I want to hear."

Schneider swiped his tablet several times and activated the holo port. The blueprints hovered in the air in front of them. "There are fans here and here."

He pointed a thick finger. "But if you enter here, through the vent in the First Officer's quarters, located portside, you will have unobstructed access. However, several turns will be difficult to manage. The sheet metal has sharp edges, and you will likely make considerable noise."

Micah swallowed. "Sounds a tad more difficult than they make it look in the movies."

Jericho smiled grimly. "Real life usually is."

"Hope you're not claustrophobic," Silas said, sounding an awful lot like he hoped Micah was.

"You won't be able to open the grille over the bridge as the screws will be on the outside," Schneider warned.

Jericho shook his head. "I have a workaround. He doesn't need to get in the bridge, just close."

Micah bit the inside of his cheek, forcing down his anxiety. He focused on the blueprints, trying to memorize the twists and turns in the narrow, convoluted ductwork.

"What if they hear him?" Silas asked. "Won't they just shoot at the ceiling and blow him to smithereens?"

Micah tried not to imagine being trapped in a tight, confined space, bullets ripping through the sheet metal all around him. "What he said."

Jericho frowned. "How close can he get without entering the actual bridge space?"

Schneider drew a line with his finger. "Approximately seven feet of ductwork extends beyond the interior wall before the vent located here."

"Seven feet. That'll still work." Jericho smacked Micah on the back so hard he almost pitched forward into the desk. "I guess you'll live through this after all."

"Great," Micah wheezed.

"Not much will filter into the vent and it'll dissipate in less than five minutes, but it will probably still hurt like hell."

Micah swallowed. "What?"

"You'll need a mask. Unfortunately, I only have a flimsy paper one."

"What are you talking about?" Micah wasn't sure he wanted to know.

Jericho pulled something flat, shiny, and disc-shaped out of his backpack. A drone. Smaller than the neighborhood guardian drones, this drone was the size of a large dinner plate.

He pressed a button, and an LED light in the center flashed blue. He pried open the back panel. Micah glimpsed its guts—wires and electrodes and other stuff Gabriel would know, but Micah never had an interest in.

Pain speared him at the thought of his brother. He shoved it aside. He took a closer look at the drone. "Wait. Is that thing weaponized?"

Jericho smiled. "Protectionary measures only, I assure you. This has a modified tear gas canister. And it's going to save our asses."

42

GABRIEL

"You let him take her!" Helpless rage boiled through Gabriel. "You know what he's going to do to her!"

Simeon shook his head. His face was strained, dark smudges beneath his eyes. "I didn't have a choice, Gabriel. I need you to keep it together. Remember the cause."

"How could you do this?" He stared at Simeon, the man who'd basically raised him, who'd been like a father. Now he was a stranger. The man who'd paid for his school lunches, who taught him how to handle a classic car, one without auto-drive.

His friend, mentor, and protector. Simeon, who had promised they'd all be heroes, who'd sworn only the guilty would die, and even then, as few as possible.

Simeon promised Amelia wouldn't be hurt. Then he'd tortured her himself, with his own hands. Amelia had warned Gabriel, and he hadn't believed her. Gabriel had trusted Simeon. Simeon, who had lied about everything.

Simeon refused to answer him. He stalked to the bridge starboard windows and looked out at the storm. He pulled out his satphone and spoke in a voice too quiet for Gabriel to overhear. Cheng and his men huddled together, their heads bent, muttering into their own satphones.

"I'll get you what you want." Declan Black leaned forward in the captain's chair.

Bitterness coiled in Gabriel's belly and slithered up his throat. He'd believed in this cause since he was fourteen. But first, he'd believed in a man. A man who wasn't who he said he was. A man who couldn't possibly stand for the ideals he'd preached for the last decade.

Gabriel felt himself crumbling. "You don't know the first thing about what I want."

"You want her."

The ship rolled. Lightning lit up the bridge windows.

"I can get you what you want."

Revulsion clogged Gabriel's throat. "Lies of a broken and desperate man. Even if she made it off the boat alive, she wouldn't want anything to do with you. Not after this."

"Yes, she will. She'll have to."

He remembered Amelia's words as she slumped in the patio chair, trembling and exhausted, the sky darkening, electrons sizzling, the wind whipping all around them. She'd shared her deepest secret, her weakness.

And Gabriel had betrayed her.

Black read his face and smirked. "Amelia developed feelings for you, didn't she? She told you about her little *condition*."

Gabriel despised the sound of her name on that man's lips. It didn't matter that he was her father; he was a monster. "Shut up."

"You know I'm right. She needs the medication or she's dead or a vegetable. Every seizure destroys more of that pretty brain of hers. If she makes it off the ship, she'll find me. And you can be there, right by my side."

"If I let you go, you'll just kill me." He masked the desire springing up inside him, the hope that Amelia might live through this, that his betrayal hadn't killed her.

"I have a need for those with certain . . . skills. There is a place for you."

There was no place left for Gabriel. Not here. Not anymore. Not with a monster like Black. Not with a deceiver like Simeon. Not with Amelia, who Gabriel had betrayed and destroyed. Not with Micah, who was too good to ever forgive him now.

Gabriel was trapped in a shadowy no man's land of rage, self-loathing, and hatred.

He made the decision in an instant. Once it was made, there was no turning back. In one swift motion, he lifted his gun, swiveled, and aimed it at Simeon's head.

Simeon looked up. Surprised disbelief and outrage sparked in his eyes.

"Hey!" Hollis shouted. "Stop!"

Gabriel pulled the trigger, the gunshot echoing in his ears. Simeon fell almost soundlessly. His body lay twitching on the floor, then went still.

"What the—?" Hollis swung around.

Across the room, Cheng raised his pulse gun and shot Hollis. The laser pulsed wide, striking her left shoulder. The smell of singed flesh filled the bridge.

Hollis stumbled, then righted herself, shrieking as she gripped her limp, lifeless arm. Before she could raise her own gun, Cheng shot her three more times.

Hollis triggered the rifle as she fell, slugs hammering the floor, the wall, and the ceiling only a few feet from where Gabriel stood.

"Thank you for that." Cheng grinned, his scar wrinkling his left cheek. "I was about to kill that self-righteous ass myself."

Gabriel stiffened. "I didn't do it for you."

"You can still redeem yourself," Black said fervently. "You can make the right choice."

"There is no redemption." The words were bitter as poison in his mouth. He widened his stance and pressed his gun against Declan Black's head.

"I'm afraid I can't let you do that." Cheng aimed his pulse gun at Gabriel. So did the three men behind him.

Black's face paled, but his voice remained steady. "Choose your actions carefully. Kill me and Amelia's treatment goes with it. Is that what you want?"

"Amelia's dead. You and Simeon made sure of that."

"Put the gun down, boy." Cheng took a step toward him.

"He deserves to die. I thought that's what we're here for." Gabriel's hands were slick, the gun trembling.

Cheng shook his head, a slow smile creeping across his face. "That was our original objective. We were hired to support the New Patriots in capturing the ship and eliminating several high-value targets, mainly the leadership of the Unity Coalition. Declan Black was the primary target.

"But that objective changed. Simeon was weak. His unfortunate distaste for torture and dispatching women limited his effectiveness. His New Patriots are idealistic and disorganized, not cut out for a task such as this. We, however, have no such qualms. And the situation has changed. We are nothing if not flexible." Cheng turned to Declan. "It's time to dispense with these little games. Mr. Black, we have a chopper waiting. You're coming with us."

Gabriel gaped at him. "What about the rendezvous point? The extraction? The boats?"

"Our boats aren't coming. They never were."

"Wait—what?" Confusion thickened like fog in Gabriel's mind. He couldn't comprehend the words he'd just heard. They didn't make sense. "No boats are coming?"

Cheng started to turn away, as if he were bored of the conversation. "Are you an idiot? That's what I said."

"What about your own men?"

Cheng shrugged. "They're nothing special. I will have a thousand more just like them by tomorrow."

The realization dawned slow and ugly. They'd been betrayed, both the New Patriots and the pirates-for-hire left to die on a burning, sinking ship—just like everyone else. His legs went weak. "We were never meant to survive the mission."

"Not even Simeon knew," Cheng said. "Our client saw to that."

"Your client?"

"You think this whole thing was some idealized statement in the name of freedom? Only one thing is at the root of an act like this. Power. Bought and paid for with cold, hard cash."

Declan's face darkened. "That lying, double-crossing sack of sh—"

"Our client took care of loose ends," Cheng said. "And killed two birds with one stone. I wasn't sure of the endgame before Black's little confession. But it all makes sense now. The New Patriots are patsies, an easy mark to take the blame. The truth about Black and BioGen's role in the release of the bioweapon virus will remain a mystery—as will the identity of the people who hired him. And you'll all be dead, so who can say what really happened here? Quite brilliant, actually."

He turned to Gabriel. "Now, put your gun down so we can finish this childish nonsense."

Gabriel kept the gun pressed against Declan's head, every muscle tensed. He couldn't lose his balance when the ship rocked, or it would all be over in a moment. He clenched his jaw, fighting down panic. He had to think. Had to be smart. "Soon as I do that, you'll shoot me."

Declan started to rise.

"Don't move!" Gabriel said.

Cheng advanced around the console, stopping on the other side of the captain's chair, his gun still aimed at Gabriel's head. Gabriel and Cheng faced each other, Declan between them.

"Put the gun down," Cheng said. "It's over."

"You first," Gabriel said to Cheng. "You can kill me, but I'll get Black, and all his secrets die with him—including the cure."

"I'm a trained killer, boy. Who do you think will win this shootout?"

Gabriel dug the barrel against Black's temple. "Are you willing to test that hypothesis?"

An explosion shook the floor beneath them.

Cheng smiled. His scar seemed to throb in the dim light, like a living thing. "Looks like the party's starting early."

"Hostiles!" One of Cheng's men pointed at the security monitors. Gabriel caught a glimpse of movement on the hallway camera out of the corner of his eye.

His finger tightened on the trigger.

43

MICAH

Micah had never been more claustrophobic in his life. The sheet metal walls closed in on him in the darkness. He choked on stale, dirty air. Dust caked his throat and prickled his nostrils.

The mask pressed against his nose and mouth so tight that it was hard to breathe. He kept choking back a sneeze.

The corners of the ducts were sharp as razor blades. The old cuts in his palm and fingers mingled with several fresh ones, all of them stinging. He'd sliced his forearm and right thigh as he slithered his way around a corner.

Everything was black. He couldn't see above, behind, or ahead of him. He couldn't get the image of rats scurrying over his hands out of his head. He crawled through an HVAC duct system, not a sewer. Still, the sensation of dust mites brushing against him made his skin crawl.

He wriggled forward, using his elbows to pull the rest of his weight. He gripped the smooth metal of the drone in his hands. His glasses kept slipping down his nose, but he had no way to fix them.

Two lefts. A right. A left. Almost every time he moved, he accidentally banged a knee or shoulder against the sheet metal walls. He winced, biting the inside of his cheeks.

If the terrorists heard him, the whole plan went pear-shaped.

Schneider assured him that since he wasn't crawling directly over the bridge, a few dings and thumps should be sufficiently muffled. Should be.

Fear thrummed through him. But there was no going back. *The best way out is always through.* He repeated the Robert Frost line in his head, his heart beating double time.

He felt his way around the final left turn, bending his body into a twisted, convoluted L-shape, his stomach and thighs scraping against the sharp corner. It snagged his shirt, and pain sliced the skin above his belly button.

Sounds filtered through the vent. Voices shouting. One of them he recognized as sure as his own face in the mirror. *Gabriel.*

Gabriel shouldn't be here. He was supposed to be down in the Oceanarium with Amelia, safe from all the death and destruction and chaos. Ice went through him, stabbing all the way to the bone.

Micah closed his eyes. Would Gabriel be killed in the crossfire? Did it make a difference? Could he risk his brother's life to save everyone else? Did he even have a choice?

He couldn't reconcile this hard, angry Gabriel with the brother who'd rescued him from bullies over and over, who'd cradled Micah in his arms that day at the hover park. Gabriel who'd sat on his bed and stroked his hair the times he contracted pneumonia. Gabriel who snuck him oranges and candy bars when they didn't have the money.

His brother. His family. The only real family he had.

Gabriel, who might be dead seconds after Micah released the drone. Micah would never get to say all the things he still needed to stay. *How could you? I'm sorry* and *I love you* and *always*, all in the same breath.

More shouting.

A gunshot blast.

It didn't matter. It couldn't matter. This one heinous act overshadowed all the good in Gabriel. No matter how many times Gabriel protected him in the past, Micah couldn't protect him now.

It was more important to save innocent lives. It had to be. He couldn't value his brother's life over so many others. Too many lives were at stake. It was the right thing.

Grief welled up, but he forced it down. He couldn't let himself feel the staggering pain, not now. All that would come later. If he survived.

He sucked in his breath, more dusty air gagging his throat.

Almost there. He recalled the complicated HVAC blueprints, trying to guestimate his location. Crawl five feet past the turn. No further, or risk being riddled with bullets like a fish trapped in a claustrophobic metal barrel.

Dim light filtered through the vent two yards in front of him. He could barely make out the shape of the drone gripped in his hands. He fumbled for the switch and activated the thing as Jericho instructed.

A spray of bullets punctured the air duct, not two feet ahead of him. He froze. More shouting from below. Time was up. He had to act. His mother's words came back to him. *Be good. Be brave.*

He whispered a prayer as he released the drone and gave it a gentle push. It whooshed silently, hovering a few inches above the duct. The drone landed on top of the grate, clicked, and let out a soft hiss.

Smoke spewed into the bridge. Chaos erupted.

Micah closed his eyes. As the sound of gunshots filled his ears, his mind repeated the same word over and over.

Always.

44

AMELIA

K ane dragged Amelia by her hair down a long hallway. He opened a door and shoved her inside. She caught glimpses of a conference room with a large table and chairs, a living room with brocaded sofas in nautical colors, a large holoscreen on the far wall. The captain's quarters.

Kane pushed her through another doorway into the bedroom. He threw her into the king-sized sleep pod, the lid already wide open. Her head bounced hard against the curved side. Her clutch knocked out of her hand.

Then he was on her, breathing stinking tobacco-breath in her face, yanking at the jewel-encrusted straps of her dress.

Her vision blurred. The bowed lid of the sleep pod shimmered above her in bursting shades of pink, yellow, white. Her stomach lurched. A migraine. It was fitting—every terrible thing coming down on her at once, like a dreadful punishment for every sin she'd ever committed.

She was going to die. Not with a bullet. A far worse way. This man was hurting her. He enjoyed hurting her. And when he finished with that, he would hurt her more. She smelled it on him, in his pungent sweat. She felt it in the tautness of his body, in the way he drank in her fear with those vicious, viper eyes.

Time slowed. She saw everything. The blinking blue nodules of the sleep pod. A smudge of a handprint on the glass doors leading to the veranda. A priceless Picasso painting hung on one wall. And Kane looming over her, the pores enlarged in his skin, the cords standing out on his neck, that awful, snarling smile.

She felt everything. The cushioned, silken base of the pod rubbing against her back. His hands like giant scrabbling spiders on her neck, her shoulders. And her brain—on fire, pulsing, throbbing.

Her whole body trembled, shuddering against the pain and terror and revulsion.

She was alone. Abandoned. No one would come for her. She was just a tool, a pawn to use and discard. Everyone used her. Here, finally, was the worst way to use a person.

This animal would take everything from her: her dignity, her sense of self, her safety. Her life.

"You awake, girl?" he growled. "Don't disappear on me."

She groaned, tried to pull away. "Please . . ."

He slapped her hard in the face. His grin widened. "Let's have some atmosphere, shall we? What are you partial to, jazz? Piano? Oh, I know. How about the violin?"

He leaned away and said something to the AI. Music flared through the stateroom.

Amelia recognized Bach's Chaccone from Partita no. 2, a demanding piece she'd been working on for years. The sweetly bitter, ominous notes of the violin flowed through her, swelling through her aching skull. The walls of the stateroom shimmered with shivering tendrils of smoky purple, sapphire blue, and shades of night—indigo, dusk, and deepest black.

"There, that's better. Now, where were we?"

The hammering inside her head intensified. Pain throbbed in her brain, needling her scalp and the base of her neck.

Use what you have.

She blinked, forcing herself to focus.

Use what you have.

She was helpless. She'd been given up by her father, by Gabriel. They had no more use for her. They didn't see her. She thought they had—she'd tried to make them—but she was wrong.

The bright lights seared her eyes, the music a pulse of pain. The migraine streaked through her skull, cracking her open, splitting her into pieces. It felt like dying. Over and over again. Dying and returning to life, only to die again.

Use what you have.

Her mind tried to leave, to drift away, to escape the horror, but the pain wouldn't let her. It chained her to the present.

But this pain she knew. This pain was her oldest, most bitter friend. A pain she suffered through, over and over. Endured. Survived.

Her migraines didn't kill her. The seizures didn't kill her. She outlasted them. She beat them.

She knew pain. And she knew how to survive it. She'd survived pain her whole life. She could do it again.

Use what you have.

Amelia opened her eyes. Splotches of colored lights swam in her vision. But she could see enough. She could move.

Kane was wrong. He thought he tortured her by blasting her favorite music, but the violin was hers. No one could take it from her. Not her father, and not this low-life scum.

Bach's Chaccone was a dance, but it was a dance full of grief and pain, hauntingly beautiful in its paradox. She could dance through her pain. She could *fight* through it.

As the music soared, she gathered herself the way she gathered herself before a performance. She coiled her strength inside herself.

And then she struck. She clawed his face, catching his cheek and part of his left eyeball. He reared back, howling.

She rolled to the side and launched herself out of the sleep pod. She hit the marble floor and scrambled to her hands and knees.

She leapt to her feet and sprinted for the door, half stumbling as vertigo gripped her, the floor rolling violently.

He lunged at her from behind. He was fast, too fast. He seized her around the waist and dragged her back, throwing her to the floor.

Her skull hit the ground, cracking her teeth together. Fresh agony ruptured behind her eyes. Kane smashed his fist into her face. Everything went dark and blurry. He hovered over her, a grotesque shadow.

She smelled his rage. It stung her nostrils like the stench of burning rubber, something dark and bitter. He grabbed her arms and pinned them above her head.

Acid surged up her throat, but she fought it down. Terror mingled with the adrenaline spiking through her. There was no time to be afraid. She gathered her strength and kneed him in the crotch.

He fell back, clutching himself. "I'll kill you for that!"

She rolled to the side and tried to get to her feet, but the pain gripped her head in a savage vise. Convulsions rippled through her. She fell to her knees. She'd never reach the door.

Use what you have.

She turned, franticly clawing at the floor, scrambling on her hands and knees toward the sleep pod. Acid churned in her gut, the wave of nausea almost knocking her flat. Her vision swam in and out of focus. She blinked furiously.

Where was it? *Where was it!*

She heard him behind her. He was coming for her. Enraged and hungry for violence, for blood.

There it was. Beneath the bed. She cried out with relief.

She saw him out of the corner of her eye. He lunged for her, lightning fast and lethal, the flash of a blade in his hand.

The world became silent. The music faded to nothing. Sound drained away. She couldn't hear a thing. Could hardly see. She used her hands, her sense of touch, the way she always did when the pain roared down on her like a train, tracks quaking beneath her feet.

He leapt on top of her, his knife at her throat. He pressed hard until the blade sliced through the top layers of her skin. Blood trickled down the hollow of her throat.

His eyes gleamed, sharp and menacing. "Die, you little b—"

"You first," she said.

Amelia stabbed the auto-injector into his right eyeball and depressed the plunger.

45

MICAH

Micah huddled in the darkness of the HVAC duct, his muscles aching. His eyes burned and watered from the remnants of the tear gas. The particles that filtered through his paper mask seared his mouth, tongue, and throat.

But he'd escaped the worst of it. He waited, tense and trembling, utterly helpless as he listened to the fierce gunfight below him.

It seemed like an eternity before the grate screwed off and dim blue light radiated into the duct. He crawled forward with his elbows and pushed his head out of the vent.

Strong arms grabbed him and pulled him the rest of the way. He dropped from the vent to the floor, landing unceremoniously on his butt.

Jericho hauled him to his feet. "Look what the cat dragged in."

He doubled over, coughing and spitting. He rubbed his face, and his hand came back smudged gray with dirt and dust. He wiped his filthy glasses on a semi-clean corner of his shirt and slipped them back on.

The smoke had dissipated. The room stank of vomit. There were bodies. His heart seized. "What happened?"

"Two escaped with Declan Black as a hostage." Jericho's nostrils flared, his eyes jagged with rage. "We couldn't risk harm to Black.

Watched the assholes just walk out of here." He explained how he'd followed them at a safe distance up to the top deck. A helicopter had hovered over the lido deck, a ladder whipping in the wind. Black's captors had escaped, abandoning the ship and its passengers—including their own men—to burn.

Schneider's men freed the remaining hostages and moved them to the hall. They were limp, unconscious, except for a woman who coughed violently, her eyes streaming with tears from the gas.

Schneider stood at the bridge console, working on getting communications back up and steering them out of the storm. The ship still rolled, but not as sharply as before. The rain slashed the windows, but with less ferocity.

Soon, the storm would be over. But it wasn't finished yet.

Schneider hit one long blast to signal an emergency evacuation, then punched the red button on the PA system. "This is CSO Schneider speaking. We have retaken the bridge. Repeat, we have retaken the bridge. All crew report to your emergency evacuation stations. Passengers, as soon as it is safe to do so, please make your way to the starboard lifeboats on Deck Four.

"And for those of you who have attacked this ship and the good people on board, the U.S. Navy has been notified, and they are en route. There are no boats coming for you. I repeat, your leadership has abandoned you, escaping via chopper. If you release your hostages and make your way immediately to the portside lifeboats, no one on this ship will attempt to stop you."

"You and Silas head for the lifeboats," Jericho said. "We're going to take the muster stations and free the remaining hostages."

"You better hurry." Schneider swiped a screen on the console, his frown deepening. "Fire zones one, two, and five are compromised. The explosions have flooded two compartments. More than three, and we sink. I've closed the watertight doors below deck and the fire-resistant doors, but the fires are hot and spreading. We don't have much time."

"We'll get rid of those bastards one way or another," Jericho said.

Micah opened his mouth, about to ask about Gabriel's fate, but he hesitated. If they knew his brother was a terrorist, would they continue to trust him? Would they suspect him, too? Or worse, just shoot him to be safe? No. He would have to find out himself.

A sharp, metallic stench filled his nostrils, mixing with the stink of gunpowder. He forced his gaze to the floor. Several bodies were scattered around the bridge. He counted nine dead. Two more were mortally wounded, sure to bleed out in the next few minutes.

His stomach curdled as he stepped over the bodies, searching each one for Gabriel. He wasn't there. Micah checked and rechecked each body. Two more lay crumpled behind the main console.

Neither of them Gabriel. His brother was not among the dead.

Impossible. He'd heard Gabriel's voice.

"Looking for someone?"

Micah stiffened.

Silas slouched against the wall, staring at him with those dark, penetrating eyes. He'd been watching him the whole time.

His stomach dropped. "Why would you say that?"

Silas only smirked. "He's down the corridor."

Micah didn't ask who. Silas knew. The way he'd been looking at him all night, scrutinizing him. But now there was no confusion. Just smug, contemptuous recognition.

"Is he—?"

"Restrained and under guard. So he can stand trial for his crimes. But he's alive." Silas arched his brow. "That a good thing? Or bad?"

Anger shot through him. Silas hit much too close to the mark. Micah didn't know what he wanted. *Alive.* He wanted his brother alive. Beyond that, he had no idea. He shouldered past Silas into the corridor.

Three rescued hostages sat in the hallway. One man moaned, clutching a bullet wound in his stomach. One appeared unconscious, and the woman sat blinking, numb, maybe in shock.

And there he was. His brother, the terrorist. Gabriel slumped against the wall a dozen yards further down the corridor. Hands cuffed in front of him, his crisp officer's uniform sullied with blood, some blotches faded to brown, some still bright red. One of Schneider's men stood guard several feet away.

Could he go to him? Could he bear to confront Gabriel, to look into that face he knew as well as his own, had loved more than himself? He blinked, fighting back the wave of grief and despair.

Someone grabbed his pant leg. One of the hostages, her dark hair wild around her face. He recognized her despite the blood and the mascara smudging her cheeks. "Mrs. Black."

"You were in the Oasis dining room. When it happened."

"Yes, ma'am," he said in a strangled voice.

Silas crouched in front of his mother. "Are you okay?"

Mother and son looked at each other. Mrs. Black's face held a complicated expression Micah couldn't read: a blend of relief, hope, fear, and regret. She lifted her hand as if to reach for Silas.

It fluttered for a moment in the space between them before she let it drop into her lap. She rubbed the red marks on her wrists instead, smiling shakily. "Silas. I've been praying every second for you and Amelia. I'm—I'm so thankful you're okay."

"You too."

"It was horrible. I was so scared, every second. And then he took her —" She looked from Silas to Micah, as if she'd awakened from a terrible nightmare only to realize it was still happening. "He took her!"

Silas stiffened. "Took who?"

"Amelia! She was here, in the bridge. They hurt her—" Her mouth contorted. "That monster took her."

His chest tightened. The fear that nagged at him in the ducts settled in his gut like a block of ice. Micah had left Amelia in the Oceanarium. He'd believed Gabriel wouldn't hurt her. Not an innocent girl. He couldn't have.

But Gabriel did. He brought her to the bridge and handed her over to brutal thugs, to killers. Micah was so naïve, stupidly trusting in the brother he thought he knew. But maybe he never did.

Maybe you could never truly know another person beyond what they wanted you to see. Or beyond what you wanted to see in them.

"Where is she?" Silas asked, his tone sharp enough to cut glass.

"I don't know!" his mother said.

"Think! You were there!"

"I don't know!"

"What did he look like?"

"He—he was big—strong. He had eyes like . . . like he was doing things to you, in his mind. Oh, Silas. He's going to kill her!" She covered her mouth with her hands, stifling a sob.

Silas leapt to his feet and turned to Micah. "Where would you go, if you were gonna—" He grimaced, unable to finish the sentence.

Micah bit the inside of his cheeks so hard he tasted blood. "I don't know where he'd take her, but I know someone who would."

He strode down the corridor. The floor jerked, and he steadied himself against the wall. Fury rose in him, blotting out the pain, the betrayal. He would mourn later.

Gabriel's eyes were closed. Micah kicked his leg. "Wake up!"

His eyes fluttered open. "Micah. You're safe."

The affection in his gaze struck him like a savage punch to the gut. "No thanks to you."

Gabriel lifted his bound hands and tilted his chin at the guard standing a dozen feet away, talking into his walkie-talkie. "Tell him you'll relieve him. He doesn't know who you are. We can get out of here, grab one of the lifeboats before anyone knows we're gone."

Micah's heart pulsed like a bruise. He could hardly bear to look Gabriel in the face. Disgust and revulsion warred with loyalty, tenderness, love. And grief, over everything, like a towering tsunami bearing down on him. "You did this. You helped kill all these people."

"I'd take it back if I could, I swear to you. It was a mistake, a terrible mistake."

He couldn't listen to Gabriel's wounded voice. Couldn't let his emotions get in the way. "Where's Amelia?"

A shadow passed over his brother's face.

"Where is she? Answer me!"

"Dead," Gabriel said in an agonized voice.

"Gabriel, please!"

"Captain's quarters. He took her to the captain's quarters. But it's too late for her, Micah. I'm so sorry. I never meant for this. Never. You have to believe me—"

"I did believe you. I believed you wouldn't actually hurt anyone. But you brought her here. You let them take her."

Gabriel's face contorted. "I'm sorry. For everything."

Micah stood and backed away.

Desperation shone in Gabriel's eyes. "Just us?"

The word *always* disintegrated on his tongue. He couldn't listen anymore. His heart would shatter if he did. "You're my brother. You'll always be my brother. I love you, but I can't save you."

"Micah!"

"I'm sorry." It felt like a betrayal, turning his back on his only family, the brother he loved more than himself. It felt like losing his own soul. Like everything he'd ever loved crumbled to dust in his hands.

"Let's go!" he called to Silas, his voice breaking.

Silas came toward him, hefting his rifle. He pointed it at Gabriel, though his gaze was locked on Micah. "Aren't you a traitor like your filthy rat of a brother? Why should I listen to you?"

Micah swallowed back the howl of outrage and grief and horror. "Because I know where she is. You want to save her?"

Silas scowled, but he nodded.

"Micah, I'm sorry—" Gabriel pleaded. "Forgive me."

But Micah and Silas were already gone.

46

WILLOW

W illow clutched the rifle to her chest with one hand and gripped Benjie's small fingers in the other. She led the caravan down several flights of stairs. Nadira hurried behind her, the other two staff members taking up the rear.

A massive explosion shook the walls and trembled the stairs. The lights flickered then went out, plunging them into darkness. Several children cried out.

"It's okay," Nadira said.

"Lo Lo!" Benjie squeezed her hand.

"Just wait." A moment later, the dim emergency lights along the floor switched on. She blinked, willing her eyes to adjust to the murky gloom. Suddenly every shadow seemed alive, taunting her. "Okay, let's go. Hurry!"

They followed her down another set of stairs to Deck Six. The smell of smoke filled her nostrils. She leaned over the stairwell railing and glimpsed a dark gray haze seeping up the stairs from below.

That way was blocked. They would have to take the Royal Promenade to the aft stairwell down to the lifeboats on Deck Four.

The ship lurched violently, and she stumbled, holding onto the wall for balance for a moment before forcing herself to move again. She rounded the corner fast, several steps into the foyer when she froze.

Movement. A glimpse of a shadow to the right.

She gestured for Nadira to stop. Nadira retreated to the stairs, but Willow and Benjie didn't have time. Her gaze spun, frantically searching for safety. The elevator alcove was across the foyer. It was the best option.

She yanked Benjie's hand and dashed across the open space, rounding the corner of the alcove. She pressed her finger to her lips. Benjie nodded, eyes wide with terror.

She peeked around the alcove wall. Nadira and the children were out of sight. They must be huddled on the stairs, blocked from view by the stairwell wall. Safe, for the moment.

If whoever was coming just walked straight through, without turning to the stairwell to the left or the elevators to the right, the dim lighting and the shadows might hide them. They might survive this.

Then she saw the blood illuminated by the emergency floor lighting. Her bloody footprints, dark and conspicuous on the gold carpet. The cuts on her feet from the coffee bar display case had been bleeding all this time, and she hadn't even noticed. The prints led straight to the alcove they were huddled within.

The sound of heavy footsteps drew closer. She shrank back against the elevator door, her heart thudding in her chest. Benjie covered his mouth with his hands.

He stared at her in desperation, his face reddening. He had to cough. *Not now. Please not now.*

She pressed her hands over his. He shook from the effort of holding it in. Her own throat closed like a vise, cutting off her breath.

The footsteps stopped. He'd seen the blood. This very second, his gaze followed the footprints straight to the alcove.

Then he stood in front of her, only a few yards away. Even in the dim lighting, she saw him clearly. He wasn't wearing a ski mask. He had blonde hair and a long, horsey face. He lifted his rifle.

"Stay back!" Hopefully Nadira and the other kids would run back up the stairs while the terrorist's attention focused on her. But she couldn't worry about that now. Not with the muzzle of an automatic rifle pointed straight at her.

She swallowed, her heart punched into her throat. Her palms were damp, Benjie's hand slipping inside hers. Benjie's cough exploded from his chest. He choked, half-coughing, half-sobbing. She clutched his hand tighter.

"You don't have to do this!" Her voice shook. "The ship is burning. We're all just trying to escape with our lives. You can let us go."

"None of you elitist scum deserve to live," he spat. He advanced, mumbling curses under his breath and jabbing the gun at them like a spear. His eyes were wild and bloodshot. Blood stains splattered his shirt and smeared his neck.

He had no wounds. It wasn't his blood.

He was going to kill them. Not because he had to. Because he could.

Time seemed to slow. Terror screamed at her to run. And maybe she could. She was fast. She could weave and dodge. Maybe she'd get away.

But Benjie wouldn't. He was too small, his legs too short. He wouldn't be able to escape.

Unless there was a distraction. Unless this vicious bastard had a more appetizing target. She could save herself, but she couldn't save them both.

The decision took only a moment. She knew what her mom would want her to do. *Take care of them.* She was *Ate*. It was her responsibility.

"When I tell you—" she squeezed Benjie's hand, "I want you to run. Don't stop. Pretend it's magic. Pretend if you're fast enough, you'll disappear."

I love you. And I'm sorry. But there wasn't time to say those things. She let go of Benjie's hand.

Her gaze never left the terrorist's face. Fear churned in her gut, but also something else. Resignation. And something like peace. *Take care of them.* To save her family, she had to be willing to do anything.

This was it. Now or never.

She stepped in front of her brother.

47

MICAH

Micah and Silas raced down the starboard corridor to the third door, marked with a gold placard titled, 'Captain Liebenberg.'

He tried the handle. "It's locked. Schneider will have a master key."

"We're out of time!" Silas rammed his shoulder against the door. It shuddered but didn't give.

Inside, someone screamed.

Micah's breath stilled in his chest. They'd found her. She was alive. But the terror in that scream iced his veins.

"Amelia!" He pounded his fists against the door. He backed up and ran at the door again.

"Use your rifle!"

Silas swung the rifle around and smashed it against the old-fashioned brass door handle. It broke off after four tries.

Micah and Silas kicked the door until it crashed open.

There was a living room area, a holoscreen, and an opened door to what he assumed was the bedroom. Dimly, he heard music blaring, but his brain hardly registered any of these things. He and Silas raced into the bedroom.

Two bodies grappled on the floor beside the sleep pod. For a horrific moment, he couldn't tell what was happening. Then his vision focused.

Amelia crouched over the body of a man—Kane. He moaned in pain, clutching at his face. She stabbed him with something as she screamed in outraged terror. He shoved her off with a flailing arm, but she hurled herself at him, stabbing him again and again in the neck, chest, and shoulders.

Silas ran to her. He grabbed her under her arms and lifted her off Kane.

She howled, turning and lunging at Silas, her weapon clutched in her hand. Silas caught hold of her wrist before she could stab him, too. "Amelia! Stop! It's me! It's me!"

Her scream died in her throat. She blinked, recognition dawning in her face. She sagged against him. They collapsed to their knees, Silas drawing her close, murmuring something into her hair.

Micah's own heart throbbed in his throat, but he dared not intrude. Amelia needed Silas, now. Micah was just glad that she was alive. "Music off." The menacing tones of the violin faded away.

Silas pulled his sister back at arm's length to examine her. Her dress was torn in several places and ripped off her shoulder. Deep bruises shaped like handprints marred her neck. Blood bubbled from a shallow cut at the base of her throat. A purplish bruise formed over her right eye, her teeth smeared bright red.

To Micah's surprise, Silas grinned at her. "What a mess you are, princess."

She half-laughed, half-choked. Her face contorted, like she was about to dissolve into tears. But she didn't. Her mouth flattened, her eyes going hard. "He was going to kill me."

"I know."

"I stopped him."

"You did."

She pulled away from him and stood, swaying on her feet. Silas jumped up and steadied her. "Come on. Let's go."

She shoved her hair out of her face. "He needs to die."

They both looked at Kane, bloodied and unconscious. Micah kicked at the man's arm, knocking it away from his face. Blood and clear goopy liquid oozed out of his right eye.

"You did that, sister?" Silas said in awe.

"I did." Her voice grew stronger. She lifted her chin and stared at her brother. "I'm going to kill him."

"No, you're not."

"Yes. I am."

She tried to pull away, but Silas gripped her upper arm. "You've been through enough. Let me do this."

They stared at each other for a long, silent minute, so much passing between them that Micah felt like an intruder. He glanced away, his gaze landing on Kane. "Silas!"

Kane writhed on the floor, his eyes rolling back in his head, white foam bubbling out of his mouth. After a moment, he went still, his body twisted grotesquely.

Amelia stared at the body, her face white. "Is he dead?"

Silas checked, pressing his fingers against Kane's neck. He nodded.

Her hands curled into fists at her sides. "Good."

Acid roiled in Micah's stomach, but he fought it back. He had no idea what was in the syringe to kill a person like that, but it didn't matter now. Amelia had done what she needed to do. Now Micah needed to be strong, to be brave. They weren't safe yet. "It's time to go."

"Micah, help Amelia. I've got the gun."

She allowed Micah to put his arm around her shoulders. He tried to be as gentle as possible, but she still winced. The ship lurched, and they staggered. Micah steadied her. "I'm sorry."

She looked at him for the first time, a fragile smile tugging at her lips. "Last time we met, didn't I say that to you?"

He pressed her black purse-thing into her trembling hands. "About that. I never should have left you. I should've—"

She shook her head. "It's done and forgotten."

Deep shame filled him, as if he alone were responsible for his brother's actions, for all the terrible things that had happened, for what Kane

248

did to Amelia, for all the dead mothers and fathers and children. Because in a way, he was.

He let his love blind him. He'd believed in the goodness in people, in his brother. And now, surrounded by all this death and darkness, he didn't know what he believed anymore.

He led Amelia out of the captain's quarters and into the hallway. "I should've done things differently. If only I—"

"Micah." Her voice softened. "I trusted him, too."

He nodded grimly, but the shame didn't dissipate. It never would.

Before they reached the stairwell, another massive explosion rocked the ship.

48

WILLOW

Willow stepped in front of her brother, shielding him with her body. She lifted the rifle with both hands, gripping the barrel and raising it like a club. "Run!"

A bang exploded in her ears. She screamed.

The terrorist stumbled, his face contorting in a stunned grimace. His gun wavered as he stared down at the red spreading across his chest.

He staggered, then fell to the floor.

A moment later, a guy dressed in black combat gear stepped out from around the corner. He had a long, wolfish face and a sour expression. He smirked, cradling an automatic rifle in his arms. "You do know that's not how you're supposed to use a gun, right?"

Her legs turned to water, and she crumpled to her knees. Benjie raced back to her, bursting into tears. She dropped the gun and wrapped him in a fierce hug, both their bodies trembling.

She looked up at the guy. "Thanks for the tip. And, you know, saving us."

He looked down at the body, nudging the guy's arm. "I needed the target practice." His voice was light, but his face paled, his lips a thin, bloodless line.

Benjie coughed, wheezing for air as she stroked his hair. "Here, get your inhaler from your backpack. It's okay, everything's okay."

"Technically, it's not." He reached down and grabbed the dead terrorist's rifle.

Two other people limped around the corner behind him, one in the standard dark-clothed terrorist garb. She leapt to her feet, pushing her brother behind her.

The first guy rolled his eyes. "Relax. I'm Silas Black, by the way. Meet my sister, Amelia, and I forgot this one's name."

"I'm Micah," the second guy said. Willow recognized him from the Oasis dining room. She'd noticed his boyish handsomeness in his tux and white gloves. Now, he was covered in smudges of dirt and blood, his expression strained.

Micah's arm looped around Amelia Black's shoulder, holding her up. Her face was bruised and bloodied, her hair a tangled mess around her face.

"Is she okay?" Willow asked.

"None of us are okay," Silas said.

"I'll be fine." Amelia's voice was raw, but she lifted her head and met Willow's gaze.

"We need to go, guys," Micah said. "We're headed for the lifeboats. Come on."

"Just a second." Willow called for the rest of the kids and the caregivers to come down the stairs. Several small, terrified faces peered around the corner of the stairwell.

Silas scowled. "You've got to be joking. There's no way in hell we're babysitting a bunch of snotty-faced rug rats on a sinking death-ship. Just, no."

"We can't abandon little kids," Micah said. "We'll figure it out."

"They'll slow us down and make too much noise. They'll get us all killed. There are still psychopaths all over this ship." He kicked at the dead man's body at his feet. "Enter exhibit A."

"You're the psychopath!" How could someone think that way? He was just another rich asshat, a pompous elitist with no compassion, no conscience.

Silas's face darkened. He took a menacing step toward her. "You forget just who knows how to use a gun here."

"We're taking them with us," Micah said. "No discussion."

"Fine." Silas sneered. "We'll leave you with the brats. Have fun."

"Silas." Amelia's voice was hoarse. Her brother stopped. A look passed between them. "We're going. All of us."

The PA system cackled. "This is CSO Schneider. We are abandoning ship. I repeat, abandon ship. Please follow standard evacuation protocols—"

Another explosion trembled the floors, the walls, the ceiling. A couple of the kids stumbled and fell. Willow leaned against the elevator for support. The floor seemed to slide beneath her feet. Not rolling. Tilting.

"I smell smoke," Benjie said in a quavering voice.

He was right. They all smelled it, a stench like burning rubber, something foul and dangerous.

Fifty yards down the Royal Promenade on the right, the heavy fire-resistant door that led to the next section hadn't closed properly. Fire burst into the promenade, black smoke billowing toward them. Flames licked the walls, the floor, the ceiling. "Time to go!"

A loud groaning, scraping sound filled the air. The floor tilted again. The ship listed. Willow grabbed Benjie's hand. "Run!"

The group half-ran, half-staggered left along the Royal Promenade, toward the aft stairwell. Shards of glass and chunks of wall and ceiling littered the floor. Bullet holes punctured the gold mermaids in the fountain.

Behind the fountain, the grand staircase had fractured, the glass spidered with jagged cracks. Several stairs were missing, the others shattered.

Smoke clouded the air in a murky, deepening haze. The stench was stronger now, stinging Willow's nostrils, gagging her throat. She stepped over a splintered, gilt-framed painting, what was once an authentic Jackson Pollock.

They edged around an enormous fallen chandelier, a motionless body trapped beneath the broken crystals. The group reached the closed fire-resistant door separating them from the aft stairwell. Micah pushed the green button. A red light over the door flashed, and the alarm blared.

Willow turned to Micah. "Didn't the *Grand Voyager* holo ads promise to make all my wishes come true?"

Micah snorted. "We might have oversold ourselves a bit."

"So did the Titanic," Amelia said.

Willow grabbed Benjie with her free hand and pushed him through the opening. "Dream vacation, my ass. Let's get the hell off this ship."

———

By the time Willow and the others made it to Deck Four, dozens of panicking passengers crowded the deck, impatiently waiting to board the lifeboats.

Several officers and a few men in plainclothes flanked either side, weapons up and ready in case of another attack. Crew members prepared the lifeboats and handed out life preservers.

The slick deck pitched beneath her feet, tilting downward. The rain battered her head. It should have been dark without lights, but tongues of fire burned through the outer decks on the floors above them, casting everything in an eerie orange glow.

Flitting, shouting shadows surrounded them. Willow gripped Benjie's hand tighter and stumbled through the surging crowd, searching every face she passed for her mom.

But she wasn't there. She wasn't anywhere.

Instead, Willow bumped into Celeste. The girl just stood there, her wet hair curtaining her face, her eyes shiny with terror.

"Get in line for a lifeboat!" Willow shook Celeste's shoulders. Celeste nodded dully.

"They won't let us through!" Nadira said.

Micah helped them shove a path through the panicked, jostling crowd to the closest lifeboat.

"Children first," the crew member manning the boat ordered, stopping a blonde, middle-aged woman from climbing aboard.

"Do you know who I am?" she sputtered. Her mascara dripped down her cheeks, her hair plastered to her skull. "I'm Meredith Jackso—"

"No one cares." Willow pushed the woman aside and lifted Benjie onto the boat.

The ship shifted with a great groan, tilting at a steeper angle. Benjie's legs slipped into the gap between the lifeboat and the side of the ship. He jerked out of her grasp. She grabbed at his arms, but her fingers couldn't grip his slick skin.

"Benjie!"

From inside the lifeboat, someone lunged forward, grabbed Benjie by his Star Wars backpack, and hauled him up and over the lip of the hatch. He fell in a heap on the floor of the boat.

A familiar face peered out at her.

"Finn!"

He grinned crookedly. "Come on in."

"Hurry up!" someone shouted.

"Let us on!" Bodies jostled her. Someone elbowed her hard in her spine. Hands clawed and shoved at her back.

Then Micah was there, standing between her and the crowd. "Go!"

She nearly slipped as she and Nadira helped the rest of the children. Finn leaned out of the hatch and grabbed each kid, lifting them to safety.

"Climb in!" Micah pushed Nadira into the boat and turned to Willow.

"But my mom—!" Could Willow escape not knowing if her mom was dead or alive? Her mom could still be on the ship. What if she was trapped somewhere and needed help? What if—

Gunshots blasted from somewhere above them. Everyone screamed.

The crowd throbbed, slipping and skidding across the slanting deck. Several people knocked against the railing, lost their balance, and fell, plunging into the ocean below.

"There's no time!" Micah shoved her. "Go!"

Maybe her mom had made it onto one of the other lifeboats . . . but her hope dwindled with every explosion that rent the sky.

Benjie. She needed to stay with Benjie. It's what her mom would want. She took a deep breath and climbed into the boat. When it was full, Micah released the gripes and securing wires. He guided two crew members onto the lifeboat and started to close the hatch.

"What about you?" she asked.

"I'll take the next one." The hatch slid shut. The shouting and the roaring wind dimmed. Everyone huddled together on the benches, soaking, trembling, terrified. Benjie and one of the little girls buried themselves against her sides.

The boat swayed as it lowered toward the sea. It released, dropping the last few feet to the water. A wave swelled beneath them, and the boat bucked as the crew started the engine and motored away from the sinking *Grand Voyager*.

"Mom!" Willow twisted around, searching the passengers' strained faces. "Has anyone seen Marisol Bahaghari?"

But no one answered. Her mom wasn't here. Dread settled in her stomach, hard as stone.

A few benches over, someone vomited. The sour stench filled her nostrils and she clenched her lips, willing herself to hold it together. She needed to be strong for Benjie.

Another crew member bustled around, handing out Dramamine and bottled water. When the lady next to her tried to wave it away, the girl insisted. "It's to keep you from becoming dangerously dehydrated."

"That and the smell," Finn said.

Willow tried to smile, but she couldn't. Her face felt like a mask, skin stretched over bone. After they'd gotten far enough from the ship, she dared look back.

The *Grand Voyager* looked like a ghost ship. The once magnificent white hull listed to the side, alight with the hungry, flickering glow of the flames chewing through the middle decks. Black smoke billowed up into the sky like the breath of a great dragon.

But the water would swallow the dragon. The ocean didn't care how mighty and splendid the *Grand Voyager* was, how wealthy and powerful its passengers. The ship would go down, every inch of it, devoured by the cold, indifferent sea.

Willow tore her gaze from the sinking ship. A second lifeboat headed toward them. A third boat released from the cradle too early. Instead of lowering on the cables, it dropped the last fifteen feet. But they were all free of the ship.

Another explosion ripped the top decks, fire and smoke spewing into the darkness.

Finn sat across from her, exhausted, his eyes as scared and lost as her own. But he was alive. Whatever hell he'd been through, he was alive. They both were.

"Where's Mom?" Benjie sat up. "Where's Zia?"

She closed her eyes for a moment, willing herself to be strong. She pulled him close and rested her forehead against his, the way her mom always did whenever one of them was frightened or sick or sad.

Her mom might be in another lifeboat. It was possible. But somehow, she knew. She felt it deep in her bones. Her mom was gone, just like Zia.

"No one can hurt them now, I promise," she said to Benjie. "You don't need to be scared anymore. I'm going to keep you safe."

He nodded and nestled himself in her lap like a puppy. In moments, he fell asleep.

If only she could sleep, too. Her eyes were gritty, her thoughts thick and foggy. Every muscle in her body ached. But Benjie slept the sleep of the innocent.

She wasn't innocent. The memory of her sister's eyes, blank and empty as marbles, burned through her. Zia had died because of her. She'd died alone and terrified. All because of Willow's selfishness. She'd spent all her time and energy resenting her family instead of loving them.

What she wouldn't give now to hear Zia's donkey laugh or listen to another of her mom's lectures on family responsibility. Her mom, who always sacrificed her own needs for her kids. Her mom, who only worked so hard to take care of them.

She stroked Benjie's hair as she blinked back tears, her heart aching with grief and regret. She couldn't cry. Not for herself. She didn't deserve it.

49

GABRIEL

Jericho shoved Gabriel through the crowd, the gun pressed against the small of his back. His hands were bound in front of him, the hard plastic digging into his wrists. Rain pelted him. The wind battered him against the railing.

The blazing fire above them battled the lightning forking through the clouds. The sky seethed like a living beast swooping down to devour them all.

"Move it!" Jericho herded him past the first line of people shoving and jostling to board the lifeboat. The understaffed crew couldn't manage the calm, orderly emergency evacuation they'd trained for. The repeated shout, "Please remain calm!" was lost in the din. The storm, the boiling sea, the listing deck, and the flames transformed the passengers into a writhing throng of panic.

The ship tilted. Everyone screamed, stumbling and slipping against the railing. Several of the barrel-shaped life raft canisters popped loose from their storage on the deck. Gabriel leapt aside as one bounced past him and crashed over the railing.

Beside him, two crew members lowered the fourth lifeboat on its cables. Gabriel sensed his brother's presence before he saw him. He twisted around.

"Don't move!" Jericho jammed the gun against his spine.

Gabriel barely noticed. "Micah!"

Micah bent over the controls as the davits and cables lowered the lifeboat until it was even with Deck Four. He glanced up at the sound of his name. His curls plastered against his forehead, water fogging his glasses. His gaze met Gabriel's and he froze, his face contorting.

Micah jerked his head and broke eye contact, turning back to the lifeboat. He opened the hatch and helped the first few passengers climb inside.

Gabriel blinked the rain out of his eyes. *Impossible.* And yet there she was, not ten feet away, Silas propping her up as Micah grasped her hand to pull her into the boat. Lightning ripped the sky, revealing her pale face, the bruising and the cut on her lip.

But Amelia was alive—dirty and wounded, but gloriously alive.

She looked at him, their eyes meeting for one long, terrible moment. And what he saw was not the hatred that he deserved, but confusion, pain, and loss.

Remorse filled him, a regret so wide and deep it swallowed him whole. He'd betrayed the only two people in his life he truly cared about. Micah, the brother he loved. And Amelia, the girl he cared about, might have loved, if only he'd had more time. If he'd given them more time. If he hadn't deceived and deserted her.

He'd fed his own desire for hatred and revenge more than anything else. More than justice. More than love. And in doing so, he'd betrayed Amelia, his brother, his cause, and ultimately, himself. Self-loathing coiled within him, dark and deadly.

Gunfire rained down. The bullets tore into the deck, exploding into splinters of teak. The terror-stricken crowd surged, knocking more people over the railing.

Jericho spun around, searching for the gunman. Bullets chewed into the hull behind Gabriel. Several panels of the glass railing shattered.

Three people to Gabriel's right crumpled, red water pooling at his feet. One of them was a girl, five or six years old, wearing only a bright yellow bathrobe. Her dark hair fanned around her head like a halo, her dim eyes staring up at him.

Gabriel turned his head and vomited. That little girl hadn't asked for any of this. *Who gets to decide who is innocent?* She was innocent. Now she was dead. She was Simeon's collateral damage. She was *Gabriel's* collateral damage.

He did this. All these people, all this pain, terror, and death. This was his fault. He saw it now so clearly, now that it was too late. His soul broke under the crushing weight.

The rain battered him, so cold. The seething sky so close. The shattered sea rose up to meet him. Ravenous, waiting. He stepped to the railing.

"Gabriel! No!" Micah said.

Someone grabbed his arm. Jericho jerked him back from the edge. "You don't get to escape justice that easily." He shoved Gabriel toward the lifeboat. "You'll pay for your sins."

Gabriel bowed his head. There was no price, no punishment, no atonement that would cover his sins. He'd been a fool to ask his brother for forgiveness. There was no forgiveness, not for him. He would find no solace, no peace, no redemption.

Not in this life or the next.

50

WILLOW

Willow watched the first hints of gray tinge the dark windows. The fingers of dawn painted the sky in the softest shades of indigo blue. There was no trace of the storm, no boiling clouds, no vicious waves.

The sea was still and flat as a sheet of glass.

"You okay?" Finn slumped across the aisle, his back against the window, his arms crossed over his chest. His eyes were blood-shot and rimmed with red, like he'd been crying in the night. Specks of dried blood dotted his right cheek.

A part of her wanted to ask what had happened to him, but she didn't. She wasn't ready to reveal her own secrets.

Every person in this boat would be haunted by the nightmare of this day for the rest of their lives—the things they'd seen, the people they'd lost, the things done to them and the things they'd done. She knew she would.

Her arms tightened around Benjie. She wouldn't let him go. Not for anything. Benjie was her only family now. He was her responsibility. He was her heart.

"I'm alive," she said.

Finn nodded. "That has to be enough."

"We have to make it enough."

He gestured at her clothes. "I guess you really do hate dresses, huh?"

She looked down at herself, the navy blue fabric ripped in several places, smeared with dirt and blood. She rubbed the cuts and bruises on her aching feet. "I sure don't miss those pain-in-the-ass heels."

Finn snorted. They exchanged strained smiles.

She noticed something in the window behind his shoulder. A gray smudge on the horizon, darker than the fog surrounding it. "What's that?"

Finn turned and looked, cupping his hands against the Plexiglas. "My lady, I do believe you've sighted a ship."

She couldn't quite believe what she'd heard. "A ship."

She glanced at Finn, her own hesitant hope reflected in his eyes.

They watched the ship grow closer in the early morning light, the sky shaded apricot and rose. It was a U.S. naval ship. And it sailed straight toward them.

Rescue.

51

AMELIA

Amelia pressed against her mother. She couldn't stop shaking. The migraine had dissipated to a dull ache at the base of her skull. Her body ached with exhaustion, like she'd been climbing a mountain for days.

She stared down at her numb hands. They didn't belong to her. It was someone else who plunged that needle into Kane's eye. Someone else who stabbed him, over and over.

But she was alive. She'd saved herself.

Silas sat across from her, staring off into nothing. It wasn't like there was anything to look at in this barren, plastic-draped room. Everything was white or gray, sterile and bland.

Since they'd been rescued by the Navy yesterday, the hundred and thirty-six survivors were confined to a massive room-like plastic tent. They were given water bottles and served several meals on brown plastic trays. They had access to a six-stalled bathroom and a few showers.

The first time she had limped to the bathroom and looked at herself in the mirror, she was shocked. Hair: tangled, knotted mess. Face: dirty, bruised, and swollen. Dress: torn and stained. Nails: ragged. She'd examined the greenish-yellow bruising on her ribs and stomach, gingerly touching the tender flesh.

But she was here. Simeon wasn't. That asshole Kane wasn't. Her father wasn't. She was. She raised her chin and met her own gaze in the mirror. This time, she smiled for herself.

But that was hours ago. Now, they just waited. Everyone sat on plastic chairs or hunched on the floor, huddled in blankets. She sat with her mother and Silas against the wall in the far corner.

Jericho sat somewhere off to the right, giving them privacy. Tyler Horne and Senator López were here, and Celeste and Meredith Jackson-Cooper. A few feet away, Willow slept with her little brother curled in her lap, a ratty backpack clutched in his skinny arms.

Micah slumped on the other side of Benjie. He was as sleep-deprived as Amelia, judging by his hollow cheeks and red-rimmed eyes. She hadn't spoken to him, but she could read the sorrow and devastation etched across his face.

Everyone was scared, confused, shell-shocked, grief-stricken. They had all lost someone. Muffled sobbing drifted over the drone of the ship's engine.

The only people who'd come into the sealed room wore bulky contamination suits. They didn't meet her gaze through their masks. They tended to the wounded and provided first aid. They examined her clutch with the single auto-injector but didn't take it. Not yet.

Whenever anyone tried to ask them questions, they just shook their heads. "We're following protocol. Someone will be in to speak with you shortly," was all they'd say. That and, "Please remain calm."

Silas glanced at her, cocking one eyebrow. He didn't constantly ask her if she was all right, like her mother did. But he studied her, scrutinizing her face, searching for something. She met his gaze. He was the brother she loved, the one who put himself between her and her father, over and over. Though he never said a word, he still made sure she was okay.

But she wasn't, not yet.

Ever since the attack, she couldn't sleep. Her eyes burned and her head throbbed, but every time she tried to rest, she saw that face behind her closed lids—Kane's venomous eyes, that hideous, lecherous grin. She could still feel his hands—huge, strong, scrabbling like spiders. She could still smell the stench of his breath, the heat of it on her cheeks. She couldn't get the stain of his touch off her skin.

If she managed to drift off, she jolted awake, her heart beating savagely against her ribs. Kane haunted her sleep, but Gabriel haunted her waking moments.

She kept seeing him in her mind's eye, in the rain and the chaos of the deck. Gabriel, desperately pleading for something she couldn't give him. She hadn't seen Gabriel since two naval officers led him away in handcuffs within moments of their rescue. She didn't know what would happen to him now.

She shivered and wrapped the Mylar blanket tighter around herself.

Her mother stirred and opened her eyes. "Amelia." Her voice filled with relief. Every time she woke up from her restless dozing, she was frantic until she laid eyes on her daughter. "We survived. We're all here."

"Not all of us," Silas said.

She licked her lips. Part of her wished she didn't need to know, that she could pretend it all away. But that was impossible. "Why are they keeping us in here?" she asked again.

This time, her mother answered. "They want to make sure we're not infected."

"Because of what's happening on the mainland," Silas said.

She rubbed her charm bracelet. "This is all because of Father, isn't it?"

Her mother gave her a hard look.

"You don't have to keep protecting me." Her tone came out sharper than she intended. "In case you haven't noticed, we're well beyond that."

Her mother sighed. "Keep your voice down, please. We must keep this between us. We don't have all the answers. Not yet. The attack on the *Voyager* must have been planned for months."

"But how—"

"There are political groups who have openly hated and threatened us for almost a decade. Your father planned the Unity Coalition's Prosperity Summit on the *Grand Voyager* for the same week every year. It wasn't like we made ourselves a difficult target." Her mother's hand strayed to the hollow of her throat.

"There's more," Amelia said.

Her mother took a deep breath. "Yes, there's more."

"The New Patriots said the universal vaccine was used as a cover to distribute a bioweapon." Amelia stared at her mother, trying to read her face for any signs of deception. "They said the engineered virus was meant to kill a hundred thousand innocent people. Father admitted it. How could he do something like that?"

"Shhh." Her mother tilted her chin at the people closest to them. But everyone else seemed to be sleeping. They sat in the far corner, which afforded as much privacy as this fish bowl allowed. "When you blame the poor for their misfortune—like your father did—it dehumanizes them. It becomes easier to justify atrocities if their plight is their own fault. And if they're less than human . . ."

"Did you know?" Silas asked.

Her mother grabbed her hand and squeezed. "I swear to you, on your life, I had no idea. I never would've—I believed we were safe. Your father—he protected us. I didn't know."

Revulsion filled her. She yanked her hand away. "But you know what he's like."

"You have to understand, Amelia. The world is such a dangerous place. He offered safety."

"Safety?" Silas asked. "Is that what you call this?"

A line appeared between her mother's brows. "It wasn't supposed to be like this."

Amelia couldn't stop thinking about all the people, all those thousands of lives. All those mothers and fathers and children and babies, all suffering, all dying in agony.

The worst part was how those people trusted the vaccine, believed in it, waited for hours to give it to their sick children. All those health workers administering the shots with a smile on their faces and gentleness in their touch, saying, "This will only hurt a bit." Because they didn't know. How could they know they were administering grief and horror and death?

She bent double, acid burning the back of her throat.

"Amelia! Are you okay?" Her mother reached for her purse. "Do you need your medication? I have your pills—"

"I'm *fine*. What about the cure? The cure the New Patriots wanted to help all those sick people?"

"They didn't want the vaccine for the sick. They wanted it for themselves."

"What?"

Her mother closed her eyes. When she opened them again, they were full of anguish. "Amelia, honey, I don't want to upset you—"

She stiffened. "Just tell me."

"The bioweapon—it didn't just infect the people who received the virus through the shot."

Dizziness rushed through her. She started to get that feeling, like when the aura came before a migraine. A warning. "Tell me."

"The engineered virus inserted into the flu vaccine—it mutated. It's contagious."

"Contagious," Amelia echoed.

"With a vaccine that utilizes a live virus, like measles or polio, viral shedding is possible. But this—something happened. I'm not an expert, but I believe the engineered virus merged with the H17N10 bat strain of influenza in tens of thousands of already infected people who lined up to receive the universal vaccine.

"When the two viruses infected the same host cells, they underwent reassortment, combining their genetic material to create a new strain— the Hydra virus. I don't know much more than this. But right before communications went down on the *Grand Voyager*, the CDC declared the Hydra virus a pandemic."

"What are we supposed to do now?" Amelia asked, fighting down panic.

Her mother clasped her hands together. "We have faith. We do anything we can to help. We pray for the sick and their families—"

"How can you say that?" Silas's mouth twisted. "How can you talk about faith after what he's done?"

Her mother's eyes filled with tears. "I hope I've taught you—"

"What you've taught us?" Silas glowered at their mother. "You taught us to respect and obey a monster."

She looked from Silas to Amelia, her face crumpling. "You both must hate me. And maybe I deserve it. But you don't know everything. I need to tell you—"

But Amelia had heard enough. She couldn't stand to be near her mother, couldn't stand to look at her. Her mother was weak. She'd always been weak. Amelia saw that now.

She'd been blind before, so determined to please her father, she hadn't seen him for what he was. She'd tried to be as meek and docile as her mother. She hadn't seen what it was doing to her own soul.

Even with Gabriel, she'd been blind, letting herself see what she wanted to see—someone to rescue her, so she didn't have to do the hard work of rescuing herself.

But she wasn't blind now. She didn't have to be weak and docile anymore. "Just stop."

"But Amelia, you don't understand—"

The entrance to the quarantined area opened, and two figures in contamination suits lumbered in, wheeling in an old-fashioned flat screen TV. Their hazmat suits made them look alien and intimidating. "Ladies and gentlemen," the first one said in a loud, throaty voice.

All around her, people sat up, rubbing their exhausted faces. A few seats down, Willow hunched protectively over her little brother. Their eyes locked. Amelia tried to offer up a reassuring smile, but her mouth, her whole face, was frozen.

"We understand your shock, confusion, and questions," the woman in the hazmat suit continued. "You've been through a tremendous ordeal. However, due to the circumstances, we must take extreme precautions. Our doctors will conduct further examinations on each of you later today. Thank you for your patience and please remain calm."

"Give us some damn answers!" someone shouted.

"Is this because of that Hydra plague?"

"What's going on?"

"You can't keep us in here!"

"I have been authorized to brief you on the current state of emergency. As you may have gathered, the Hydra virus is a particularly virulent strain of Influenza A. It has also mutated in . . . unexpected ways."

"What's happening?" a man asked, terror in his voice.

"All state and national agencies are working in conjunction to contain the disease. President Sloane has ordered all domestic ports closed, and domestic and international flights have been grounded."

A murmur spread through the room. "*President* Sloane?" Tyler Horne asked.

The woman nodded. "President Morgan succumbed to the virus the night before last. President Amanda Sloane was sworn in immediately. Her first act was to declare a national state of emergency."

Another audible gasp.

"President Sloane announced yesterday that the Hydra virus was released upon the United States as a biological weapon."

No one moved. No one breathed.

"The effects have been . . . catastrophic. We'll release information as we receive it, but for now, we've been authorized to show you part of President Sloane's emergency address." The woman turned on the television and stepped aside.

On the screen, the new president stood behind her desk in the Oval Office. She leaned forward, her hands splayed on the desk. She was a tall, svelte woman in her mid-fifties, her auburn hair clipped short around her ears, her gaze somber. She looked like a person who was strong and capable, someone able and ready to handle the crisis. "I'm shocked and saddened to announce that the *Grand Voyager* cruise ship sank yesterday after it was attacked by terrorists. As of now, we do not know how many survived. This was an intricately planned and organized two-prong attack.

"The murder of so many of our shining beacons of industry as well as several wonderful and dedicated members of Congress and their families is an unpalatable act. It will not stand unavenged. The murder of millions of American men, women, and children via a deadly biological weapon is a heart-breaking atrocity we shall never forget. This too, we shall avenge with the full force of our military power.

"We have reason to believe the criminals behind these acts are one and the same, the homegrown terrorist group known as the New Patriots. I pledge to you tonight that we will find each and every perpetrator of these horrendous attacks. We will show them the exact meaning of American justice.

"But tonight, we are a nation in mourning. You did not vote for me, but I am still your president, the leader of this magnificent country. I will not rest until we contain this bioweapon. We will not stop until our country is safe again.

"As my first act as President, I gathered an emergency session in Congress and oversaw the passage of the Safe and Secure Act. This bill empowers us to track down and capture the wicked persons responsible for these atrocities. The bio-identification Vitalichip will enable us to identify and help those who are ill and protect those who are not, saving as many American men, women, and children as possible."

The President paused, staring out at the viewers with a stony determination. "Our hope and faith in the American dream is not diminished tonight. The world's prayers are with the United States. God be with us."

The TV went dark. A second later, the room exploded into panicked confusion.

The hairs on the back of Amelia's neck prickled. "That's not right—"

Her mother gripped her arm so tightly her nails dug into Amelia's skin. "Shhh!"

An image of Gabriel flashed through her mind. Gabriel leaning over her, his face brimming with emotion, his dark eyes glossy with pain. "But it wasn't them—"

"Stop talking. Right now."

She stared at her mother in shock. She couldn't remember the last time she'd seen her so fierce, her eyes filled with a desperate determination. "What—?"

Her mother leaned in close, her breath hot on Amelia's ear. "No one here knows what your father did. Not even Jericho."

She stiffened. "Gabriel knows."

"Then we pray he says nothing. Do you have any idea what these people will do to us if they find out?"

"No. I—"

"There are others involved, high in the government. You remember all those disturbing calls that agitated your father so much?"

"But it wasn't the New—"

"Keep quiet," her mother said, iron in her voice. "Of course not. But it was someone. Someone with enough power and influence to organize a terrorist attack on a cruise ship full of powerful and influential people. Someone determined enough to poison a hundred thousand people and frame a terrorist group. The microchip contract alone will be worth billions. There's more going on than we know. We're in an extremely dangerous position. Do you understand?"

Amelia nodded. Her brain buzzed with the implications of her mother's words. Her father hadn't acted alone. But then, who was behind it? And what about the attack on the *Grand Voyager*?

Were they covering their tracks, tying up loose ends by destroying everyone who had any intimate knowledge of the engineering of the Hydra virus? And what would happen to her family if Gabriel revealed the truth about her father?

But her mind stopped there. It was too much to take in at once.

"Ladies and gentlemen!" the woman in the hazmat suit said. "Our doctors will begin seeing you soon."

"How long do we have to stay here?"

"We're not sick!"

"That boy is coughing! You locked us in here with the infected!"

"When are we going home?"

"Everyone will be tested!" The woman raised her hands. "You must remain calm."

A shiver ran through her, a cold that reached deep into her bones. When *were* they going home? And the bigger questions, the words she could hardly bring herself to think, let alone speak aloud: Was there a home to go back to? And if there was, what dangers awaited them there?

And what about her medication? She only had one auto-injector and one month's supply of pills in her mother's purse. If her father was really, truly gone . . .

"It's the end," Silas said flatly. "The end of the world."

She shook her head. She couldn't believe that. She wouldn't. "No. It's not."

She remembered her mother's saying about glass, how it was beautiful but weak, but it could be strengthened by heat—made strong by fire.

They'd tried to break her. The terrorists. Kane. Gabriel. Her own father. But they couldn't. None of them could.

She hadn't shattered.

Whatever came next, she would face it.

They all would.

The End

ALSO BY KYLA STONE

ACKNOWLEDGMENTS

I'm been lucky enough to have wonderful support from family, friends, fellow writers, and readers. I am eternally grateful to everyone who read the manuscript and provided feedback—a few of you read various versions multiple times.

Many thanks to my awesome beta readers. Your thoughtful critiques and enthusiasm were invaluable. This book is a hundred times better because of you: Anna Baker, Cody Mauro, Elaine Roth, Elizabeth Oakes, Lauren Nikkel, Kimberley Trembley, Michelle Browne, Leslie Spurrier, Jazmin Cybulski, Tasmin Bowerman, Melissa Eddings, and Barry and Derise Marden.

To Danita Mayer and Britney Goodman for the time and care you spent on excellent developmental editing. To Michelle Brown and Holly Jenkins for lending me your eagle eyes with copyediting and proofreading.

Thank you to Miltiadis Kapodistrias for answering my questions about working on a cruise ship and for not freaking out when I started in on where the bombs should be located. And especially to Becca Cross, for being an amazing friend and early reader of all three of my books.

To my husband, for patiently listening to plot and character conundrums for months and stepping in to help with suppers and grocery shopping before deadlines.

And to my kids, for being my everything.

ABOUT THE AUTHOR

Kyla Stone is an emerging author of contemporary young adult fiction and sci-fi novels. She lives in Atlanta, Georgia with her husband, two children, and two spoiled cats. When she's not writing or spending time with her family, she loves to read, hike, draw, travel, and play games. Her favorite food is dark chocolate.

Kyla loves to hear from her readers. For news and new releases, visit her at:

www.FaceBook.com/KylaStoneBooks

www.Amazon.com/author/kylaStone

Email her at KylaStone@yahoo.com

SNEAK PEEK OF FALLING STARS: THE LAST SANCTUARY BOOK TWO

FALLING STARS CHAPTER ONE

Eighteen-old-year old Amelia Black thought she knew how to survive. She was wrong.

The world had changed drastically in only a few short weeks. She didn't know how yet.

So many questions, and she didn't have the answers to any of them. Until now. Soon, they would see the outside world for the first time in almost six weeks.

Amelia leaned against the wall of the military transport. The hard metal bench beneath her vibrated. People pressed on either side of her.

The truck slowed, bumping over ruts in the road.

"What now?" her brother Silas asked. He lounged on the bench across from her, his legs draped over a plastic-wrapped cardboard box labeled 'Medical Supplies: Syringes'. Dozens of similar boxes were stacked along the front end of the truck and secured with rubber straps.

There were no windows. Air conditioning piped through a vent near the front, but the air still felt hot and stuffy. They'd been riding for hours since departing the naval base in Jacksonville, Florida, early that morning.

The brakes squealed as the truck rumbled to a halt.

"What's going on?" Amelia asked, though she didn't expect an answer.

Their convoy included eight transport trucks: four filled with medical supplies, two filled with canned food, MREs, and bottled water, and two transported civilians.

Four camouflaged military jeeps took the front and rear of the convoy, the soldiers decked out with combat gear and pulse guns.

"How much longer?" eight-year-old Benjie asked beside her.

Willow Bahaghari squeezed her brother's hand and grinned. But her grin was forced, her eyes tired. She pushed her thick black hair behind her ears. "It's probably just something blocking the road. This will all be over soon, I promise."

Amelia sighed. If only that were true. It still felt strange not to be quarantined, trapped in the same small space day after day, surrounded by the white walls of a medical tent.

They'd been quarantined for eighteen days—four days on the naval ship that rescued them from the sinking *Grand Voyager*, then another fourteen days once they'd arrived at Mayport Naval Station in Jacksonville.

Several high-value government officials and powerful CEOs had been airlifted to an undisclosed location the day they'd cleared quarantine. The rest of the one hundred and thirty-six survivors waited five more days for a supply transport to take them to Fort Campbell in Kentucky, a military base relocating the survivors of the Hydra virus.

"Can I wear one of those?" Benjie asked. He pointed at the CDC epidemiologist sitting on Amelia's other side. Dr. Martinez wore a bulky yellow hazmat suit, every inch of her covered by the suit, gloves, and a helmet sealed at the neck.

Dr. Martinez had taken bloodwork from them every day for the last fourteen days. She was in her mid-forties and spoke little, her expression always grim. She folded her hands in her lap. "Personal Protection Equipment will be issued to you when you reach your relocation destination."

Benjie scrunched up his face. He was cute, with brown skin, large dark eyes, and black hair sticking up all over his head. "I don't want a new home. I like my old one."

Amelia's gut tightened. She agreed with him. She missed her own sleep pod and her light-filled studio, where she practiced the violin for three hours every day.

But the world had changed drastically in the six weeks since they boarded the *Grand Voyager*—that much was clear.

She despised all this not-knowing. What was out there? What was happening? How many people were sick? Why wouldn't they tell the truth?

"Why can't I go home?" Benjie asked again.

Willow squeezed his hand. "Benjie, hush."

Dr. Martinez pressed her lips together behind her helmet. "They'll explain once you reach your destination. Until then, that information is classified."

Benjie sighed and clasped his arms around his ratty backpack. "That's what everyone says."

Dr. Martinez hesitated. "I am sorry."

Willow shifted. "I've gotta pee," she said under her breath. "How long 'til we get to wherever the hell we're going?"

Amelia shrugged. "I don't know."

"It'll take forever at this rate." Willow gestured at the walls of the transport. "What do you think it's like out there?"

"Your guess is as good as mine." Amelia didn't know how bad it was. None of them did.

The *Grand Voyager* survivors were anxious to return to their homes, find their families, and find out what the hell happened.

Amelia knew what her mother would say. *At least we have each other.* Amelia had her mother and brother, which was more than most people.

Willow had lost her mother and sister. Willow's friend, Finn Ellington-Fletcher, a giant black kid with a gap-toothed smile and a penchant for goofy humor, had lost his father. Others lost their entire families, gunned down by the terrorists, burned in the explosions, or trapped and drowned as the ship sank, consumed in smoke and flames and terror.

"I thought you might have a higher clearance," Willow continued. "Seeing as you're the daughter of Declan Black."

Her father was the famous founder and CEO of BioGen Technologies and the chairman of the Unity Coalition, a conglomerate of powerful biotech and national defense corporations. BioGen manufactured and distributed the universal flu vaccine to combat the raging bat-flu epidemic.

Only a few people still living knew the truth.

Her father had also designed the Hydra Virus, releasing it as an act of bioterrorism in a calculated attempt to pass his rights-reducing, citizen-tracking Safe and Secure Act. The new president blamed the attack on the domestic terrorist group, the New Patriots. Consumed by fear, the government had passed the Safe and Secure Act in an emergency session, just as her father predicted.

But the plan backfired. The virus, meant to kill one hundred thousand people deliberately culled from the disposable poor, mutated instead. It underwent reassortment, recombining with the bat-flu to create a deadly, highly contagious supervirus.

Her father—though not the mastermind—had designed and implemented the entire thing.

An international terrorist syndicate had taken her father hostage. Was he still alive? Did she even care?

She did, in spite of everything.

She rubbed the diamond-studded charm bracelet on her left wrist, the one he'd bought for her thirteenth birthday. Part of her wanted to rip it off and throw it away, but for some reason, she couldn't. Even though he'd betrayed her, betrayed them all.

"No," she said finally. "I don't know anything."

Willow shot her a dubious look, shrugged, and turned back to her brother. "Suit yourself."

The truck started again, jolting forward. Amelia's shoulder bumped the wall. She rubbed her shoulder and scanned the people in the transport—Enrique López, the Mexican-American senator from New York; Tyler Horne, the hotshot inventor of the RFID microchip VitaliChip; her brother Silas and her mother, Elise; and Micah Ramos Rivera, Gabriel's brother.

Gabriel Ramos Rivera rode in the second transport truck, A prisoner in handcuffs guarded by a half-dozen soldiers and her father's former head of security, Ed Jericho.

Gabriel. The guy she fell for against her better judgment. The enigmatic, brooding Puerto Rican hothead with the bronze skin, dark smoldering eyes, and irresistible smile.

The ruthless rebel and New Patriot who'd hijacked the *Grand Voyager*, taken her hostage, and betrayed her—who willingly and knowingly gave her up to Kane, a psychopathic terrorist who'd enjoyed killing. Who took pleasure in others' pain. Who'd taken pleasure in her own.

Kane and his scrabbling hands, his beady eyes, his vicious leer as he hovered over her. That asshole tried to break her. He almost succeeded.

He still invaded her nightmares at night. She always awoke gasping, her heart a wild, frantic thing in her chest, her thoughts a tangled knot of terror. Amelia closed her eyes, shoving those thoughts out of her head.

The truck suddenly slammed to a stop. Amelia crashed into Benjie, knocking him off the bench. Across the aisle, Micah and Silas jolted awake, gripping the bench to keep their balance.

Outside the truck, someone shouted.

"What was that?" Benjie asked, eyes wide. Amelia and Willow exchanged nervous glances. Whatever it was didn't sound good.

Dr. Martinez clutched her hands together in front of her chest. "I'm sure it's fine. Just a routine checkpoint." But her voice quavered.

Gunfire exploded outside the truck, somewhere to Amelia's right. Shouting filled the air. "Get down!" Someone screamed.

Her heart squeezed, her breath stilling in her chest. Why had they stopped? Why were the soldiers shooting? What was happening?

Tyler Horne leapt to his feet, his perfectly coiffed blonde hair matted against his head. "We're being attacked, aren't we?"

Dr. Martinez said nothing. More shouting filled the air. Something struck the side of the truck. The wall shuddered. Amelia jerked forward.

"Tell us the truth, damn it!" Tyler Horne took an aggressive step toward the doctor.

Senator López stood and blocked Horne with his outstretched hand. "Stay calm. Panic won't help anything."

A bullet punctured the left side of the transport above Horne's head.

The passengers screamed and ducked, scrambling off the benches along the walls and crouching low. Amelia covered her head with her arms, the hairs on her neck standing on end.

Beside her, Willow pushed Benjie down and covered his body with her own. "Stay down!"

More shots rang out. Loud bangs and thumps shuddered the truck, as if people were shoving it from both sides. Maybe they were.

Angry shouts filled the air. It sounded like they'd surrounded the truck. The back doors clanged and jerked, but they didn't open. They were locked from the inside.

"They want the supplies, don't they?" Micah adjusted his glasses nervously. His brown eyes were huge in his boyish face, his dark wavy hair damp on his forehead.

"Why the hell won't you say something?" Willow asked Dr. Martinez, her voice rising. "*This* can't be classified, too!"

"Yes," Dr. Martinez admitted, fear and defeat in her voice. "It must be an ambush. The roads are—dangerous. There are no hospitals, no stores. People are desperate."

Amelia's mind couldn't focus on the words. No hospitals? That didn't make sense.

Another bullet punched through the transport walls like they were butter. The attackers were using armor-piercing rounds. The next stray bullet would hit someone. "Maybe we should give them what they want."

"She's right," Silas said. He had their father's intensity, the same sinewy frame and lean, wolfish face. "Open the doors."

Horne pointed his finger at Silas. "You're insane if you think you're going to let them in here. They're shooting people!"

Silas bristled, his smoke-gray eyes glittering. "You're not in charge here."

"Just give them the supplies so they'll stop shooting at us," Micah said.

"You don't understand." Dr. Martinez twisted her hands. "We need those supplies for research and medical personnel at the base. We can't just give them—"

"Screw this." Silas leapt to his feet. He crouched low and lurched over cowering bodies to reach the back doors.

Micah followed close behind. The truck rocked and they stumbled, righting themselves and lunging for the doors before anyone could stop them.

"Don't open that door! You aren't protected!" Dr. Martinez rose to her feet just as another bullet punched through the wall inches from her head. She shrieked and dropped to the floor.

Amelia craned her neck to watch Micah and Silas wrestle with the doors' locking mechanism. Her knees ached from kneeling on the metal floor. A rivet scraped her shin, ripping a hole in her khaki cargo pants. The shouts and screams from outside the truck echoed in her ears.

A chill ran down her spine. Opening the doors might be a terrible idea, but they were sitting ducks, just waiting for the next bullet to kill somebody.

Someone gripped her arm. Amelia glanced up and stared at Dr. Martinez. Her mouth pressed into a grim line, her eyes hard and unreadable. "Whatever you do, don't touch anyone."

"How bad is it?" Amelia asked.

Dr. Martinez shook her head. "I wanted to tell all of you right away, but my superiors were concerned with suicide attempts and panicked rebellion. They thought you wouldn't sit meekly in quarantine if you knew . . ."

Her voice trailed off as an ear-piecing shriek drowned her out. Amelia's blood turned to ice. "If we knew what? Tell me!"

Someone shouted as the back doors swung open. Daylight poured into the transport. The attackers yanked Micah and Silas from the truck. Four of them scrambled inside, black streaks across their cheeks and foreheads, semi-automatic rifles flailing.

Terror gripped Amelia. She couldn't focus on the doctor's words. Would these people actually kill them? What had they done to Silas and Micah? Was her brother hurt? Was he—

"It's airborne, passed through coughing and sneezing," Dr. Martinez said hastily, her words tripping over each other. She squeezed Amelia's arm with her gloved fingers. "It lives on non-organic surfaces for twenty-four hours, organic surfaces for up to two weeks. Always wear gloves and protective gear—"

An attacker with long red hair bound in a ponytail reached them and lunged for the doctor. The attacker wasn't a man but a tall, muscular woman, her face contorted in rage.

She seized Dr. Martinez by the throat, lifting her to her feet with one hand. She thrust the muzzle of her gun against the doctor's stomach.

"You people!" she spat. "You just left us to die!"

Amelia watched in shock, unable to move.

"Amelia!" Her mother moved to her, gripping her arm. "Go! Go!"

Amelia, Willow, and Benjie scooted from their seats and scrambled after her mother, weaving around the legs of a dozen attackers as they leapt onto the truck. They were just people, not soldiers. Men and women, some with combat gear, some only in dark clothes. Their faces were desperate. Their eyes blazed dangerously.

Amelia flinched as someone kneed her in the ribs. Hands scrabbled over her, scratching at her arms. Someone else seized her SmartFlex and tried to rip it off her wrist.

"Let go!" She jerked free and kept moving, stumbling toward the back of the truck. The rest of the attackers ignored her. They were focused on the boxes of medical supplies.

The sound of a gunshot ricocheted inside the truck.

Dr. Martinez moaned.

Amelia twisted in her mother's grasp, trying to see what happened. But the icy dread in her gut told her she already knew. The woman with the ponytail had shot the doctor for no reason.

They ran for the wide-open doors.

Made in United States
Troutdale, OR
04/28/2024

19508822R00181